W9-BZZ-169

LOOSE TONGUES

LOOSE TONGUES

Chris Simms

This first world edition published 2018
in Great Britain and the USA by
SEVERN HOUSE PUBLISHERS LTD of
Eardley House, 4 Uxbridge Street, London W8 7SY
Trade paperback edition first published
in Great Britain and the USA 2018 by
SEVERN HOUSE PUBLISHERS LTD

British Library Cataloguing in Publication Data
A CIP catalogue record for this title is available from the British Library.

ISBN-13: 978-0-7278-8810-5 (cased)
ISBN-13: 978-1-84751-936-8 (trade paper)
ISBN-13: 978-1-78010-991-6 (e-book)

All Severn House titles are printed on acid-free paper.

Severn House Publishers support the Forest Stewardship Council™ [FSC™],
the leading international forest certification organisation. All our titles that
are printed on FSC certified paper carry the FSC logo.

Typeset by Palimpsest Book Production Ltd.,
Falkirk, Stirlingshire, Scotland.
Printed and bound in Great Britain by
TJ International, Padstow, Cornwall.

To Abi. Without you, this novel would not exist.

Thanks to the lovely folk at Severn House; you make the process of publishing a pleasure!

PROLOGUE

He liked the sight of liquefying wire. The way he could alter something so dramatically, it filled him with hope for the future. Sharp fumes from the soldering iron rose up, causing his nose and lips to twitch. It was the closest he ever strayed to a smile.

The space where he worked had been a garage, once. But it had housed no car in a long time. This was where his tools were hoarded. Full cabinets and crowded shelves. A workbench pock-marked by years of hard labour, its edge clamped in the iron grip of a vice. Next to it towered a vertical drill, the machine's bit pointing down like a cruel proboscis.

The garage was windowless. Hanging from a peg on the side door was a courier driver's uniform: plain navy trousers and a matching jacket. Insignia on the sleeves and a silver winged logo above the chest pocket. Small details that gave the impression of someone official. He'd purchased it from a fancy dress shop in Chicago for $39.99.

Suspended above his head was a double strip light, its contented hum only showing itself during pauses in the programme playing on a nearby radio. The presenter asked a question in his mature, measured tones. The studio guest's voice, in contrast, was shrill and increasingly insistent.

There can be no flexibility on this. Absolutely none. How could a society that classes itself as civilized even consider it? I mean really, how could it? The whole thing is just another example of the victim-blaming that occurs every day in our male-dominated—

He pressed a button, cutting her off mid-sentence. He hoped for some relief, but as the song playing on the next station wound to a close, the DJ began to speak. The female DJ.

Sorry if I'm harping on about this, listeners. But ten litres of wine, per person, per year? Just tipped down the sink? Ten. Litres. I'm getting quite emotional here. Those bottles weren't half empty, people, they were half full! Oh, oh, the sheer waste! Lara, in Timperley, has texted to say that she sometimes pops the cork on a red, only to realize—

He clicked again, more aggressively this time. The radio fell silent. Annoying loud bitches, would they never shut up?

He let the quiet settle in then turned his attention back to the console. It was a little larger than those used by genuine delivery drivers, and he'd sheathed its casing in rubber, just to be safe. But a casual observer would never know the difference.

Its upper surface was dominated by a glass touchscreen. This was where they'd believe a signature was required. The stylus for writing it was metal. A wire ran through the coiled plastic cord attaching it to his creation. That wire then connected to a row of nine-volt batteries concealed in the casing.

The beads of solder he'd just applied had now cooled. The Royer circuit he'd built inside it was complete. Further along the workbench was a polystyrene block. Embedded in the block was a metal coat hanger bent into the shape of an upturned hand. The clips of a meter had been attached to what represented the thumb. Everything was set.

He put his glasses on and took a breath in, composing himself. Then he lifted the console clear and spoke politely to the wall. 'Delivery, madam. Yes, for this address. If you could please sign for it here.'

He slid the stylus from its holder and laid it across the palm of the improvised hand. The internal mechanism of the stylus had been taken from a 100,000 volt Micro Stun Gun he'd purchased during the same trip to Chicago the previous month. He'd booked his flight the day after receiving final confirmation that his employment had been terminated at the college in Manchester where he'd worked for the last twelve years.

He regarded the stylus for a moment longer then pressed a button hidden from view on the device's underside. A bright blue flash lit the room and the stylus jumped up as if trying to yank itself free of the plastic leash.

He calmly put the console back on the mat, took his glasses off and leaned forward to read the meter.

4.21 milliamps.

Enough to send an adult female flying backwards. Enough to send her crashing to the floor, completely powerless. Enough so he could then silence her. Forever.

ONE

A head poked out of the door and looked left then right. 'In you come, ladies and gents, boys and girls.'

The officer who'd spoken was well in to his forties, veins in his temples accentuated by a haircut that had left little more than fuzz.

Sean Blake got to his feet, as did the rest of the group. They glanced awkwardly at one another, each of them clutching a cardboard box. Who was going first?

'Jesus,' the officer sighed, a palm pressed against the door to stop it swinging shut. 'Marko, lead the way, will you?'

The person beside Sean immediately stepped forward and disappeared into the incident room. Sean glanced at the remaining two people. As both were female, he took a step back to let them through first. But the nearest one – who he guessed was about the same age as him – gestured with her chin. 'You're the detective.'

With a shrug to show he didn't think that trumped manners, Sean stepped into the noise beyond.

The incident room held over a dozen workstations: cups, photo frames, paperwork and other paraphernalia scattered around most of them.

An officer on the far side of the room stood. 'Anyone got a Samsung charger I can borrow?'

'Christ, Ted. Again?'

'Yeah, sorry.'

Troughton pointed. 'The two empty ones, over there, in the far corner. Ladies, civilian support is off to the right. I think your table's the last one.'

As Sean followed his fellow detective constable across the room, he could feel the eyes of the other officers settling on him. His black brogues, not even two days old, had his toes in a terrier-like grip. *Shit*, he thought. *You're walking like a weirdo. Stop it.*

The other detective had broad shoulders and a confident way of moving. At about six foot two, he was a good four inches taller than Sean. The difference in height made Sean even more aware of his own stocky build: when feeling uncomfortable, he tended to hunch forward. He knew it made him appear defensive or wary. Even a touch aggressive.

Beside one of the workstations was a window. His new colleague made immediately for it. Box held above the desk, he glanced back. 'You OK with that one? When I was here before, they had me sitting here.'

Sean took a quick look at the rejected workstation. A filing cabinet butted into the space beside the chair. Definitely the arse end of the deal. The other detective's assumption rankled with him. 'No.'

He'd already placed his box down. 'Sorry?'

From the corner of his eye, Sean saw the nearest two detectives' heads turn.

'This side has miles less room. I don't really want it, either.'

'Oh.' The other detective's hands stayed on his box.

Sean plonked his on the chair and extended a fist across the desks. 'Rock, paper, scissors?'

'Rock . . .?'

'You never played it?'

'Yeah, but years ago—'

'On three, then. Come on.'

Reluctantly, Wheeler lifted his knuckles.

Sean checked the other man's eyes. *He'll choose rock*, he thought. *People used to getting their own way usually do.* 'One, two, three.' He straightened his fingers to signify paper.

The other detective only had a middle and forefinger extended. Now smiling, he made a snipping movement.

Shit, Sean thought. 'It's yours,' he stated, transferring his box to the desk. 'I'm Sean Blake, by the way.'

'Mark Wheeler.'

They were still shaking hands when the officer who'd directed them across appeared. 'Right, you've been given your login details before coming up here?'

They both nodded.

'Good. Marko, I don't need to give you the low-down of where things are.' He paused. 'In fact, you can let Sean know. It is Sean, isn't it?'

He gave a nod.

'I'm Inspector Colin Troughton, office manager. You'll be dealing mostly with me. Marko, how did that last rotation of yours go? What was it again?'

'Financial investigations, over at Chester House.'

'But you preferred the hustle and bustle of the Serious Crimes Unit?'

'Any day.'

'Well, you obviously made the right impression when you were here. Congratulations. And, Sean—' the man's voice underwent an almost imperceptible shift – 'I gather this is also your first stint as a detective constable?'

'Yes, sir. It is.' He caught the glint of something in the other man's eyes. Amusement, perhaps? Probably, Sean concluded, guessing his tie was wonky or a tuft of his wavy black hair was sticking up; it was usually doing something it shouldn't.

'There's a briefing in ten minutes, so get yourselves sorted out. I'll check the girls know what they're doing.'

Sean didn't sit down; his eyes had been drawn to the noticeboard on the end wall. A pair of photos dominated the display. The faces of two women. He already knew their names: Pamela Flood and Francesca Pinto. Pamela Flood's body had been found five days ago in the front room of the flat she rented. She was in an armchair in the front room, but that hadn't been where she'd died. Lividity beneath the skin of the buttocks and abrasions under the armpits suggested she'd been dragged into the front room and propped in the chair post-mortem. Unusual, but nothing more than that. What had pushed her death into the category of bizarre was the fact her mobile phone had then been forced so far into her mouth, it had lodged at the back of her throat.

'Hear the detail about Francesca Pinto they're holding back on?'

Sean looked across the desks. Mark flicked back his fringe of blonde hair then beckoned him towards the noticeboard.

From the facial photos alone, the contrast between the two women was obvious. Francesca Pinto looked well-off. Her skin was clear, make-up tastefully done, hair properly styled. She had been smiling when the photo – probably sourced from a partner or family member – had been taken. Her teeth were white and even. Something worth showing off. She also looked about ten years younger than Pamela Flood, though, Sean knew, they were almost the same age.

Pamela Flood looked like she'd had just about enough of life. Her skin sagged and her eyes were dull and tired. Dark curls – too regular to be natural – hung low over her forehead and each ear. Her mouth was partly open, even though she wasn't smiling. Her bottom row of teeth was visible, and they looked more like a row of rickety fence posts. Brown and with gaps.

Francesca had been found two days ago. The fact her body had been arranged in the same way as Pamela's had led to the investigating team's rapid expansion – and the two detectives' arrival that morning. Sean came to a stop beside Mark. 'Her phone was also in her mouth, wasn't it?'

'Yeah,' Mark replied, hands in pockets, eyes on Francesca's face. 'But her handset was a newer model. Bigger.'

'Bigger?' Sean glanced at his colleague, wondering how that was significant.

Mark nodded. 'To fit the phone in her mouth, her tongue had been cut out. No sign of it at the scene.'

TWO

Sean saw the number on his phone's screen and felt his shoulders sag. Mum. Ringing now, of all times. His new appointment was letting her relive her own time in the police . . . still, ignoring the call was unthinkable: she might need help. The familiar procession of grim possibilities started to parade through his mind.

Mum sprawled on the kitchen floor, her walking frame on its side.

Mum marooned midway up the stairs, the chairlift having stopped working.

Mum stranded at the end of the front door's ramp, the batteries in her wheelchair dead.

He was glad Mark Wheeler was still over at the noticeboard, now talking with a couple of detectives he must have met during his previous rotation. Turning his seat so he was facing the filing cabinet, Sean accepted the call. He could hear a low rumble and, above that, a knocking sound. It was growing more urgent. 'Mum? Everything OK?'

'Sean? Are you there?'

'Yes, Mum.' The usual surge in his temples as his heart began to thud. 'Can you hear me?'

'Oh, there you are. It's clearer now.'

'I said, is everything OK?'

'I'm on a bus, surprise, surprise. There's a terrible rattle each time we pull away. The driver says it's the panelling.'

The noise subsided.

'That's better. Can you hear me?'

He sat back, tension melting. 'So you're all right?'

'Yes, I'm fine.'

Checking no one was close enough to hear, he whispered, 'Mum, it's my first day.'

'That's why I'm ringing! To wish you luck.'

'You already did that. This morning, before I set off?'

'Well, yes. But still. So, you're there, in the incident room?'

'Yes.'

'Have you got your own work space?'

He focused on the filing cabinet inches from his face. 'Kind of.'

'And there's only one other DC brought in, aside from you?'

'Mum, I'll tell you all this later.'

'It's just . . . I'm so proud of you, Sean.'

He glanced over his shoulder. Mark was walking back towards their desks. 'Thanks. There's a briefing in about twenty seconds. Got to go.'

'Of course. Is everyone there? Who's doing the briefing?'

'Talk later, bye.'

Janet Blake continued to look at the screen of her phone even though the call to her son had ended. Detective Constable Blake. He'd kill her if he knew that's how he was now listed in her phone. Smiling to herself, she recalled the look of amazement and joy on his face when he'd been notified that, within just two months of completing his aidship to become a detective, he'd been allocated a place in the SCU, with a team working a double murder.

That smile slipped slightly when she reflected on the phone call she'd made to her old colleague at Ashton station, Tony Shipton. Tony had done well in the years since they'd walked a beat together. In fact, he'd risen to the rank of Assistant Chief Constable – one of only a handful in the whole of Greater Manchester Police. He'd always said he'd do her a favour if he ever could: now she'd cashed in that promise and got her only son a huge step up the career—

A voice further down the bus had become so loud it broke Janet's chain of thought.

'I said that to her. 'Course I did, Linds! I said to her you're bang out of order doing that and she said it was first come, first served, but she's full of shit, as we both know, so I said you got to it before Steve even put it up and you know I wanted the extra shift on that Saturday, the sneaky fucking bitch.'

Janet could have rubbed her hands together. The hours she spent going round and round bus routes had a soporific effect: conversations like this were a bloody godsend. Her wheelchair was up at the front of the bus, facing sideways towards the driver. Trying to appear casual, she took a glance at the rows of seats to her right. The bus only had a smattering of passengers. The woman was three rows back, now nodding vigorously. Pointy face, twisted in a grimace, maroon-coloured hair cut in a severe bob. With the fingers of her free hand, she was attempting to balance a packet of twenty Lambert and Butlers on the railing of the seat in front. Janet could just see the red of a lighter poking out from the woman's curled palm. She'd be lighting up the instant she got off.

The seat across the aisle was taken by a good-looking man in his mid-forties. He had on a dark green bomber jacket that was spattered with dry paint. From the frown on his face, he was unable to ignore the woman, too.

'Yes, yes, yes, and that. Yes, I know she did. I told you, Linds, she's a sneaky fucking bitch. What can I do? Steve? Soft as shit. Gives him the pout and that's it, she gets away with it every bastard time. Tomorrow? Staying in bed for most of it. Danny's not back till next week. Somewhere up near Newcastle. Yeah, house to myself. Bliss. Then I'm back in on Saturday, but only until lunch. Yeah, Linds, I know it's shit, but what—'

'Hey.'

A male voice. Word too loud to be speaking on the phone.

Janet adjusted the bulky folder of survey forms balanced across her lap and took another look. This could get interesting. The good-looking guy was leaning across the aisle towards shrew-face.

Now he'd moved, Janet could tell that, beneath the jacket's padding, the guy was heavily muscled.

'Turn it down, will you? I can hear every word of this and it's making my head ache.'

The woman lowered the phone from her face to give him an open-mouthed stare. 'You what?'

'You talking to Linds. I really don't want to know.'

'You hearing this, Linds? Some bloke's just had a pop at me. Unbelievable.'

He shook his head. 'I'm not having a pop. I'm just asking you to keep it down. The whole bus is having to listen. You're swearing like they gave out badges for it at school.'

Janet looked away so no one could see her smile. The man had a faint accent. German or similar.

'You've got a problem with me talking to my friend? How about you take your problem and fucking do one? There's plenty of other buses behind this one. If you don't like what you hear, get one of them.'

The man crossed his arms, sat back and slowly shook his head. 'You should really watch your mouth. Anyone told you that?'

'Linds, it's my stop, I'll call you back.' She stuffed the phone in her pocket and started to stand. Five feet two and stick thin. 'You fucking threatening me?'

'I didn't threaten you.'

'Yes, you fucking did.' The bus was beginning to slow as she started for the exit doors midway down the aisle. A man – late fifties, greying hair – was also getting off. Now he found himself trapped behind the woman as she turned back to the bloke in the bomber jacket. 'You should close them flappy ears of yours and button that lip. Listening in on people.'

The seated man's ears flushed red. Janet noticed they did stick out quite badly. 'No ch-ch—' he fought for his words. 'N-n-no choice, the tongue on you.'

As the bus pulled to a stop, the woman's face shone with playground glee. 'No ch-ch-ch, no ch-ch-ch. Learn to sp-sp-speak before you start on someone, dickhead!' The doors opened and she stepped off the bus. She was immediately at the window, her middle finger pressed against the glass, eyes drilling the man.

He stared straight ahead, face now poppy-red.

THREE

'First up everyone, we'll be spreading the workload a bit with some new members to the team. We have Detective Constable Mark Wheeler, who many of you will no doubt remember from his recent rotation here. A pleasure to have you back, Mark.'

He bowed his head while attempting a modest grin.

'And Detective Constable Sean Blake, who's joining us from across the river in Salford. That right, Sean?'

'Yes, sir.'

'Well, my congratulations for having survived that. Better class of criminal in Manchester proper, we like to think.'

A few people chuckled and Sean managed a smile.

'Next, we have two CSWs to join Maggie's team. Helen Johnson and Katie May. Have I got that right?'

Sean looked to the side of the room. Both women were nodding back. Sean noticed that Katie was blushing. Their eyes touched and he gave her an encouraging nod.

'Good. Welcome all. Now, to business.' The officer half turned to the noticeboard. 'I called this briefing a bit later because we were waiting for approval on the warrant for Pamela Flood's sometime partner, Ian Cahill.'

He tapped the mug shot of a nasty-looking bloke that had been pinned alongside the image of the murdered woman.

'We now have that. Word came in that Cahill's been using a property in Middleton. He's there right now, tucked up in a nice warm bed. We have a car outside his house. As you're aware, Cahill is already well-known to us. Previous convictions include ones for assault, so a Tactical Aid Unit will be going in to make the actual arrest. We'll have a presence there as back up and to go straight in and search the property once Cahill's been carted off.'

He consulted a clipboard on the table beside him.

'Detectives Fuller, Morris and Moor, it's your lucky day.' He paused as a thought occurred, then his eyes cut to Mark Wheeler and Sean Blake. 'You two? Are you up to date with your officer safety training?'

Sean nodded, as did Mark.

'Good. Nothing like a live op for bonding a team: you're coming, too. Stab-proof vests for everyone at the scene. DS Fuller? We'll need the evidence collecting kit.'

He lifted an arm and rotated a wrist to expose his watch. 'The TAU boys have a rendezvous at the end of Cahill's road in twenty, so we need to get going. Two cars, myself and DS Fuller driving. The rest of you? Keep to your allocated actions and I'll see you back here soon.'

'Sir?'

Sean glanced across to see that a stoutly built female in a brown skirt and white blouse had asked the question.

'Yes, DS Dragomir?'

'Has anything to connect Cahill to Francesca Pinto yet come to light?'

Sean let his gaze linger on the woman for a second longer. Her light brown hair was cut in a short, sensible style and the frames of her glasses seemed too thick. The accent, he guessed, was Eastern European. Bulgaria, Slovenia or something similar.

The leading officer looked briefly at Pinto's photo, as if the murder victim was able to hear his answer. 'Woodhill's – the firm of solicitors where Francesca worked – are still checking their records to pinpoint when and where she and Cahill crossed paths. It won't take long to dig the information out.'

Sean found himself in the back of a dark green Volvo being driven at an uncomfortably fast pace by DS Fuller. The flesh at the base of his skull bulged out above his thick neck. Directly in front of them was an identical vehicle that contained Detective Chief Inspector Ransford and Detective Constables Morris and Moor.

Sean kept glancing down at his hands, disappointed how they were slightly sweaty. He couldn't quite believe they were on their way to arresting the prime suspect in a double murder case. It was exciting – but it also felt surreal.

He glanced up to see Fuller's beady eyes on him in the rear-view mirror. 'All right back there?'

Sean gave a silent nod, before deciding a proper reply was more appropriate. 'Yeah, fine thanks.'

'Good stuff. You were looking a bit queasy for a second. You don't get carsick, do you?'

'No. Just . . .'

'Feeling like you've been swept up in a whirlwind?'

'Yes.'

Fuller nodded. 'It's not always like this, believe me. But we don't believe in comfort zones in the SCU. Or passengers. Especially not passengers. Keep on your toes, always show willing, and you'll fit right in.' His head turned towards the front seat where Mark Wheeler sat. 'So, Marko, fraud investigations not your cup of tea?'

Mark lifted his chin and directed a relaxed smile towards the vehicle's ceiling. He was, Sean thought, like a star pupil. Football captain, head of year and an A-grade student, all rolled into one. Someone being groomed for the top.

'Too much sitting at a desk, staring at numbers. I was nearly nodding off.'

Fuller grinned. 'Yeah, bollocks to that. Bringing in the bad guys: nothing beats it.'

They hit a knot of traffic that slowed them to crawling pace. Sean let his gaze trail along the pavement beyond his window. A solitary schoolboy was cramming a cereal bar into his mouth, his book bag almost sliding off the hunched shoulder of a too-big blazer. *I remember that*, Sean thought. During his school years, there often wasn't enough milk in the fridge for them both. Since Janet was housebound during most of that time, he'd just grab something from the corner shop and stuff it on his way to school.

Next, he saw a man in his early thirties looking stressed. In one hand was a bunch of keys he was managing to jangle loudly with every rushed step. He made a woman going in the opposite direction pause by positioning himself in her path. Words were rapidly spoken. The woman shook her head apologetically, having to step round him. He raised a hand in passive protest then continued on his way.

Their car moved forward and Sean twisted in his seat, certain he'd seen the bloke somewhere before. They reached a set of lights and rolled to a stop. Sean realized, in a few more seconds, the man would catch them up. He half lowered his window to listen.

'Excuse me, love. Love? Listen, I'm really sorry, but I just came out of a job interview and my car's been towed! I'm fifty pence short for the bus fare out to the compound. That's all.'

The Northern Irish accent put a drawl on his little speech, as if – given a choice – his words would be happier to stay in his mouth. Sean took another look: Daniel Thompson. The straggly hair might have been grown out, but no doubt it was him. *It must have been*, Sean thought, *ten months since I arrested him for breaking into an amusement arcade.* The poor bloke had crowbarred an entire row of fruit machines open, all of which had been emptied earlier that afternoon. Crime was never going to make him rich, that was for sure.

'Ah, cheers, love. You're a saviour, seriously.'

Thompson waited a couple of seconds then began to manoeuvre himself into the path of someone new.

'Really sorry, pal. I just came out of a job interview to find my car's been towed. Thing is, I need—'

'Thompson!'

His head whipped round.

Sean had already wound the window fully down. Using two fingers, he drew a bead from his eyes across to the other man. *I'm watching you.*

Thompson blinked a couple of time before realization dawned. 'Constable Bl—' He swiftly regained his composure. 'Day off, is it. No uniform?'

Sean brought him closer by crooking a finger. 'Bought yourself a car and learned to drive since you got out?'

Thompson smiled sheepishly. 'You're a sharp one, Constable Blake. It's my cousin's. I only borrowed it, you see.'

'That right? So what's the make?'

'It's a you know – one of them Japanese ones . . . Toyota?'

Sean's eyes were on the set of keys. 'Really? Because I don't see a fob for a Toyota in your—'

'Hey!' Fuller barked. He was peering between the two front seats, hostile stare on Thompson.

The young man had to bend down to make eye contact. 'All right, over there?'

'Fuck off.'

The friendly twinkle vanished from Thompson's eyes and he immediately stepped back, a wheedling note lifting his voice. 'No need to get all—'

Fuller accelerated through the green lights, now using the rearview mirror to look at Sean. 'Who was that?'

'I crossed paths with him a bit when I was working in the Pendleton nick.'

'Yeah?' Fuller didn't sound interested. 'Forget lowlifes like him, DC Blake. They're not your shout anymore.'

Sean leaned forward. 'Even if he's right in front of me, ripping folks off?'

Fuller sighed. 'Small fry. Not your concern.' He floated a faint smile in Mark Wheeler's direction.

Sean was just able to see his fellow detective constable's eyebrows lift in tacit agreement. *Cheers for that buddy*, thought Sean, sitting back.

'So,' Mark announced, 'how come this guy is our man?'

'Cahill?' Fuller shoved his bottom lip out. 'Pamela Flood had taken out a restraining order on him. CCTV from a camera on the house a few doors down from hers shows Cahill making his way along the street at three in the morning. One of those infrared jobs; got him plain as day.'

'When was this?'

'Hours before she was killed. He shouldn't have been within a kilometre of her house and, when originally questioned, claimed that was the case. We now also know he called her earlier that evening.'

'You managed to pull in his phone records?'

'No. With it being a murder investigation, we obtained all of hers. He rang asking to be taken back. They ended up having a proper go at each other. By the end of the call, he's threatening to kill her.'

'Actual threat?'

'"I will slit your fucking throat."'

'The romantic old so-and-so.'

Fuller laughed.

The rear of Cahill's property ended at a five-foot-high wooden fence. Fuller peered over it then sank back down out of sight. 'All the curtains upstairs are drawn. Bloke's about to get the mother of all wake-up calls.' He tried the back gate and found it wasn't locked. 'Result. We'll get closer. If he does exit the property, we can bring him down before he takes a step.'

Before leaving the station, they'd all changed into casual clothes and trainers. Sean's stab-proof vest was digging into his armpits.

He sank to his haunches and tugged at its lower edge. Beside him, Mark Wheeler moved an extendable baton from hand to hand. *Finally*, Sean thought, *a trace of nerves. Just a trace, but enough to prove he's human.*

DS Fuller checked his watch. 'Right, thirty-six seconds and the front goes in. We'll hear a load of shouting as the TAU pile up the stairs. Let's get in position.'

As he slipped through the half-open gate, the first thing Sean noticed was a children's trampoline. Way too big for the garden, it was practically touching the back of the modest property. In the other corner was a small conservatory, double doors that, when open, would give access to a cramped patio. Empty beer bottles and cans floated in the tray of a rusty barbecue.

Moving quickly, they approached the house and pressed themselves against the rear wall, out of sight of anyone peering from a first-floor window. DS Fuller gave a thumbs up, then mouthed he was checking the side of the property for any door there. He skirted carefully round the trampoline and disappeared from sight.

Sean frowned. What was a trampoline doing in the garden? In the briefing at the end of the road, he was sure it had been stated Cahill lived alone. There were no kids in—

A massive bang sent a tremor through the bricks behind him. Another. The TAU had started swinging their Enforcer against the front door. *Must have extra locks on it*, thought Sean, looking up to see a bedroom window had swung open. A pair of bare feet then lower legs, calf muscles stained by tattoos, appeared.

Another bang, this one accompanied by the sound of splintering wood.

Above him he could now see muscular thighs, then black boxer shorts with the words Calvin Klein repeating round the waistband. From inside the house, a chorus of shouts.

Police! Do not move! Stay still! Police!

The muffled thud of boots going up the stairs. Sean looked down; the trampoline was directly beneath the window. Cahill's legs were now fully out. His lower back appeared as he started sliding himself across the windowsill.

'He's going to jump down!' Sean yelled, trying to drag the trampoline away from the house. But the metal frame's lower edge came up against the patio. The trampoline abruptly halted and

Sean fell back into a sitting position. Next to him, Mark Wheeler was fumbling with the release mechanism of his baton.

Now hanging by just the fingertips of one hand, Cahill twisted and dropped, knees flexing as he made contact with the elasticated surface. The next thing he was launched forward, directly at Mark. The two men went down, arms and legs intertwined. Cahill's right elbow came back and he started peppering Mark's neck with pathetic little rabbit punches.

Sean scrambled on to all fours, ready to dive at Cahill. Each time the man's elbow came back, an arc of blood followed it. Was there a weapon in Cahill's fist?

Mark's arms fell away, allowing Cahill to raise himself to his knees. His head swivelled. Flecks of red covered his face and neck and the whites of his eyes seemed too bright. Time seemed to slow down as Sean stared back. From Mark's mouth came the sound of a bath draining dry.

A voice, from the open window above. 'Get him!'

Cahill's eyes lifted and a stubby screwdriver with a sharpened point fell from his grip.

'Get him! Move!'

As Cahill started sprinting towards the open gate, Sean jumped to his feet. He took a step forward but the sight of Mark Wheeler stopped him. The skin of his colleague's face was like greaseproof paper. His eyes had rolled up into his head and the spurts of blood coming from the side of his neck were rapidly losing strength.

A compress. He needed a compress. Something to cover all the wounds at once. He began tugging the Velcro straps at the waist of his stab-proof vest. Beneath it he was wearing a cotton sweatshirt. That would have to do.

He felt himself being shoved aside as DS Fuller's voice rang out. 'Paramedics, paramedics, we need paramedics!'

FOUR

J ust before nine thirty in the morning: the perfect time to pay someone a visit. Those with jobs were confined to their workplaces, children were shut away in school, retired folk had yet to venture out. The streets were quiet and, more importantly, there was room to park.

He swung his white Peugeot van into a space further down the road from flat 54a. On the passenger seat beside him was a package, complete with label, which he'd prepared the night before. Once he knew her address, finding her name on the internet had taken no time at all.

After checking the pavement was free of people, he pulled the baseball cap low on his head, picked up the package and his console from the passenger seat and climbed out of the van.

Yesterday, when he'd followed the woman home from the bus, he'd been able to get a good look at where she lived. A ground-floor flat of a semi-detached house. A huge caravan occupied every inch of one neighbour's drive. The other was screened off by a laurel hedge at least eight foot high. The chances of being observed were minimal.

He walked with purpose; a man with a schedule to keep. Head down, he marched up to the front door and pressed the bell. Waiting for an answer, he contemplated her behaviour the previous day on the bus.

Her screeching voice and the foul language she'd flung around. No better than an ape soiling its cage. He felt his grip tightening on the package and had to relax his fingers before he damaged it. *Come on! Drag your lazy carcass out of bed.* He pressed the bell again. Women who thought they could talk to men like that. How he loathed them. He thought about the crude, raucous females who'd started to attend his classes at the academy.

They weren't interested in learning how to be electricians. To them, his classes were just an opportunity for idle chat, flirting and playing on their phones. The moment his hand struck the feisty little blonde's face was still crystal clear in his mind. Her look of utter shock, a sweet moment of silence – then chaos.

'*Oh my God!*'
'*No way!*'
'*You cannot do that!*'
'*Did he just hit Shelley?*'
'*Get her away from her, man!*'
'*You are bang out of order!*'
'*Shelley, are you OK?*'
'*A slap? You are in deep shit.*'
'*He actually hit her?*'

'*I said get away from her!*'

'*I can't believe this!*'

'*Come on, Shelley, we're getting out of here.*'

The clatter of plastic wheels approached along the pavement behind him. He kept his back to the street, bowed his head and remained very still. The adoring murmurs of a mum as she passed the end of the drive, a buggy pushed before her. If she had seen him on the front step, all she'd have clocked was a dark blue uniform.

He pressed the bell a third time and kept his finger on it.

A shadow shifted beyond the frosted glass. A pinkish blur materialized from the gloom and he heard the shuffle of her feet. 'Yes, all right! Stop the fucking ringing!'

He lowered his finger and waited.

Her voice, ragged and irritated, came through the door. 'Who is it?'

'Signed-for package. Julie Roe?'

The lock rattled and the door swung open. She was in a hideous dressing gown the colour of bubble-gum, bare feet and ankles in view. Her eyes were puffy and that absurd maroon hair stuck out at one side. If she remembered him from the bus, it certainly didn't show on her face.

One hand was pinching the sides of her dressing gown tight at the base of her throat. Her other hand held a mobile phone. Even as she spoke, she couldn't help checking its screen. 'A package?'

Christ, he thought. *Conscious for less than a minute and already glued to the bloody thing.*

'That's correct. It's signed-for. If I could just get a signature from you, here?'

She wrenched her eyes from her phone, blinked a couple of times and then coughed. He tasted her stale breath in his mouth. 'Who's it from?'

'No idea. I just require a signature on the console.'

'Had to come on my day off,' she murmured. 'Fucking typical.' She held a hand out.

'Thank you.' He slid the stylus from its clip.

FIVE

The handset gave his mum's voice a plastic buzz. He sighed, eyes fixed on the ceiling above his bed. He'd been awake for hours.

'Sean?'

He let his head fall to the side. The little walkie-talkie on the bedside table made it easy for her to get his attention, wherever either of them was in the house. At times like these, he wished he'd never had the idea of getting them. He wished he was asleep. He wished he could turn over and pretend the previous day had never happened. Why did he even try and become a detective so early in his career? But he knew the answer to that.

'Sean?'

He'd been so close to getting his stab-proof vest off.

'Sean, it's after nine o'clock. You can't still be—'

'Morning, Mum.' He was up on one elbow, handset held before his face.

'Good morning to you. There's a cup of tea for you down here, and I'm doing some eggs.'

'I'll be there in a minute.'

He dropped the handset on the duvet and leaned his head back. The images refused to fade: blood bubbling from Mark Wheeler's parted lips. Miniature geysers spurting from his neck. Four or five. The wet hiss each eruption had made. When DS Fuller had looked up to shout, Sean saw that Mark's blood had hit him in the face. A dribble on his chin had made Fuller look like he'd been feeding on the stricken officer.

The journey back to the station had been oddly silent, even though everyone in the car had been speaking. Then he'd been led up the stairs to a small meeting room. Ransford spoke to him briefly before making way for two other men. Forms were laid out in front of him. A drink appeared. Hot chocolate, like he was a child. Eventually, Ransford came back.

He was carrying two written statements. One from the TAU

officer who'd shouted down from the bedroom window and one
from DS Fuller. The TAU officer had stated that, when he looked
into the back garden, Sean had been partly under the trampoline.
It appeared he was trying to avoid tackling Cahill, who had leaped
down from the first-floor window.

'No,' Sean replied. 'That's not right. I was trying to drag it out
into the garden. I saw Cahill coming out of the first-floor window
and was trying to cut off his escape route.'

'And when he attacked DC Wheeler, you failed to act
because . . .?'

'Failed to act? It happened so fast. Cahill let go of the window
ledge. From my position on the grass, I saw the underside of the
trampoline stretch down. Next thing—'

'You were beneath the trampoline?'

'Partly. I fell back as I was trying to pull it away from the wall.'

Ransford didn't look impressed. 'Carry on.'

'Next thing, they're both beside me on the grass. I thought it
was his fist connecting with Mark's neck area. It was only when
I saw blood—'

'The TAU officer stated that, even after Cahill dropped the
implement, he had to instruct you to prevent his escape.'

'I . . . well . . . I was about to.'

'But only after he'd shouted at you?'

'I'm not sure.' Sean could hear his voice starting to waver. 'I
mean, I was getting to my feet, about to give chase.'

'But then you stopped.'

'When I saw the extent of Mark's injuries, yes.'

Ransford shuffled the sheets of paper in his hand. 'DS Fuller
states that, when he entered the back garden from the side area
of the property, there was no sign of Cahill and you were, I
quote, "frozen". Looking down at Wheeler – nothing more.'

'No, that's not right, either. I knew the flow of blood had to be
stemmed. But there were multiple puncture wounds, all close
together. Pressing down on one would only widen the adjacent ones.
That's exactly what happened when DS Fuller applied his hands to
the wounds. I was attempting to remove my stab-proof vest so I
could create a compress with the sweatshirt I had on underneath.
At that point, a TAU officer arrived with a first-aid kit.'

'This was when DC Wheeler entered cardiac arrest?'

Sean nodded.

Ransford was silent for a few seconds. 'I see.'

Sean watched him as he reread what was on the sheets of paper in his hand. 'I think we need to hear from Mark Wheeler. He's the only person who can clear this up properly, and that's obviously not . . . listen, this hasn't been easy for anyone. I think it's best you head home, have some time to get your head straight. I'll contact you tomorrow.'

The walk to his desk felt like he was wading through treacle. Everyone was engrossed in their tasks: on phones, studying screens, consulting with colleagues. Eyes flicked to him for a second, then moved away.

Only the woman – Dragmar? – had come across. She'd placed a hand on his shoulder, asked how he was. As he'd made his way to the main doors, he noticed Fuller was at his desk. The man kept his eyes averted. So did DCs Morris and Moor.

The walkie-talkie clicked. 'Sean?'

He retrieved the handset. 'Coming.'

'Have you got the radio on up there?'

'No.'

'There's just been an announcement about Mark Wheeler. He's not dead. Critical, but he's alive.'

Sean sat up properly. 'He is?'

'They just said so. On BBC Radio Manchester.'

'He's alive? They said that?'

'Yes!'

Sean bowed his head in thanks.

SIX

S he lay on the floor like a shop dummy, arms and legs still vibrating from the charge. Funny how they did that, he thought, closing the front door behind him.

Knowing her muscles would cease to spasm in another few seconds, he hooded her then drew the string tight about her throat. He preferred an opaque bag: see-through ones allowed eye contact, which wasn't pleasant.

A moment of welcome silence, as if she was thinking. Then the thin polythene began to crater across her mouth as she tried to drag in air. The crinkly noise sped up and he held her arms tight at her sides. Next, the legs started to thrash, heels hammering against the carpet.

Not long now.

He took the opportunity for a look around. The lounge was immediately to his right. Big telly and fat sofa. No sign of any books, as expected. A framed photo on the wall at the base of the stairs. Her and a female friend sipping from cocktails in a neon-lit bar. A closed door to his left with a cheap plastic plaque.

Salle de Bains.

He didn't think she'd have spoken French. Probably just a memento from a holiday. Maybe the Danny she'd mentioned on the bus had treated her to a city break. An EasyJet flight to Paris, or Nice, or maybe that place over on the east coast. The one popular with lots of British.

The thump of her feet was growing less insistent.

Nantes, that was it. Convenient for getting to the coast. There was an island you could get a ferry to. Pleasant place, though a bit crowded. Very nice beaches.

She became still, at last.

As he'd walked up to her front door, he'd noticed the front room curtains were drawn. So he rose to his feet and, humming to himself, wandered in. On the table before the telly was an empty bottle of wine and four – no, five – cans of vodka and cranberry. Two were lying on their sides. An ashtray crowded with butts.

As he'd thought, not a single book in the place. All the shelving unit in the corner contained were DVDs. *Friends. League of Gentlemen. Twilight. Pretty Woman. Mean Girls.* All the signs of a slovenly lifestyle.

The armchair was ideal, though. High backed and with wide armrests. Getting her in a good position would be easy.

He went back into the hallway, loosened the string and slid the bag off her head. *Not got much to say now, have you?* Miniscule blossoms of blood, fragile as snowflakes, dotted her eyeballs. Sadly, they'd soon lose definition to become ugly smears.

He reached into the pocket of the dressing gown to remove her phone. It was long and narrow. Even though her mouth could accommodate it quite comfortably, he'd already made the decision about taking their tongues.

The sight of them, in their jars on the shelf in his garage, was something he liked to . . . he searched for the appropriate word. Savour? He almost smiled. Very droll. His first attempt had been clumsy. For a start, he'd only realized it would be necessary to cut it out after he'd propped her in the chair. He'd not come equipped with a knife, so had ended up searching through her kitchen and she didn't have one with a serrated edge.

As with everything in life, he said to himself, *you could improve.* That was something he always told his students. He removed the side of the console and laid the panel on the floor. Taped to its inner surface was a wooden-handled fold-out knife. He liked its design, especially the small, crescent-shaped groove on one side of the blade. He inserted the nail of his thumb into it and pulled the six-inch length of metal clear. A row of tiny teeth ran along its lower edge.

SEVEN

His mum was at the cooker, slowly circling a wooden spatula in a shallow pan. Scrambled eggs. Something she always did when she felt he needed pepping up.

Her left forearm was resting across the top of her walking frame and her right hip was jutting out. He wondered how long she'd been on her feet; too much standing and her lower back would be making her wince by lunchtime.

'I can do that, Mum.'

She spoke over her shoulder. 'The toast's about to pop up. You can be in charge of that.'

'Sure?'

'Yes, this is almost ready.'

A brief clank from the toaster proved her timing was spot-on. They both worked in silence for a while as the radio played a tune. Once the toast was buttered, he laid the slices on a plate and took a seat. At the scrape of his chair, she turned the gas off and lifted the pan from the hob. A well-oiled routine. The kitchen was small enough for her to be able to place the pan on the table without taking a step.

'Cheers, Mum.' He tipped the pan up and the scrambled eggs slid onto his toast. After taking a sip of tea, he reached for the pepper.

'Tracksuit?'

He glanced up to see her manoeuvring herself down opposite him. 'No point in getting dressed properly. They told me to take some time off.'

'Some?'

'I'm not sure. He said he'd be in touch.'

'And do you feel the need to be at home?'

He hunched a shoulder. 'I'm certainly not feeling one hundred per cent. Not after what happened.'

'I'm sure the rest of the team isn't, either. They will have been working until god-knows-when. And they'll be back in there now, you can be sure of that.'

It occurred to him that, as he'd left the office, DS Fuller had been at his desk. DCs Morris and Moor were at theirs, too. They'd all been busily working. Playing their part. Was he the only one who Ransford had sent home?

She tipped her head towards the radio. 'Your colleague survived. That weight is lifted.'

'Yeah, but . . .' He shook his head. 'We went over all this yesterday.'

'We did – and what happened in that back garden was not your fault.'

'You might think that.'

'And if you suspect people on your team think differently, that's all the more reason to be in. You have to get things straight with Ransford, and fast. Fight your corner, Sean!'

He took a gulp of tea. She was right. She was always bloody right.

'Sean, you had a shocker of a first day. I know that. But what they'll be looking for now? A willingness to get stuck in, believe me. And you're not showing that by sitting here . . .'

'Feeling sorry for myself. Right?'

She pursed her lips. 'I didn't say that. We all have set backs, we all have things go wrong. But it's how—'

'We deal with them that counts.' *Number two from Mum's list of favourite speeches*, he thought. The prospect of stepping back into the incident room turned his stomach. He gave up sawing through his toast and took another gulp of tea instead. 'Think about it this way, then,' she announced. 'The bastard tried to kill one of yours. Everyone – and I mean everyone, Sean – now has one thing on their mind: catching him.'

His mind turned to what had happened to his mum. The incident that had ended her career in the police had very nearly killed her. As a teenager, he'd spent far too much time imagining scenarios where he got revenge on the driver. If she was deliberately trying to stir up those memories, it had certainly worked. He pushed his breakfast aside. 'I'm going back.'

He kept his eyes on Inspector Troughton's desk as he made his way across the incident room. Half the people present were too busy to notice his arrival. Now closer, he realized the person the office manager was speaking to was DCI Ransford. Sean fought the urge to slow down. It would be so easy to alter direction and avoid this. As he reached the office manager's desk, the two men looked up.

'Sir,' Sean announced, addressing his DCI, 'I'm reporting for duty.'

Ransford cocked an eyebrow. 'I signed you off.'

'Can't sit at home, sir. Not with this going on.'

'You feel OK?'

'I'm fine.'

Ransford held his eyes for a moment longer. If he was convinced, it wasn't showing. If anything, he looked slightly irritated. 'Very well.'

'Anything more on Mark?'

'Still sedated and will be for a while. Could be nerve damage, could be a lot of things.'

Sean gave a solitary nod. 'Can I have a word in private at some point, sir?'

Ransford shook his head. 'Not now, DC Blake. Maybe later.'

Troughton pointed to the corner workstation. 'Take a seat, I'll be across.'

Sean turned swiftly to catch the tail-end of DS Fuller's hostile stare.

On reaching his workstation, Sean stole a glance to Mark Wheeler's side. The cardboard box was still there. Sean could see the tips of three trophies inside. *I've never won a bloody trophy for anything*, Sean thought, as he removed his jacket. He draped it over the back of the chair and squeezed into the narrow space. It felt like eating alone in a busy restaurant. Certain the whole room was watching, he turned his computer on and logged in. As he contemplated what the hell to do next, Troughton appeared.

'I doubt you've heard about Cahill.'

Sean looked up. 'No – the radio didn't mention any arrest.'

'That's because he got away. Once out that back garden, he vaulted over into a neighbour's and, two more gardens along, got lucky: their garage was open. We think he took some overalls, a pair of work boots and a jacket. After that, we're struggling.'

'Jesus,' Sean whispered. 'He vanished?'

Troughton placed a pile of printouts on Sean's desk. 'We could do with these being checked.'

Sean gave him a quizzical look.

'Bank and credit card statements, plus expense account records for Francesca Pinto. Anything to indicate contact with Ian Cahill. Funds to or from a source with no clear reference – you know the stuff. Flag up anything iffy. Come back to me if you can't pinpoint what it is.'

Sean wasn't sure what to say. This was the sort of work normally allocated to a civilian support worker. 'Aren't we getting out there and trying to locate Cahill?'

'Oh, there are plenty of detectives doing that. But DCI Ransford said you're to stay in here.'

Sean hunched over the paperwork; his face felt like it could have lit the room. Judgement had obviously been passed and they didn't think he could be relied on out in the field.

He was almost at the end of the second sheet when a commotion broke out on the far side of the room. An officer was on his feet, hand waving in the air. *Cahill*, thought Sean. *Have they found him already?*

Ransford appeared from his side office. 'What is it?'

'Call patched over from Trafford Division, sir! The body of an adult female has just been found. Same as Flood and Pinto.'

EIGHT

The electric hum rose as the train's speed increased. Beyond the plate glass, the end of the platform slid by faster and faster. Around him, people were settling into their seats, arranging what they needed for the journey ahead.

A two-tone note sounded and a voice announced that the next station would be Stockport. He liked travelling on trains, the reassuring way they powered along, the calming effect of the carriage as it gently rocked. Train journeys, he concluded, should be tranquil experiences – and they would be but for stupid women who insisted on speaking.

He closed his eyes and listened to the wash of voices around him. Two females, in seats somewhere ahead.

'Hang on, how could it go back into my account?'

'When it happened to me, it's recredited automatically. It's very quick, she said. About thirty seconds.'

'Really?'

'Yes.'

'Thirty seconds?'

'I don't know how they do it, but it's very quick.'

'That is quick. I wonder if it even spilled out? Maybe it was the bank's money, not mine. There was nothing on my statement about it coming out.'

'I don't know how they do these things, but it is very quick. She said that.'

'Recredited?'

'Yes.'

He turned his head slightly, better to zone in on a male voice to his left.

'Can Gavin put that information somewhere near the end of the presentation? Second to last slide, maybe. For today, yes. No. The client will want it as a PDF.'

Deeper, modulated, authoritative: the sound of men's voices didn't bother him. From somewhere in front, he picked out another female voice.

'Butter on crumpets, jam on bagels, you silly so-and-so! If the butter's dripping, that's good, that's part of it. There's damp there again already? In that same corner? I can get it on the way home. Yes, Dettol, I know.'

A phone rang and he heard a new voice, female, soft and close behind him.

'Hi there. Oh, right. Well, he's the one who started last week. Matt. No not him. The taller one. Fair-haired. Yes, him. Well, we said to him, if he's going to be rude, it can't be to customers. Us? It's water off a duck's back with us, but not customers. No, I don't think he will. Or he just won't come back Monday, probably that.'

He opened his eyes. There was nothing of interest here. He contemplated walking through to the next carriage and listening in there. But the train was already starting to slow. Instead, he decided to disembark at Stockport. Dozens of local stopping services passed through the station. He could transfer to a different line and roam about for hours. After all, now his teaching career was over, he had all day. Sooner or later, some crass bitch would cross his path. Someone who needed to be silenced. Destiny had guaranteed it.

He stood, turned round and started making his way towards the doors. The woman who'd been talking about Matt was in her late thirties, with a round face and sloping shoulders. As more of her came into view, he saw the ponderous breasts and bulging stomach. The fingers holding the phone were pudgy. She wore a wedding ring. Glancing up, she caught his eye and automatically smiled.

He didn't know what it was about his face that made so many people do that. Especially females. Over the course of his life, more than one woman had described his eyes as kind. The only woman he'd come close to feeling affection for – aside from Mother – had said he had puppy-dog eyes. When he'd asked her what that meant, she'd said he looked a little bit lost. Like he could do with a hug. He hadn't liked the implication of that.

The woman who was on her phone reminded him of the principal at the Lightwater Academy who'd been engineering his removal from his job. Katherine Harpham. He positioned himself before the doors, as the train's speed ebbed. Her infuriating self-importance. Her lavender lipstick and honeysuckle scent. All the times she'd phoned, summoning him to her office. The whine of her voice worming its way down his ear canal and into his brain. In high-pitched, fake-apologetic tones, she'd described the series of measures she was being forced to put in place. He knew they were designed solely to make him fail. Courses in equality, diversity awareness and gender relations. Claptrap, the lot of them. Reapplying for his old job, altering the department to make one teacher superfluous to the college's needs . . .

Then he'd struck the female student and none of it mattered.

When he'd started teaching the NVQ in Electrotechnical Services, it had all been lads. Behaviour was rarely an issue. They might have larked about and swore a bit, but it was nothing he couldn't put right. The student he'd hit? She'd deserved it.

As the flat of his hand made contact with her face, it created a sound that was so sharp. Every other noise in his classroom had been cut dead. In that tiny moment of time, he wasn't sure if the hand that had done it was his. Her eyes were wide, mouth hanging open. The phone he'd caught her using beneath the desk clattered to the floor. A surge of adrenaline almost lifted him towards the ceiling. He felt immense. *That shut you up*, he'd wanted to shout. *That put an end to your denials. Your foul-mouthed lies.*

But before the words could leave his mouth, other people had butted in. Voices from all sides. People jostling him. Other females whisked their weeping friend from the room. Male students squared up to him, outraged at what he'd done. And the little shit in the corner who was filming the entire thing kept laughing.

As he looked at his reflection in the glass, the train came to a stop. He had no idea where the student was now, but he knew exactly where to find Katherine Harpham. Yes, he knew all about her pretty little cottage with its rose bushes and the secluded lane that led to it. It wouldn't take him long to drive out there. Not long at all. To see her features transform as electricity charged through her . . .

'Excuse me, are you getting off?'

His eyes refocused. The doors were open. On the platform was an elderly woman in a long beige coat. It looked expensive: cashmere, probably.

'You're in the way,' she declared impatiently. 'Are you staying on or getting off?'

He stepped down and as he passed her, bent to within whispering distance of her ear. 'Slut.'

'I beg your pardon? What was that? What did you just—'

But he was already trotting down the stairs into the underpass.

Sean regarded the sheath of printouts. The firm of twenty-four-hour solicitors Francesca Pinto worked for had found the time she'd been on duty when Cahill had been arrested: it had been almost three years ago. She hadn't gone on to represent him in court, but that's when contact between them had occurred.

All her records from that point had been obtained. She had two bank accounts and three credit cards. So far, all he'd established was that she was a creature of habit: a big shop at Sainsbury's each Saturday. A few bits from M&S on a Sunday. Lunch purchased on a Wednesday, Thursday and Friday from Pret or Philpotts. A couple of drinks on a Thursday, usually Gino's or sometimes, the Sky Bar.

Standing orders and direct debits seemed entirely regular: gas, electricity, water and council tax. Monthly gym membership with the YMCA in Castlefield. Five pounds a month to WaterAid, three pounds a month to the Tiger Trust.

He flagged up a few one-off transactions that would need to be checked.

£184 to Cross Lane Enterprises, last May.

£76 to BDDO in June.

£237 received from CP in September.

All the while, he kept sneaking glances to the main grouping of workstations where the rest of the detectives worked. Most of them were empty. He knew where they'd be: banging on the doors of all Cahill's known associates. *Where is he? Tell us what you know. The longer this takes the more grief you'll get. Knocking on your door, ringing your phone, watching you in the street, turning up at your local. It will not end.*

Those not scouring the city for Cahill were at the latest victim's house. Sean had only been able to overhear that she was young. Early twenties. Her dad had found her.

Sean had started to glance over the credit card statements when he noticed someone approaching his desk. The female detective with the foreign name.

'Hello, DC Blake, are you well today?'

The way she spoke made it obvious that her English had been formally learned.

'Yes, fine, thanks.' He waggled a finger above the paperwork. 'Going through all this.'

'Yes. You haven't moved all morning. Have you been told where the nearest toilets are? Or where you can find a drink?'

That, he recalled, had been Mark Wheeler's job yesterday. 'No, but don't worry. I spotted the canteen on the ground—'

'There is one much closer. On this floor. It's smaller, but you can usually get a seat.' She kept looking at him. 'I'll show you?'

'Oh, OK. Thanks.'

He tried to think of something to say as they walked down the corridor.

'When did you join, Sean?'

'A few years ago, but I've been involved since my teens. First, in the police cadets, then a spell volunteering as a special constable.'

'Your mission in life, then?' She smiled.

'Well, my mum was an officer. Here, in the GMP.'

'Yes, a sergeant, like me. But not a detective.'

He turned his head. 'Did you work with her?'

'No, but I know of her. She is a bit of a legend. Is it true that, on her beat, she knew everyone by their first name?'

'I think that's been a bit exaggerated. But she worked her area of Salford long enough to know a lot of them.'

'The days when we actually had proper contact with the community. How times change. What happened to her was truly terrible.'

Sean wasn't sure how to respond.

'When something like that happens, the officer's name sticks.' She pushed open a set of double doors on the left. 'Toilets through there.' A doorway was in the corner. 'The coffee bar is staffed until three o'clock each day. After that, it's the machines.'

He took in a row of vending machines lining one wall. 'OK.'

She came to a stop at the counter. 'What will you have?'

'You're all right,' he replied, patting a pocket. *Idiot*, he thought. *No change and my cards are back in the incident room.*

'This is on me, don't worry.' She turned to the woman standing by the till. 'Hi Anita, one cappuccino. Sean?'

'Thanks. The same, please.'

He looked towards the tables and saw DS Fuller and DC Morris

hunched over, heads almost touching. He quickly turned away
before they caught him staring.

'So – your surname. Drag . . .'

'Omir. Magda Dragomir. I'm from Romania, originally.'

'Really?' Immediately, he knew he'd spoken with too much
enthusiasm.

She was looking at him expectantly now. 'You know Romania,
Sean?'

'Me? Not really . . .'

'You could also be from that part of the world. With your . . .
heavy bones. Here and here.' She ran the tips of her fingers
across her eyebrow and then round to her cheekbone.

'Is that right?' he almost laughed.

'And the dark hair. It's very common in the region. Is your
father the same?'

The question caught him by surprise. He floundered for his words.
'My father? Well . . .' All he had was an old photo of the man.

'Sorry,' she cut in. 'I am always so nosy. But you know Romania?'

'Only to read about.'

'You read about Romania?' She looked puzzled.

There was no way of avoiding the question. Not without
appearing evasive. 'The Carpathian Mountains. It's a very interesting area.'

She placed a hand on her hip and cocked her head to the side.
'Come on! You're not one of those Gothics, are you?' Her gaze
lifted. 'Is that lovely thick hair of yours dyed black?'

He couldn't help warm to her direct style. Anyone from Britain
would have edged closer to that question bit by bit. 'No, it's not.
And you mean Goths?'

'The ones who wear black clothes and big clunky boots?'

'Yes. Why would you think I'm a Goth?'

'Transylvania is in the Carpathian Mountains. Vampires? Count
Dracula's castle?' She scrutinized his hair another time.

'No,' he grinned. 'But I do like wolves. The Carpathians are
home to the largest wild population in Europe.'

She arched an eyebrow. 'Not werewolves?'

'No. Just wolves.'

'And we have brown bears. Wild boar, even lynx.'

'I know.'

'But no vampire bats. Sorry.' She handed him his coffee. 'What do you like about wolves?'

He looked away for a second. 'I don't know, really.'

She touched her fingers to her sternum. 'You feel that they are close to your heart?'

He nodded politely, not quite sure what she meant.

'I think that is so for a lot of people. Have you ever seen one in real life?'

'No.' He eyed her more closely. 'Have you?'

'No.'

He was tempted to tell her about the Snowdonia Wolf Sanctuary. The live camera feed on his computer, but Fuller and Morris were making a beeline towards them. He felt himself stiffen.

'Interesting, isn't it?' Fuller said in an artificially loud voice, waving a copy of the *Metro News*. 'It's not what you know . . .'

Morris gave a rehearsed nod. 'Same everywhere, isn't it?'

Fuller dropped the copy of the free newspaper on the end of the counter. 'Certainly is, mate. Certainly is.' They carried on out the door.

Their comments had been clumsy. Obviously staged. Sean stepped back to better see the newspaper.

The main story was about the recall of a new model of mobile phone. Below that was something about a member of the cabinet and her son's appointment as managing director of a research group she had established.

'They will calm down,' Magda said, leading the way towards the doors. 'Emotions are all up for now.'

He wondered what she meant.

'Julie, it's Linds. You still asleep? Lazy old slapper!' A pause. 'When you can be arsed getting out of bed, give me a call. I have a Groupon voucher: lunch for two in the Jamie Oliver place, top of King Street. You fancy? Talk in a bit, bye.'

The glow on the screen's handset lasted for a few more seconds. The bluish light made the blood that had clotted around the woman's nostrils and chin appear black.

Footsteps approached the silent flat, the letterbox creaked and a few envelopes fluttered down to the carpet. The postman's footsteps faded.

NINE

J anet Blake flicked the little hammer of the bicycle bell. She'd asked Sean to mount it on the armrest of her motorized wheelchair because the noise was less offensive than the thing's buzzer. Children, she'd noticed, always reacted. She suspected because it bore a resemblance to a sleigh bell, which meant Christmas, which meant presents.

But adults and teenagers, especially those engrossed in their phones, were often oblivious. Janet could tell she'd be in for a long wait before the four young men blocking the walkway heard her.

So she went to her back-up tactic.

She'd spotted the brass horn in a charity shop window and immediately knew it would be perfect. Squeezing the bulb of rubber at the end created a comical *hoo-hee* sound. Janet had heard every response, multiple times.

Watch your backs, Coco's coming through!

Selling tickets for the circus, love?

Bloody hell, thought you were the Keystone Cops.

She'd learned during her time on the force that a bit of humour made people far more cooperative.

The four lads were now looking down at her with a mixture of surprise and amusement.

'Didn't want to catch any of your ankles there!'

Taking their time, they stepped out of her way.

She proceeded towards the far side of Piccadilly Gardens. The area had been extensively redeveloped. Groupings of shiny benches, raised grassy areas and an elaborate water feature that never worked. The plan had been for it to form a pleasant open-air space in the centre of the city.

That plan had fallen flat.

At 9.25 on a Friday morning, the area had become a congregating point for those who didn't work regular hours. Or for those who didn't work at all. Her practiced eye observed the choreographed movements of various young men. The subtle nods and the slouching gaits. Little packages that slipped from one hand into another. The purchaser of drugs peeling away, suddenly keen to be gone, the seller immediately scanning for his next customer.

Janet steered her wheelchair round the corner of the building beside the tram tracks. The front office of Transport For Greater Manchester consisted mainly of ticket counters and information desks. Racks laden with timetables and price schemes for the city's interconnected network of buses, trains and trams. Ridesocial cycling routes. Leaflets suggesting day trip destinations: Bury Market, Stockport Hat Museum, the Thomas & Friends Experience on the East Lancashire Railway.

She always appreciated the return to a smooth surface of carpet. Steering round some members of the public, she glided over to the far door, where she pressed her pass against a touchpad. The door swung back and she continued down a corridor and into the large office. 'Morning, Stella!'

The woman at the first desk glanced up. 'Hello there.'

Janet's desk was set apart from the others. This gave her enough room to swing the wheelchair in. Her computer and keyboard were on a hydraulic arm that she could extend and lower to the required height.

'It's that meeting at quarter to,' Stella stated.

The organization was in the middle of its quarterly customer survey – an exercise that entailed trying to coax harassed, time-pressed or just plain exhausted passengers into accepting forms that they could complete and return from the comfort of their own home. A response rate of well under half a per cent was considered excellent.

'Whoop-di-do,' Janet replied.

Stella smiled knowingly.

Ten minutes later, they were all gathered in the ground floor's main meeting room. Len Benson had been put in charge of the survey. Prior to starting in the office, he'd driven buses for over twenty years. His paunch formed a doughy fold over the front of his trousers and the blubber that had built up around his face and neck permanently gleamed. The whiteboard behind him displayed a map of the city's transport system. A click of the mouse caused everything to fade but the bus routes.

'OK,' Len panted. 'Last day for focusing on the south-west section of the city. Janet, I've allocated you the wheelchair friendly routes going out to Parr's Wood and Heaton Mersey. That all right?'

Another day sitting in the special bay up by the driver, pressing forms, complete with prepaid envelopes, into the reluctant hands of passengers. 'Fine with me, Len, thanks.'

TEN

T he afternoon briefing took place at five, once the team was back from the third victim's flat.

Victoria Walker was a twenty-one-year-old from Urmston. She worked as a customer service representative for an Audi garage. The office where she worked was in Trafford Park, a vast and soulless industrial estate to the east of Manchester United's football ground.

Her body had been discovered by her father, who had a spare set of keys to the tiny flat that Victoria, with assistance from a government scheme aimed at first-time buyers, had just put a deposit down for.

It appeared she had been dead for at least three days.

The apartment was on the ground floor and formed part of a modern-looking development designed to give its occupants the illusion of not living in what was, essentially, a large block of flats.

Small balconies jutted out on the skewed upper floors, each one angled and screened so adjacent ones weren't in view. Victoria's apartment had its own walkway up to the front door which was set back in a deep recess created, in part, by the overhanging balcony of the flat directly above.

DCI Ransford pinned Victoria's photo to the board and stepped aside. She was, by several years, the youngest victim so far. And also very pretty, Sean thought, despite the hackneyed selfie-pout, fake eyelashes and hair in a carefully arranged tumble down one side of her face. The shoulder strap of her halter neck top had a silvery sheen.

Sean tried to stop himself from making assumptions: party girl, socializer, pre-loading with drinks before a big night out.

Ransford crossed his arms and surveyed the room. 'What links this woman to Ian Cahill? We need to know. Was her contact with him direct or through an intermediary? We know Victoria wasn't single: she'd been seeing a Ryan Hewitt for almost five years. They got engaged in February, on Valentine's Day.'

Sean found himself adjusting the party girl persona.

'Is it Ryan Hewitt who's had dealings with Cahill? Has Victoria Walker's dad?'

He jabbed a thumb over his shoulder at the section of board devoted to Cahill.

'We know he's got priors for a range of offences, most of them money-related. Credit card fraud, handling stolen goods, knocking on elderly folk's doors offering to fix their drives or clean their gutters. The search of the property he fled from has turned up some interesting paperwork. Seems his current thing is a crash-for-cash racket.'

Sean's gaze shifted to Ian Cahill's mug shot. It was the sort of thing he could see someone like Cahill being involved in; there'd been plenty of media reports on how vehicle collisions were being staged at roundabouts in order to then make massive insurance claims.

'Could he have set something up with Victoria Walker to defraud the Audi dealership?' Ransford asked, taking another step along to Pamela Flood's photo.

'We know of Flood's involvement with Cahill's previous scams. Obviously, the two had recently fallen out. So how heavily involved was she with this latest one? Could she have been the one who originally approached Victoria, perhaps proposing some kind of sting on Audi? Any records of Cahill or Walker contacting the dealership for a test drive or similar?'

He came to a stop and crossed his arms.

'If we're working on the basis Cahill needed to stop them all talking – or that he was punishing then for having talked -- who the hell were they talking with? Not us, certainly. Another criminal gang? If the murders are serving as a warning, who is the warning for? Could there be any others on his list? All this is going to need some substantial rejigging of allocated actions. Inspector Troughton.'

The office manager got to his feet. 'So, we'll be mapping the latest victim's last twenty-four hours. We're already obtaining all her financial and telecoms records. The laptop recovered from her flat has already gone to . . .'

As Troughton continued to outline the workload ahead, Sean let his eyes wander across the rest of the board. He studied Victoria Walker's and Francesca Pinto's pictures. Two women, in full-time jobs, hard-working and clearly ambitious. Both on the property ladder, planning for the long-term. What had either of them to gain from an association with someone like Cahill?

The mention of Mark Wheeler's name plunged Sean back into the room.

Ransford's head had dropped. 'No change, as far as we know. I gather the plan is to keep him sedated until he's stabilized, then start to explore if there's any long-term consequences. It's very likely he's suffered nerve damage that will severely affect his mobility, but that's not definite.' He looked up. 'His family, by the way, said anyone is welcome to drop by. I'll email the details of where you can find him in the hospital. Questions?'

'What's the situation with the press?'

DCI nodded. 'Good point. Tina?'

The head of media relations had been observing proceedings from the open doorway of the DCI's office. Pushing a pair of square lens glasses with turquoise frames up into a shock of auburn hair, she stepped fully out. 'Probably the one break we've had so far is with the news cycle. The *Manchester Evening Chronicle* has all but signed off the main stories for their Saturday edition. At the moment, editorial are aware of Pamela Flood's and Francesca Pinto's murders, but – as far as we know – not Victoria Walker's.'

She raised a finger for emphasis.

'The advantage we currently have is that Sunday editions are more features- and less news-focused. As a result, they are planned well ahead. If we can keep Victoria Walker's death quiet for the next, say, ten hours, they won't be able to shunt aside the Sunday features they currently have in place. What they will do, however, is make major amounts of space ready for Monday morning. I'm anticipating front pages.'

'So, with luck, we're spared all the extra fuss until then?' Ransford asked.

She nodded. 'Online is a different matter, but I've been keeping back a great story about a pensioner's lost wedding ring. It was found last week during a search of a known burglar's address.

Tomorrow, the ring gets handed back to a Joyce and Walter Clayton of Harpurhey. Married for over fifty years, still in the same terraced house. I'll get them to go over their wedding photos, grandkids sitting alongside them if we're lucky. It's the perfect feel-good police story. Granada have already confirmed they'll use it as their anchor story. Online will lap it up, too.'

Sean hadn't realized the part media considerations played in a high-profile murder case. What the woman had been talking about was employing a news item solely to deflect attention from another. Spin.

There was something sad about the way Ransford cleared his throat. 'So, what that means for us is this: we have the weekend to find Cahill. I want this man locked up before Monday. Anything else?'

No one spoke up.

'OK. It's a quarter past five. I know it's a Friday night, but we have been given the green light on overtime. Anyone looking to head home in the next three hours, make Inspector Troughton aware of your intention before you leave. I don't want anything that could have been resolved this evening left hanging: eight o'clock tomorrow morning, I'll be upstairs with whichever assistant chief is on duty. I want the progress report I'll be giving him absolutely watertight.'

ELEVEN

It was almost ten o'clock by the time Sean felt he could do no more with Francesca Pinto's statements.

By laboriously combing through the internet, he'd been able to establish who or what was behind most of the transactions not linked to recognizable companies and organizations.

The one that had interested him most was a series of minor payments to Grey Lane Enterprises. Most weeks, at least one transaction took place. None exceeded twenty pounds. It was, he knew, the kind of amount that characterized low-level blackmail – something Cahill was more than capable of.

Eventually, he'd established that Grey Lane Enterprises was the trading name of a Mrs Kate Lawrence, who lived on a Grey Lane, in Denton. From there, he'd worked out that the woman had purchased the franchise for a Wine Store outlet the previous year. The shop was situated on Ashfield Road. A check on Google revealed that was two streets away from Francesca's home address near Deansgate. Seemed Francesca had quite a taste for Gavi or Viognier or whatever was currently popular with well-off solicitors.

He scanned the room and counted just seven other heads, including DCI Ransford's. After filing his report on the system with a comment stating that the six remaining unidentified transactions would be followed up first thing the next day, Sean slid his coat from the back of his chair and wandered towards the doors.

'Night,' he called over to the remaining detectives, a hand half raised.

'See you,' one replied without looking up.

In the car park, he paused beside his car. Ransford had mentioned that Mark Wheeler's family were fine with anyone visiting their son at the hospital. He checked his watch: ten thirteen. Surely, no one would be there this late?

When he produced his warrant card at the nurse's station for the MRI's Intensive Care Unit, it occurred to him that, since becoming a detective constable, this was the first time he'd actually needed it.

As the lift took him up to the ICU a growing sense of anxiety began to eat away at him. He focused on his breathing, trying to keep it slow and steady. Memories of immediately after Mum's accident were popping up. Being kept back after school, waiting outside the head teacher's office because there were no relatives who could come and collect him. Being driven to one of his mum's friend's houses, not his own. She'd given him spaghetti hoops on toast for tea. He couldn't stand them, but didn't dare say. Then the hospital visit. Police officers in the corridor gently ruffling his hair, a female officer turning away with tears on her face. His mum propped up in bed, trying to act like she wasn't in pain.

Sean stepped out of the lift and looked down the corridor. The ceiling lights were so muted, shadows formed dark pools at regular intervals along the floor. The tepid air was stratified by smells: the cloying fog of sickness occasionally lanced by the scent of cleaning fluid. He remembered it so clearly. Within each bay of beds, a mass of lights shone in the darkness. They blinked with the rhythmic monotony of planes in a night sky.

The car that had mown down his mum had been driven by a thirty-eight-year-old man who had created so much noise while battering his partner, neighbours had rung the police.

Janet had been in the second patrol car to arrive at the scene. The first officers to attend had found a badly injured female lying amid the splintered remains of a kitchen table and chairs. The perpetrator seemed to have left the scene.

As Janet pulled up, he appeared from behind the row of wheelie bins in a neighbour's front yard. He jumped into a Renault Scenic. Janet's mistake had been to try and block his escape by standing in the road.

Sean reached the end of the corridor. The last room on the right was number fourteen. He took a couple of steps back and turned to the window. By not looking at the mass of lights, he was able to make out a white expanse below them. Bed covers. The bed was facing sideways to him. His eyes travelled left, towards the wall. Mark's head and shoulders were shrouded in darkness. All around him, motionless bursts of colour hung in the air.

Bouquets of flowers, he realized, suddenly aware he'd come empty-handed. All the lights winked out, temporarily obscured as a shadow crossed before them. The door opened silently and a tall, stooped man looked out.

'Have you come to see Mark?'

The resemblance was clear. In fact, the only difference was how a couple of decades had pressed the man's skin against the bones of his face.

'I'm Roger Wheeler, his dad. Please, come in.'

Sean couldn't move. He wanted to speak, but his lips refused to part. 'No,' he croaked then cleared his throat. 'Sorry, no, I was just popping by.'

The man emerged into the corridor and the door slowly closed itself behind him. 'That's very kind. How do you know Mark?' His hand was outstretched, waiting for Sean's.

'We . . . it was the first day. For both of us.'

The man's tentative smile faltered. 'You are . . .?'

'Sean . . . Detective Constable Blake.'

The man's hand dropped as his face filled with dismay. 'Why

have you come? Why?' He turned to the window, forlorn as he looked through the glass. 'Why did you do nothing to help my boy?' He looked back, rims of his eyes dancing with tears. 'Why?'

Sean tried to gesture. His arms felt like pendulums. 'I did. I was about to.'

The man's head shook. 'No. You shouldn't be here.'

'Mr Wheeler? I don't know what you've been told, but people—'

'Just go!' His voice reverberated down the empty corridor. Sean stepped back.

'Go,' he whispered, turning away.

Sean looked at the expanse of glass as the door opened. Light fell across the bed. Mark lay there, a respiratory tube curling from his slack lips.

Aside from Cahill, he was the only person who knew what had really happened in that garden. As the door swung shut, the wedge of light first narrowed then slid off the bed.

To his surprise, the television was still on in the front room. As he made for the kitchen, he heard her stir.

'Sean?'

Her voice was heavy with sleep. He knew why she wasn't in bed; she'd been waiting up for him. Just like she did on the very few occasions he went out as a teenager. 'Yeah, it's me.'

'It's late.'

He opened the fridge and poured himself some milk, automatically making a mental note of what they were running low on. He'd need to do a big shop soon. 'It is.'

'Have you been working all this time? Are you coming through?'

He finished the milk, placed the glass in the sink and bowed his head. Her concern was like being wrapped in cloth. He wanted to rip it aside so he could breathe.

'Sean, are you coming in here?'

He stood in the living room doorway. She was in her armchair, walking frame beside it. The telly's electric glow tinged the side of her face pale blue. Some sci-fi film she couldn't possibly have been watching. How long had she been asleep? 'I think I'll just head up to bed. Knackered.'

Her hand brushed at the arm of the sofa. A silent entreaty to sit. 'It's been busy, then? What did they have you doing?'

'Yeah, really busy. Actually, I need to be back in early.'

'They are going at it, then. How did it go with your DCI? You had that chat, didn't you?'

'No, I didn't get the chance.'

Disapproval twisted her mouth. 'You did ask to speak with him, though?'

Here we go, he thought. *Time for my telling off.* 'It's a triple-murder investigation. A detective's been—'

'Triple? There's been another?'

He was determined to finish. 'A detective's been seriously injured. The man we want is . . . out there. No one knows where. What makes you think Ransford has any time for me?'

'Don't undervalue yourself, Sean. You are a member of that team—'

He slapped the door frame with his palm. 'I am not a member of that team! I'm a new detective constable who's come in and first day on the job – first day – I've apparently stood by as my colleague had a sharpened screwdriver shoved in and out of his neck. I'm not a member of that team. I sit in a cramped corner, facing an empty desk and I go over old bank statements because they don't trust me and when I go to the canteen I get cryptic comments about some newspaper story and the only person prepared to talk to me is this Romanian woman who acts like she's . . .' he waved a hand, 'I don't know, an aunt or something.'

Janet's mouth was hanging open.

Sean turned round and walked towards the stairs. 'I'm off to bed.'

He stood in the middle of his bedroom and deep breathed. In and out, in and out. Little by little, the tingling in his shoulders dissipated into his arms. After a few more slow exhalations it felt like the tips of his fingers were touching lemonade. *The problem*, he said to himself for the thousandth time, *is that she never lets up. It's like having a thirteen-stone conscience strapped to your back.*

He opened his eyes.

A silhouette of a wolf, caught on a crest of the Siberian steppe, a blood moon behind it. *One day*, he said to himself, eyes on the *National Geographic* poster he'd bought as a teenager. He kept up to date on the cost of an escorted tour, staying in a yurt and driving skidoos each day through the wilderness, a local ranger leading you across the paw-punctured snow the pack had left in its wake.

One day, he'd do it. One day.

His mind was still thrumming with what he'd said to her. But guilt was beginning to seed itself. He knew that it would grow during the night. And by morning, it would have smothered any anger that might have remained.

TWELVE

She was at the kitchen table, toast and a pot of tea beside her, iPad propped against a pile of cookery books. Her chin lifted and he saw the cautious look in her eyes. Partly expectant, partly hesitant. Who would speak first?

But as soon as he'd woken, the recollection of what he'd said had made his toes squirm beneath the duvet. 'Mum, sorry about last night. What I said came out . . .'

'That's fine,' she cut in, her face immediately softening. 'It was late and you were tired. Me? I need to not be so . . . you know. Pushy.'

He smiled briefly before reaching for the loaf of bread beside the toaster.

'Tea?'

He glanced at the wall clock. 'Just got time for a quick cup.'

The radio was on low. BBC Radio Manchester, as usual.

'There's nothing about a third murder,' Janet stated. Her forefinger dabbed the iPad's screen. 'Or on here.'

'No – not yet, anyway.'

'But it's linked to the first two?'

'Exactly the same.'

As he filled a mug and carried it back over to the toaster, Janet tracked him. 'Another female?'

'Yes. Early twenties, working in an Audi call centre.'

'Here in Manchester?'

He nodded, stirring as he did so.

'Three victims. Why isn't the prime suspect's face, what's his name, Cahill? Why isn't it plastered all over the news?'

'They want to have him in custody first, retain control of the situation.'

Janet scowled. 'Retain control of the— what is policing coming to? Jesus.'

The toaster clicked. 'He can't have got far. He fled the scene with nothing on him. Someone is sheltering him, and with all the resources now being chucked at it . . .'

'Is anyone asking why?'

'What do you mean?'

'Why did he do it? Kill three women like that.'

'The prime suspect's motivation?'

'Sean, you're not on a training course. Just, why did Cahill do it? Keep it simple.'

'They're still trying to work it out.' He smeared marmalade across both slices and took a huge bite out of one.

She waited while he chewed.

'He was involved in crash-for-cash scams, some of them with the help of the first victim. Number two worked as a solicitor and had been on duty once when he'd been arrested, number three was in car sales. That's the line of reasoning.'

Janet's eyes had narrowed. 'Anything to suggest the three victims knew each other?'

'Not yet.'

She said nothing.

Sean added some cold water to his tea, gulped it back and lifted up the other piece of toast. 'I'll eat this on the way in. You'll be OK?'

'Of course. I've got an afternoon shift.'

'This customer survey thing?'

'That's the one.'

'Still making you hand out forms on buses?'

'Who knows? Could be trams today, if I'm lucky.' She gave him a wink.

'Well, I think it's out of order, forcing you to—'

'No one's forced me. I volunteered. I quite like it, actually. And besides, there's a section in the survey on ease of access for less able-bodied people: nothing like first-hand experience.'

'Let me know what food we need – I'll do a supermarket run at some point this weekend. And I'll push a vacuum round, too. I know it's overdue.'

'Why don't we do an internet order for the food? Now you're so busy—'

'They always muck-up something. I'd prefer to do it myself.'

He leaned down and, as he kissed her cheek, she raised a hand to the side of his face. 'Last night, you said that you were—'

'I was angry. Tired-angry. Trangy.' He straightened up. 'It's just because I'm new. The rest of the team aren't really ignoring—'

'But you said something about a newspaper.'

'Oh, that. There's this DS. He obviously took a shine to Mark Wheeler. I'm definitely not his friend.'

'But what was it about a newspaper?'

'Don't know. I think he was trying to make some kind of hint. The page had a report about a cabinet minister. She'd done something to get in trouble.'

'What was her name?'

'The one who always wears those big dangly earrings. Her.'

Janet gave a mystified shake of her head as she reached for the teapot. 'Ring me, will you? If you know what time you'll be back.'

'Will do.'

He was almost at the front door when she called again. 'And Sean, don't leave it any longer: sort out a minute to clear things up with DCI—'

He banged the door shut behind him.

Janet waited a few seconds then reached for her iPad and opened a search window. She knew exactly which cabinet minister who Sean had tried to describe. Ursula Fitzgibbon, safe seat in North London, Minister for Arts and Culture and married to a ridiculously wealthy fund manager.

A quick search of her name immediately brought up the news story.

Before entering politics, Ursula had set up WellSpring, an organization that helped production companies source private funding for film projects. Her son, Sebastian, a recent graduate with no industry experience, had just been appointed as WellSpring's new managing director.

Slowly, Janet raised a hand to her mouth and stared in horror at the wall.

THIRTEEN

A succession of notes filled the tram carriage. Some bitch had set her handset's ring volume far too high.

'Hello?'

The woman's voice was tight with anger.

'Yes, this is Heather Knight. You've only just arrived? Even though you said you'd be there by ten fifteen? And it's now . . . That's right, ten forty. Jesus Christ, first the cab company, now you. Where am I? On my way back to the office. I gave up waiting.'

He crept his gaze along, as if studying the row of advertisements above the windows. Save on travel insurance. Learn a new language. Relieve feminine itching. There she was, not five metres away. He focused on the window, studying her reflection in it.

Platinum hair in a side parting, not long enough to touch her collar. Eyebrows two immaculate arches. Lipstick that turned her mouth into a slash of red. A business suit. A brash obnoxious woman in a business suit. He hoped he'd be able to make this one writhe.

She jutted her chin out in preparation to speak.

'That car was serviced two days ago. Two bloody days! Something about a fault with the ABS system. Oh, right, yes.' A mocking tone entered her voice. 'Just drive the thing with a message like that on the screen. Unbelievable. So that's the official advice of your dealership? I bet BMW would be interested to hear that.'

Her free hand was grasping a ceiling rail. Oyster-coloured nails rose and fell, each one making a plastic tick.

'OK . . . hold it right there. This is what you're going to do. I left the key with the man in the Portakabin thing. Can you see it? Good. You're going to retrieve the key from him and you're going to sort that car out. Then, once it's working properly, you're going to deliver it to my home address, before Sunday evening. If that doesn't happen, I'll be reviewing our entire fleet agreement with you.'

He edged closer, while removing a small notebook from his pocket. Once it was open, he pursed his lips, as if attempting to recall something of significance.

'Please,' she interrupted, 'don't adopt a tone that implies you're doing a favour for me. No, it's gun-metal grey. The six series, over on the right? Well done! Sorry? You don't have that to hand?' She shook her head. 'Well, have you got a pen? That's something. It's number sixteen, Kersal Mews, Didsbury. Yes, Knight, with a K. Correct.'

Thank you, he thought, jotting her address down on the page. *Thank you so much.*

'Yes, this number is fine. Good bye.'

As soon as she ended the call, her phone rang again.

'Hello, you.' Her voice still held a trace of irritation. 'No, I just finished dealing with a stupid man from the garage.' She breathed deeply. 'Imbeciles. Taking the piss – or trying to. I'll tell you when you get back. You're where? In a toilet? Why are you in a toilet? What about the ones who need to ring their wife or kids?' She smiled wearily. 'I don't know. Silly boys and their stag-do rules. And you've got two more days of this? Poor little muffin, you're going be in a right state. OK. No, I finish at lunch. A bath and then season two of *The Crimson Rose*. At least half of it. Easily! Only seven episodes, about fifty minutes each. Can't bloody wait. OK. Tell Andy I said hi – oh, yes, maybe not then. Right. Just try not to, at least? Bye then. You, too. Bye.'

He slipped his notebook back in his pocket and glanced at her reflection. *I'll see you shortly, muffin.*

FOURTEEN

Sean straightened his legs under the desk. Then, pretending to stretch his arms, glanced over his shoulder. The office manager was sitting with Maggie James, the lady who led up the CSWs.

Sean looked to where the rest of the team were sitting. One of the girls who'd started the same day as him was already in. He tried to remember her name. Something to do with a month. March or May. Stacey May?

She glanced up at that exact moment and caught him staring. Shit! He held up a hand and she sent back a quick, tight smile. *Now*, he asked himself, *what do you do? Go over and talk? Yes, you should go over and talk. But what will you say?* He closed down the conversation in his head and wandered over before any more doubts could set in. 'Is it Stacey?'

Her frown caused a double-wrinkle to form across the bridge of her nose. Am image flashed: him kissing it. 'Katie.'

Idiot, he thought, rolling his eyes in apology. 'Right, Katie. I'm Sean.'

'I know.'

Her answer was oddly abrupt. She seemed uncomfortable and he remembered the way she'd blushed when introduced to the team. 'How are you finding things so far?'

She spread both hands above the sheets of paper covering her desk. 'Busy.'

'Yes, it is.'

Her eyes dropped momentarily to a particular printout.

'Well . . . I'll leave you to it.' He was about to step back when a voice spoke behind him. 'Were you after Inspector Troughton?'

He turned. Maggie James was walking past.

'He's now free.'

'Great, cheers.' He looked back at Katie. 'See you later.'

Another brief smile.

'Morning, Inspector. I wanted you to know I've gone through those last six transactions on Francesca Pinto's financial records. They all correspond to legitimate companies.'

'Record updated on the system?'

'Yes.'

'OK. Give me a few minutes to sort this lot and have a word with the allocator. Grab yourself a coffee or something.'

'No problem. Do you want one?'

Troughton held a finger to a full cup.

Sean had set off for the doors when the inspector spoke again. 'Oh, DC Blake?'

He retraced his steps. 'Sir?'

'A message came over from the ICU.' A biro waggled in his hand. 'Bit awkward, this – but best not to pay any more visits. I'm sure you understand.'

Sean blinked. 'I thought, with it being so late, no family members would—'

'Not a problem. Perfectly understandable.'

'Thing is, sir, Mark Wheeler's dad, he's been wrongly led to believe that—' Troughton's phone began to ring.

Sean tried starting again. 'I tried to explain that—'

But the office manager had already picked up the receiver. 'Inspector Troughton speaking. No need, sir, I can get that for you.'

His seat swivelled round and Sean was left looking at the man's back.

The coffee counter in the canteen had closed at noon. Sean checked his watch. Missed it by nine minutes. He altered direction for the vending machines, checking his pocket for change.

A few seconds later, a spindle of brown liquid descended into a plastic cup. The machine said its coffee was freshly ground. It was certainly making enough noise, he thought, for that to be true.

On the table beside him was a copy of yesterday's paper. Someone had almost managed to complete the crossword. He lifted it up and studied the gaps.

Wood carving implement. Four letters, second being a D.

Heaven. Eight letters, starting with a V, second to last letter an L.

Sorrow. Three letters, last one an E.

French river. Five letters, middle one an I.

Fierce growling. Eight letters, second one an N, third one an A.

He mentally jotted in the answers. *Adze. Valhalla. Woe. Seine. Snarling. Thanks, Mum*, he said to himself, thinking of the countless times she'd got him to sit with her at the kitchen table, newspaper open on the puzzles page.

He remembered the comment DS Fuller had made the day before. What the hell was going on with that? Who you know, he'd said. Sean opened out the pages and started trying to find the story.

He'd reached page nine when he heard a muffled shout of delight. He cocked his head. More voices were joining in, now accompanied by clapping. Someone let out a whoop.

He jogged out of the canteen and down the corridor. When he pushed open the doors of the incident room, everyone was on their feet. People were high-fiving each other. Ransford was in the centre of the room, punching the air.

Sean called to the nearest officer. The man's face was beaming.

'Cahill! The fucker's just been caught.'

FIFTEEN

For a while, he toyed with the idea of mocking up a label that featured a BMW logo. After all, that's who she thought she was dealing with. On reflection, he decided it could lead to her asking questions. And that would mean a delay on the doorstep. It was the only time in the process where he was vulnerable.

Where targets lived had to meet selection criteria just as strict as the targets themselves.

Women: crass, inconsiderate, high-handed, haughty or generally insolent.

The entrances to where they lived: modest.

He was amused by the contrast.

Front doors that were discreet. Hidden from view. Not making a statement. He looked for a high hedge, a large tree, a wooden fence: anything that served to obscure interaction and conceal the moment the electric charge was delivered.

Ironically, that was exactly the case with the cottage where Katherine Harpham lived. Two years ago, he'd been there along with other academy staff. It had been a beautiful summer evening and he could still picture the rose bushes that lined her front path. A deep porch with a tiled roof. She'd been in a cotton dress and sandals, hair hanging down, full of smiles. The hall carpet was, if he remembered rightly, an oatmeal brown. Thick, too. Enough to reduce the impact of landing on it with your muscles in a full rictus spasm.

He closed the van door gently, keeping noise to a minimum. His heart was beating slightly faster. He'd not delivered before on a Saturday and there were signs of activity all around. A couple of cars passing slowly on the street. Music from an open window. A dog's excited bark and a child's laughter.

He reached the turn-off for the development. A verge sign read *Private: resident parking only.* Heather Knight's flat was under the archway that led into a courtyard neatly partitioned by parking spaces.

His baseball cap was low on his head and he kept his eyes on the ground. Once out of sight beneath the archway, he risked a quick check about. Out in the main courtyard he could see that over half the parking spaces contained a vehicle. In the nearest one was a gun-metal grey 6 series BMW. The garage had obviously been keen to keep their contract. So now, no one else was due at her door. At least not for a while.

He double-checked the courtyard was free of people, and kept looking in that direction as he pressed her doorbell.

Now came the nerve-racking wait.

His hearing seemed more acute. A voice told the dog to shut-up. Inside the flat, a door opened. From out in the courtyard came an electric double-beep. Someone had unlocked a car. He stared off to his right. A man in his mid-twenties stepped out of a front door no more than thirty metres away. He was speaking over his shoulder to a woman who stood on the front step.

'Yeah, I heard: two of them.'

'But only if the packets are five hundred grams.'

'Got it.'

'And,' she said, 'reduced fat coconut milk.'

'One tin?'

'Yes.'

He held his breath. He could still walk away. Right now. All the woman had to do was turn her head and she'd be looking straight at him. Yes, he was in shadow. But he wasn't invisible. The footsteps beyond Heather's door were getting closer. He couldn't bear to abandon things. Not this close to success.

The woman over in the courtyard stepped back and the front door of the apartment closed. He breathed out. Now it was the man he needed to worry about. He tried to work out timings. The man had the door of his car open. He was getting in. He would then need to reverse the vehicle out and swing it round. It would only take a few seconds. Heather Knight needed to open her door. And she needed to do it now.

He heard a key turning in the lock. *Come on, come on.*

His heart was hammering as the door finally opened. 'Yes?'

He immediately lifted the box. 'Delivery for Heather Knight.'

A frown appeared on her face. Off the side, he heard the car's engine start. 'Really? Who from?'

'I think it was a car dealership.' He handed her the package.

She examined the label, studying her own name and address. 'The BMW one on the A34?'

He didn't dare look to his right. He didn't need to: in the periphery of his vision, a pair of reversing lights had come on. 'I didn't collect it. Sorry, but I'm double-parked out on the road. Just a signature here?'

'Right, yes.' She tested the package's weight. 'Chocolates, I bet.'

He knew it contained nothing more than some balled-up newspaper and a block of wood. He risked a quick look to the side. The car had backed out of its space. Next, it would start to edge forward and he would be directly in its view.

She tucked the package under an arm and held her hand out for the stylus. As soon as she had it in her grip, he pressed the button. The electric crackle was over in an instant. Eyes fixed, teeth clenched, she thudded against the hallway wall and keeled over. He bent down, and tried to fold her legs so they were clear of the door. Her bloody knees wouldn't bend. Stiff as planks. He had to kick them aside before he could step in and shut the door behind him.

He barely had time to suck in a chestful of air before the sigh of tyres went past outside.

SIXTEEN

'Four times?' Ransford's voice had gone squeaky.

Sean sneaked a glance over. The man's office door was half-open and he was pacing to and fro behind his desk.

'How long until that happens? Christ. OK, OK – the instant it does, I want to know.'

He put the phone down and emerged from his office. 'Get this, everyone – Ian Cahill was in a McDonald's out in Middleton. A constable coming off the night shift was in there having breakfast. Cahill walks straight past him. He makes the call and three cars of uniforms pile in minutes later. Cahill refused to lie down when ordered to do so. Instead, he stood up.' Ransford did his best to suppress a smile. 'Afraid he would attempt to arm himself, the officers—'

'What with?' Someone called out. 'A McFlurry?'

Guffaws of laughter.

Ransford raised both hands. 'All right, all right. Actually, he had a threatening-looking straw in his milkshake.'

More laughing.

'Seriously, though, he got to his feet, so they deployed Tasers. Four times.'

'Oooh, that would have hurt.'

'Good.'

'Fucking commendations all round.'

Ransford nodded his agreement. 'Yes, but while he was flipping about on the floor, he managed to smash all his front teeth out against a table leg.'

Delighted cheers filled the room.

Ransford stood still, patiently waiting for the noise to die down. 'Upshot is, he's now at the A&E getting it seen to, so it will be some time before we get to offer him our hospitality here. I'd also like to stress, we have still to find what links all three victims: keep digging, ladies and gents, keep digging.'

Sean sat back in his seat. Shortly after news of Cahill's capture broke, Troughton had pulled a chair up beside Sean's and sat down. 'These financial checks you did on Francesca Pinto's various accounts. It's nice work, Detective.'

Sean quickly checked the man's face for any hint of sarcasm. 'Thanks,' he said, cautiously. 'What's next?'

Troughton sent a glance in the direction of Ransford's office before turning back and sighing. 'What are we going to do with you?'

'Sorry, sir?'

'You're very thorough, DC Blake, and I like that. My problem is, DCI Ransford doesn't want you on outside enquiries, if it can be avoided. Not until the incident with Mark Wheeler's been resolved.'

Anger spiked in Sean's chest and he opened his mouth to protest.

'Leave it,' Troughton cut in. 'I've read your report. I've read the others, too. Until Mark can give his, we'll only be going round in circles. Bottom line is, I'm limited to which actions I can put your way. Do you understand that?'

Sean didn't reply.

'Detective, do you understand that?'

He gave a nod.

'OK. I'll do my best not to only shovel shit in your direction. Right now, I want you to look over the reports on the three victims' movements during their last twenty-four hours. See if you can spot anything that might link them to Cahill which the computer hasn't picked up.'

During his training, Sean had been taught the scope of the police computer system, HOLMES. Though it was able to process and cross-match the countless reports and tiny pieces of information that any murder enquiry inevitably generated, it had its weak points. For instance, if the indexing system used to categorize those reports wasn't used consistently, things could fall between the cracks.

'Sir, what are the chances of that actually resulting in anything useful?'

Troughton stood. 'Best I can do, Detective.'

The inspector walked away and Sean turned to his screen. The back of his neck and ears prickled. This was fucking out of order. This was shit. This was . . . he took a deep breath then let it out bit by bit. Yes, it was shit. But what could he do about it? Nothing.

He brought up the report on Pamela Flood. Whoever had compiled her timeline, he quickly concluded, had done an excellent job. Almost every second to the point of her arrival home had been accounted for. Break times at work, colleagues spoken to, shops visited, phone calls received and made, streets walked along.

He accessed the one for Francesca Pinto and started doing the same thing all over again.

Lunchtime came and went and it was only when he started into the preliminary report on Victoria Walker that a thought occurred: if he was seeking to find some kind of connecting factor, would it not make more sense to know what the two later victims had been doing in the twenty-four hours that led up to Pamela Flood's death? Similarly, it could be useful to know what Victoria Walker was up to in the twenty-four hours prior to Francesca Pinto dying. The reports didn't cover that.

He had gathered the necessary paperwork together and was about to approach Troughton with his suggestion when Ransford emerged at speed from his inner office. This was his chance to ask for a word.

'Cahill's out of A&E,' Ransford announced to a detective whose desk was by his door. 'As soon as downstairs have processed him, we'll need an interview room. I'm bringing the assistant chief up to speed.'

Sean was directly in Ransford's path as he marched purposefully towards the doors. 'Sir?'

The DCI didn't break his stride. 'Not now!'

Sean had to step back so fast, he almost fell over the wastepaper basket behind him. As he bent down to stand it back up, he caught the look of amusement on the nearest officer's face. It was the same one who'd told him about Cahill being arrested.

'Watch your step there, pal.'

Sean engineered a smile. 'Didn't pick that moment very well, did I?'

'No, not really.' He raised a hand. 'Adrian Wareham.'

'Hi. Sean—'

'Yeah, I remember from Ransford's briefing.' He looked over at the doors their senior officer had just vanished through. 'I wouldn't worry, his stress levels always go through the roof,' he said in a low voice. 'Listen – people are going for a pint after work tonight. Want to come?'

The Oddfellow's Arms was one street over, on the corner of Bosworth Road. A traditional-style boozer with, Sean noticed approvingly, only one TV screen. Adrian led him past the main bar to a side hatch, where he began trying to signal a barmaid.

Sean turned back to study the front area of the pub. A couple – both younger than him – were sitting either side of a small table. Heads bent, faces lit by their smart phones' glow. *Jesus*, thought Sean. *I hope it's not a first date.*

A server approached the table and put down two plates of food. Saying nothing, the girl immediately lifted her phone to take a photo.

'Pint of lager, cheers, Kate. Sean?'

A pint, Sean thought, without enthusiasm. But he couldn't think of a better option. 'Yeah, the same. Thanks.' He glanced around, wondering where everyone else was.

'Behind you,' said Adrian. 'They pretty much keep the entire thing free for us.'

Sean looked over his shoulder. Across the corridor was an open door. The room beyond was the sort of space that would perfectly suit a private function. Somewhere that was part of the pub, but also slightly removed. 'Half the stuff that gets talked about would give normal punters nightmares. Better to just shove us all out of the way, in there.' It was, Sean thought, the type of gesture that only resulted from putting considerable amounts of cash behind the bar. 'Nice little arrangement.'

'Well,' Adrian added, handing him a drink, 'we're always dead paranoid about being overheard, aren't we?'

Sean followed him into the room. Maggie James and her cohort of support workers seemed to have taken over the table at the far end. The rest of the room consisted of small groups of mostly male officers. Sean spotted DS Fuller in one corner, deep in conversation with Morris and a few others.

Adrian led him to a group who were discussing Cahill's long list of previous convictions: two of the officers knew him from their time in uniform. For them, it had only been a matter of time before the man had progressed to murder.

Once Cahill had been put into an interview room, there'd been another wait while he consulted with his solicitor. Or tried to consult, the oldest detective had gleefully reported. The bloke looked like he'd had a few too many injections of filler: like someone had stuck some inner-tubing to his mouth and painted it the colour that lips were meant to be.

Sean sipped at his drink, doing his best to appear at ease. He'd never found trying to interact with new groups of people easy. Especially not in the noisy surroundings of a pub. The conversation drifted onto other topics and the group began to fragment as people peeled off to chat with other colleagues.

Sean checked the time on his phone. He'd only been in the room for a quarter of an hour. Too soon to head home and, besides, he owed Adrian a drink. Looking about, he spotted Magda sitting at a table near the door. The place next to her was empty. 'Mind if I join you?'

She patted the seat enthusiastically. 'Take a seat. So, your first taste of the Oddfellow's Arms – how are you finding it?'

'Yeah, nice.' He glanced at the old black-and-white photos of Manchester on the walls. Horse-drawn carts on Deansgate. Stern-looking men in aprons outside dimly lit stores. Dirty-faced kids, playing with marbles in back alleys. 'I like this back-room business.'

'Yes,' Magda nodded. 'A good place for talking shop. What would you normally do on a Saturday night, if you weren't only just finishing work?'

Feeling self-conscious, he adjusted the position of a beer mat. Saturday nights? How to answer that. He could hardly say that most of his social life during his teenage years and beyond had been organized by Barnardo's. Meetings in musty social clubs and the odd excursion to give young carers some respite from looking after sick or injured parents.

'Is this,' Magda said, 'the sort of place you go to with your friends?'

A few faces flashed in his head. Damon, whose dad had multiple sclerosis. Lauren, whose mum had a massive stroke in her mid-thirties and now couldn't talk or walk. Richard, whose mum lost both legs to blood poisoning and whose dad was now suffering from fibromyalgia. They'd all welcome the day trips and cinema visits the charity had arranged, but none of them were able to ever truly relax and have fun: the yoke of premature responsibility had seen to that. He was about to shrug and say, actually, wine bars were more his thing. But something about the way Magda was watching him made him decide against lying. 'It was tricky, you know – after Mum was injured. She needed a lot of looking after. There were operations. Lots of them.'

Magda placed her drink down. 'Of course. I should have realized.'

'It's all right. Not the most cheerful thing we could chat about.'

'No: but I would like to know. If you don't mind . . .'

'Fine with me.'

She sat back. 'Did you not have help?'

'For the first few years after it happened. But that money ran out, eventually.'

'And then it was just you?'

'A community nurse would come by.' He glanced at her. She looked horrified. 'It wasn't that bad. She's become a lot more capable of looking after herself. We make a pretty good team, actually.'

'How old were you when she was—'

'Nearly ten.'

'You had to learn to do all the chores, did you? Around the home?'

'You mean like doing the washing? Cleaning the house? Shopping?'

She nodded.

'I did. But surely that's no bad thing? Better than being helpless. Or hopeless.'

Her eyes roamed the room. 'Like most men. And how is she now?'

Sean took a sip of his drink. 'She'll never walk properly, if that's what you mean. The damage to her pelvis and hips, it was too serious. But, as I said, she's learned to adapt. She has a little wheelchair she nips about on.'

'And is she – you know – how is her spirit?'

Sean had a sudden image of his mum tending to a small ghost. A miniature phantom she kept in a birdcage. He smiled.

'What?' Magda asked, looking confused.

Sean shook his head, still smiling. 'Sorry. It's your choice of words. They're quite funny.'

'Ah. Spirit is not right?'

'No, it is. I don't know, maybe a bit old-fashioned. Her spirit?' He paused to take another sip. He couldn't tell her his mum's spirit was crushed. That she got by, had found a job with a very understanding employer, kept a cheerful front for her colleagues. But, some mornings, he suspected the only thing that got her out of bed was a determination to see him succeed. 'She's OK, most of the time. Talking of which . . .'

He checked his phone again. If he stayed much longer, he'd need to let her know he was running late. 'So what about you? What brought you to Britain?'

She waved a hand. 'You remember someone called Nicolae Ceauşescu?'

He gave her a blank look.

'He was our head of state, until 1989.'

'Oh – you mean the one who was executed?'

She gave a grim nod. 'He was terrible for my country. Many people had to leave. Some other time I will tell you. Not now.'

'OK.' He checked his drink: hardly any left. 'Would you like another?'

She shook her head. 'One's plenty for me. I think most people will head home except, maybe, some of the—' She caught her words.

Younger ones, Sean thought. *Like me.* 'One's who aren't driving?' he asked, happy to rescue her.

'Yes, those.'

'I'd better be off, too. I'll just check if Adrian wants a drink. See you tomorrow, Magda. And thanks, you know, for making me feel welcome.'

He opened his front door on a dark hallway. *Odd*, Sean thought, checking his watch even though he knew full well it was almost seven o'clock.

'Mum?' He hung his keys up and looked in the kitchen. Empty. There was a packet of biscuits on the table, so she must have got in from work at some point. He placed a hand against the kettle. Faintly warm. So where was she? The familiar ripple of anxiety.

It was possible she'd nodded off in the front room – even though, when that happened, the telly was normally on. The room was dark, but he could just make out her walking frame by the sofa. He started patting the wall for the light switch when the walkie-talkie on the hallway table gave a crackly hiss.

'Sean?'

A jolt of adrenalin made his stomach lift. Stepping back, he scrabbled for the device and almost knocked it to the floor. 'Mum, where are you?'

'Upstairs.' Her voice was barely more than a whisper.

He placed a hand on the banister post and called up. 'Are you OK?'

'Don't come up. Just . . . ring for an ambulance.'

He started climbing the stairs, now addressing the walkie-talkie. 'What do you mean? Where are you?'

'Sean . . . don't . . .'

The stairlift was at the top. She was definitely up here, somewhere. He placed the walkie-talkie on the seat of the mechanized chair and looked about: the bathroom door was shut. 'Mum?'

Her voice came from the other side, feeble and distressed. 'I need you to call me—'

'I'm right outside the door, Mum. What's going on?'

'I slipped, getting out of the bath.'

He brought his ear away from the painted wood. 'You slipped? Are you hurt?'

'No, I'm stuck.'

'In the bath?'

'I can't lift myself out.'

'I'll open the—'

'No! Just call for help.'

'But I'm here, Mum. I can help.'

'I don't want your help!' Anger and humiliation made her voice tremble. 'I don't want you to see me like this! I don't want you to—'

He heard her sob and a lump rose in his throat.

'Just call them, Sean. Please.'

SEVENTEEN

The paramedic's meaty forearms bulged when he crossed his arms. 'You'd be surprised. What would you say, Andy? Two or three a month?'

'And then some!' His colleague was down on one knee, packing items back into a large carry case. 'They should carry a health warning, those things.'

The towel on Janet's head resembled a large turquoise turban. 'You read the ingredients and they sound so lovely.'

The paramedic who was standing gave a knowing nod. 'Until you try getting up. Then all those lovely oils aren't such good news.'

'It's the last bath bomb I ever buy,' Janet announced. 'And that's a promise.'

'Have you ever considered getting a bath seat fitted?'

She straightened the collar of her towelling bathrobe and scowled. 'I'm not that much of an invalid, please.'

The paramedic cocked his head. 'I didn't say that, Mrs Blake.'

She batted a hand. 'I'm not being serious. I don't know . . . I thought maybe once I reached my eighties, not my fifties.'

'Well, it's something to consider. Or one of those sitting baths. The chair bit is part of the mould, and there are handles dotted about. Quite fancy one myself; sit there and read the papers.'

Sean could see his mum's posture stiffen a fraction. She hated all the practical changes she'd had to make because of the incident that had nearly killed her. Every measure she took, she said once, felt like defeat.

'Sure you don't have time for a tea?' Sean asked, pouring boiling water into the pot.

The paramedic who was kneeling looked up. 'Bloody tempting, that. But we should go.'

His colleague regarded Janet. 'Sure there's no pain? No one's going to mind giving you a swift check over.'

'Saturday night in A&E?' She smiled. 'I'd rather not. Spent enough time in and out of there as a bobby.'

'A bobby, hey? When were you in the job?'

Sean wondered if speaking in a calm and soothing way was a mandatory part of all paramedical training.

'A few years back, now. I was in for almost twenty years.'

He whistled. 'Some sentence.'

'Some sentence, indeed.' She nodded at Sean. 'And now my son here is starting his. Just become a detective, he has. Not even—'

Sean jumped in before she could build up a head of steam. The pair of them would never escape. 'We'd better let you get on.'

The zip closed on the carry case and the kneeling paramedic stood. 'You're right.'

'Take care of yourself, Mrs Blake,' the other one announced.

'Don't you worry about me.'

Sean showed them to the door, his voice dropping as they stepped past him. 'Thanks for that.'

One of them paused. 'Tough one, isn't she?'

She makes out she is, he thought, returning his grin. 'You could say that.'

When he wandered back into the kitchen, she'd lost a lot of her cheer.

'You didn't need to clean it, Sean,' she said quietly, hardly able to meet his eyes.

He thought about entering the bathroom after the paramedics had washed her down and carried her through to her room. Fragments of faeces, bits of soap and the odd strand of hair had clung stubbornly to the sides of the bath. He'd scrubbed quietly at it with a cloth the entire time they were in the next room. 'It took all of two minutes.'

'That's not the point.'

'What's the problem? I can't see any—'

'No son should have to clear up his own mother's . . .' the sound of an *s* struggled to escape her lips as she searched for another word. 'You know what.'

He took his time pouring their tea. Her incontinence issues were what she found hardest to deal with. Since the car had crushed her pelvis and shattered her right leg, she'd only been caught out twice, and never in public. At least, not as far as he knew. 'You wiped up plenty of my crap in your time.'

She propped her head in her hands, sighed deeply then gazed at him over her knuckles. 'Oh, Sean. You're . . . you're . . . I don't want this for you.'

He placed the cups on the table and sat down beside her. 'What's that?'

'This.' She raised her hands and he saw how close she was to crying. 'You, in on a Saturday night, taking care of me. Sean, you're twenty-two years old and you've never had a proper girlfriend. Because of me.'

'It's not because of you.'

'It is. I hobble you. That's what I do: hobble you.'

'You and your crossword clues.'

She laughed through her nose and immediately plucked a tissue from her sleeve. 'Don't joke. It's not funny.'

He understood what she meant. All his teenage years had been spent hurrying home from school, his sense of anxiety not subsiding until he could see once more that she was safe.

She placed a hand against his face. 'Look at you.'

He tilted his head away, mock alarm in his eyes. 'Please, Mum. Don't start on about the—'

'I will! Black hair and brooding looks. Winning combination.'

'I've never heard you say that before.'

'It's true.' She sniffed loudly. 'So, what's been happening? The local news mentioned an arrest . . .'

'Yeah, they cornered Cahill in a McDonald's of all places. Can you believe it?'

'Actually, I can.'

'What, him risk everything for a Big Mac?'

'Him behaving like a plonker. Most criminals aren't really that clever, Sean. That's why they're criminals. Force of habit, staying with what they know: they don't often stray far.'

'Well, he got four shots of the Taser.'

'The one that was needed and three more for luck?'

He held up a thumb. 'Correct.'

'Has questioning started to take place?'

'Yes.'

'And what were you doing today?'

'Well . . .' He tried to phrase his reply to make him sound an integral part of the investigation. 'Once word came in Cahill was in custody, a lot of the focus turned to the victims.'

'Still searching for what connects them to him?'

'Yup.'

She looked surprised. 'What did they have you working on?'

'Helping to analyse the three women's movements during their last twenty-four hours.'

'Analyse?'

'Comparing them, looking for anything to suggest they were working together.'

'You mean phone contact?'

'I did make a start on their phone records.'

'Surely that's already been done?'

'I'm double-checking. In case something was missed.'

She slid him a dubious glance. 'OK. Anything of note?'

'Mum, you know discussing the specifics of an—'

'Oh come off it. I'm police, too.'

'Were,' he corrected.

She glared briefly. 'You know what I mean. How am I going to compromise anything? Besides, a fresh pair of eyes and all that . . .'

He sighed. 'No phone contact between them. Not on the phones we've recovered, anyway.'

'And each victim's movements have been mapped by triangulating their phone's signal?'

'Of course. Nothing overlapped.'

'And the phone calls of all three have been plotted on a timeline?'

'Yes. Victim one: routine was normal. She finished work at the usual time, caught her regular bus home, stayed in for the evening. Similar story with victim two: jumped on the free city centre shuttle bus to work, spent the day in the office, back home to Deansgate, went for some food, nipped into a wine bar. Victim three turned up for work, ate lunch at her desk, travelled back home to her new flat.'

'They all had jobs, then?'

'Yes. Variety of work. Zero-hour contract in a shoe shop, full-time professional and a call-centre operative.'

'How close were their places of work?'

'They weren't. Not walking distance during a lunch break, if that's what you're thinking.'

Janet stared off into space and, for a while, the only sound was the tick of the kitchen clock.

'You didn't mention how victim number three got home,' she announced, turning to him.

'Didn't I?'

'No. Victims one and two: bus. Victim three?'

'Tram. All of two stops.'

'Buses and trams.'

'Is that significant?'

'No idea. I doubt it. How they came to be involved with Cahill—'

'Is something only he can answer,' Sean said.

Janet nodded. 'And you'll find that out tomorrow, I'm sure.'

'Let's hope.' He patted his thighs. 'Right, bed for me.' As he got to his feet, he heard her murmur something. 'What was that, Mum?'

She gave a minute shake of the head. 'Sorry?'

'You said something.'

'Did I? Thinking aloud, that's all.'

'What was it?'

She breathed in deeply. 'It would be very interesting to see the actual transcripts of their calls. I know how it works: so far, everyone's been instructed to look at who the victims spoke to, yes?'

Sean nodded.

'But no one will have been paying much attention to what they said. Not properly, anyway.'

He rarely got a sense of how keenly she missed her job, but this was one of those times. 'You think that could be worth it?'

'Could be. Who knows?'

He studied her for a moment longer, wondering if he could sneak any transcripts out for her to look at.

Once he'd closed his bedroom door, he stood in the centre of the room and listened. She said she was turning the lights out and coming up, too. The low whirr of the stair lift soon started.

Then he heard her shuffling progress down the corridor. The toilet flushed, water gurgled in the pipes and her bedroom door clicked shut.

The signal that, finally, he could relax.

Moving quietly, he approached his iMac in the corner of the room. The screen came to life and he logged on to the Facebook group that consisted of him and a few carers of a similar age. Over the years, their number had steadily dwindled. The first thing he saw was a request for help from Alice, who lived in Rochdale with her blind mum.

Agh! The corners of Mum's new shower are getting covered in this horrid black stuff. She can't see it, but I can. Any suggestions? I've tried bleach, but it comes back within a week.

Sean reached for the keyboard. *Hi Alice, you'll need a mould removal spray. About five quid? It works better if you cut an old cloth into strips and spray them with remover. Lay the wet strips over the black bits and leave overnight. Let me know if that works.'*
He came back out of that post and noticed another below it.

Guy's gone.

Sean felt a lurch of abandonment: the same he always felt when one of these messages appeared. Knowing what was coming, he opened the panel up.

Hey everyone. I wanted to let you all know, Dad finally passed away two days ago. It's cool; the hospice was amazing and he was totally free of pain all the way to the end. He'd often said he was ready to go, so please don't feel sad! It's a weird time now, suddenly in this house and all on my own. Well, not really on my own – people are popping by all the time, but you know what I mean. Anyway, I'm taking a breather by heading off to Thailand and Vietnam fairly soon! Then on to Australia where I plan to work for a while, but don't think you've heard the last of me because I will be checking in to see how you're all doing and to gloat about the weather. Heh, heh. That's all for now, got loads to sort out. Stay strong, you hear? And, honestly, I'm OK. Guy. XXX

Sean started to type, but couldn't see the letters that were appearing on the screen. Wiping the tears from his eyes, he began again.

Guy, I'm so relieved it all went smoothly for your dad, I know how much he'd been suffering. He was some fighter, from what you said. You take care and enjoy that trip because you deserve it!

And let us know what those beach parties are like! We'll be thinking of you.

He pressed send and bowed his head, knowing how things would pan out. Guy might send a few messages to begin with. But, as time went by, he'd get busier with other things. He was beginning a new part of his life, and that's how it should be. Their little group had just shrunk again.

He rotated his shoulders a few times, logged out and then picked a particular icon from the toolbar at the bottom. The webcam display in the enclosure of the Snowdonia Wolf Sanctuary. He went to the view within the sleeping area and observed the long bodies stretched out on a layer of leaves and hay and moss. Cree and Yurok, the alpha couple and their clump of puppies. Makah, the beta male nearby. Four more adults, but no sign of her. He clicked on the exterior view.

Nothing moved among the small copse of pines at the far end of the enclosure. He clicked again. She was standing beside the pool of water, head hanging low as if wondering how a slice of the night sky had been laid across its still surface.

EIGHTEEN

The gun-metal grey BMW 6 series eased to a stop on Darlington Avenue and the driver lifted the printout off the dashboard. Kersal Mews. This was it.

He climbed out of the car, removed the polythene wrapper from the driver's seat, then crouched to slide the paper from the footwell.

His boss had been very specific: the woman was a fire-breathing bitch who probably feasted on men's balls for breakfast. Be polite and don't leave so much as a speck of dust in her vehicle.

He checked over the sleek exterior. They'd even given it a complimentary polish. He cast his eye over the printout once more. Heather Knight, number sixteen. There were two front doors under the archway that led into the main courtyard. Number sixteen was on the left. Before ringing, he peered into the courtyard beyond. Audis, a Porsche, a Mercedes SLK. Another BMW 6 series, also grey. A couple of VW Beetles. Everyone said Didsbury was dead posh and trendy. He walked out into the morning sunlight, looking for number sixteen's slot. He could leave the car there. It was in the opposite corner, but some twat had parked a white Range Rover diagonally across a pavement bit and its bumper was jutting into sixteen's space. He imagined the woman's reaction when she got hold of the owner. When he rang her front doorbell, it made a noise like piano notes.

After standing there for over a minute, he tried again.

Nothing. *Fuck's sake.* Wondering why he couldn't just post the keys through the letterbox, he ambled back to the grass verge and called Martin. 'Hi there. Yeah, I'm here, but she's not answering her door. Twice. A minute, easily. It's permit parking out on the road and she has a space in the courtyard bit, but some four-by-four is blocking it. Have you got a number for – you have? OK, I'll wait outside her door.'

He had just reached it when he heard a phone start to ring from inside the flat. After seven repeats, it stopped. He crouched down and lifted the letterbox. Neat hallway, a row of watercolour sunsets along the wall. The ringing started again.

The noise was floating through the open doorway immediately on the right. He started trying to angle his head to see in when he heard a door open behind him. A man in one of those wanky wax jackets. He was wearing a tweed flat cap and was peering inquisitively at him.

He straightened up, aware of his shaved head and tattooed neck. He never thought he'd be glad of his naff work fleece with the word *Gleesons* stitched across the left breast. 'I'm trying to drop off her car. Have you seen her?'

Beyond her front door, the ringing continued.

'No, sorry.' The man turned round and closed the door to his flat, then checked it was properly locked.

He rang Martin as the man in the tweed cap walked out onto the road.

His boss didn't bother with any preamble. 'It's just going to her answerphone.'

'I know, I could hear it from outside.'

'Happy to issue demands, then disappears. Arrogant fucking slag.'

'What do you want me to do?'

'You'll have to bring it back. I'll try her again before we close.'

*   *   *

Sean conducted a quick survey of the incident room as he came through the doors. Over half the desks allocated to detectives were still empty.

The one who had invited him along to the pub was beside the photocopier, watching sheet after sheet emerge from the machine. Sean had to pause a moment before the man's name came back: Adrian Wareham.

Hoping the previous day's friendliness had survived, Sean approached him. 'Morning.'

The man glanced up. 'All right?'

'Yeah, you?' Sean replied, encouraged. 'What's the score with Cahill?'

He lifted a shoulder. 'Just giving it "No comment" so far.'

'Is he going to be charged?'

'With the women's murders?'

Sean nodded.

'Not enough evidence. Ransford's keeping his powder dry. So far, he's only being held on the attempted murder of DC Wheeler.'

Sean inadvertently glanced over to his colleague's empty desk. 'Any update from the hospital?'

'Still under sedation. Apparently, a consultant is checking him over today.'

Sean nodded again. 'That's good, I suppose.'

'I suppose.' The copier came to a stop and the officer took the stack of sheets out.

'Have they even mentioned the victims' names to Cahill?'

'No: he's just been asked to give his whereabouts for the estimated times of their deaths.'

'And?'

'He says he was just round and about in Manchester.'

Sean thought for a moment. If Cahill was claiming only that, he was putting himself as potentially in the vicinity of all the victims' houses when they were killed. 'Has he got no one to vouch for where he was?'

'He reckons he swung by a petrol station on the morning Francesca Pinto died. CCTV is being retrieved.' The officer sat down and reached for a stapler. 'Our problem is time of death. None of them are precise.'

'What did he say about that footage of him on Pamela Flood's road?'

'No comment.'

'And the phone recording of him threatening to kill her?'

'I'll give you three guesses.'

'Figures.' Sean checked the time. It was now after ten o'clock. Though Cahill had been apprehended just before eleven in the morning the previous day, he wasn't actually taken into custody until five that afternoon. In line with the PACE Act, he'd need to be formally charged with something in the next seven hours.

The other officer saw Sean studying his watch. 'DCI Ransford's called a press conference for later this afternoon. About four – in time for the early evening news and so that the papers can get their Monday editions ready.'

'What's the plan in the meantime?'

'They'll keep at him. See if he lets anything slip.'

NINETEEN

The aroma of baked grease and charred food had ingrained itself to the oven's inner surfaces. He rested his weight on his elbows to relieve the muscles in his lower back. Twisting his head in the confined space, he spoke into his shoulder. 'Almost done.'

He could only see her lower legs. Woollen stockings disappeared beneath the hem of her long skirt.

'I can't thank you enough, Brian.'

'It's my pleasure.' As he lifted the screwdriver once again, crockery chinked behind him. The thread of the last screw bit and he gave it another half-turn, just to be sure. 'That's it,' he announced, shuffling backwards, thankful to be able to finally lift his head higher than his hips. 'OK, a quick test to check it's working. If you could flick the switch back on for me?'

'Yes, of course.' Her slippers scraped across the tiled floor and there was a single click. The indicator light on the cooker glowed orange. 'Is it on?'

'Certainly is, Edith.' He turned the dial for the main oven and the interior fan began to whirr. The sound steadied into a hum and he held a hand into the compartment. Heat soon started to waft between his outstretched fingers. He sat back on his heels. 'I'm sure that's fine, but we'll leave it running for a minute or two.'

'A cup of tea, then? And a slice of cake?'

'That sounds wonderful,' he replied, getting to his feet.

She smiled coyly. 'It's only a ginger cake. Nothing special.'

'Nothing special! Let me be the judge of that.' He knew the pride she took in her baking. It was why she'd been so anxious for her oven to be fixed.

'And it's a few days old, now.'

'I'll just wash my hands, if I may?'

'Of course. The hand towel is the one on the left-hand hook.'

He glanced at the coil of metal he'd laid out on a sheet of newspaper. 'Shall I dispose of the old element for you?'

'If you don't mind?'

'Of course I don't.' Not bothering with the handwash beside the sink, he dripped a bead of washing-up liquid onto his palm and began rubbing his hands together.

'That family who've moved into the large detached house at the end of Windlehurst Road? The ones whose surname no one can pronounce?' Edith's voice now contained a hint of disapproval. 'They're knocking the garage down. Mrs Payne – she lives at twenty-three – she went to check the plans in the local library and it's for a much larger garage, but she thinks it might really be used as a bungalow.'

He held his hands beneath the tap, knowing the type of response she'd be waiting for. 'They like to all live together, don't they? In-laws and whatnot.'

'Yes,' she agreed, voice bolder. 'Who knows how many they'll try and cram in? Could they really use it as a bungalow?'

'No. Planning permission will have been for a garage. There are all sorts of extra hoops to jump through if it will be for living in.' He selected a towel on the left-hand hook and started to dry his hands.

'Oh, that's a relief. I'll tell Mrs Payne. She was very distressed.'

'Well, she has no need to worry.' His reflection showed faintly in the window before him. His hair, mostly grey now, was slightly ruffled. He smoothed the side parting back into place. Nice and neat.

'But if they do it sneakily, how would the council ever know?'

'I imagine we'd tell them,' he replied, turning round. He didn't add that he quite liked the way their types lived. At least the women dressed properly and kept themselves to themselves. You didn't see them roaming the streets in skimpy tops and tiny shorts, swigging alcohol, screeching and cackling like hyenas.

Edith nodded uncertainly. 'Sit down, Brian, please.'

The chair at the head of the table had already been moved back. He took his seat and watched as she added milk to a couple of china cups. Then she lifted a teapot that was embossed with a pattern of roses. His neighbour was now in her eighties – a good three decades older than him – and her movements were slowing, growing less sure. The spout of the teapot connected with the rim of the cup. As she righted it, a dribble of tea ran down and dripped onto the cake. He pretended not to notice.

'So, while I'm here with my toolbox: any other jobs to be done?'

She placed the teapot down and brushed both hands on her apron. 'I don't think so. Would you mind . . .?' She glanced at the knife.

'Of course.' He surveyed her kitchen. The room was immaculate. Everything in its place, nothing frivolous or bought on a whim. Most of her appliances were years old. 'How's your boiler? Is it working fine?'

'Yes, thanks to you.'

He pressed the knife into the cake.

'Actually, I have noticed rainwater running down beside the drainpipe.'

'Which one?'

'By the front door.'

'That one connects with the gutter above the bay window. It's probably become blocked with leaves from Graham's sycamore. They create a terrible tangle. I'll fetch my ladders after this.'

'I don't want you to take any risks.'

'It's not high, don't worry. Best to resolve the issue now, while the weather's mild. If rainwater's flowing over the brickwork, it'll cause cracking and all sorts of bother once winter sets in.'

Once he'd drained the last of his tea, he placed the cup back in its saucer. 'Lovely, Edith. Now, I'll pop across for those ladders.'

'Thank you. And I'll wrap you the rest of this cake.'

'No, no, I couldn't—'

'Nonsense. I can't eat it. Take it into the staffroom, I'm sure they'll finish it off.'

'Finish it off? Edith, when I bring your cake in, there's a stampede.'

The modesty of her laughter made him smile.

They lived on a cul-de-sac of nine identical houses. His was the first on the left, opposite Edith's. The driveway was short and, as he walked up it, he regarded the foil package in his hands. Even if he'd wanted to take it into the staffroom, that would never happen now: his job had been taken from him by that bloody Harpham woman.

By the time he'd unlocked the garage's side door, anger was making his temples hum. He stood below the strip lights and thought about the bitch who'd put him in the position of having to pretend to go to work each morning. The humiliation of it.

He bent down and placed the cake on the concrete floor. Give this to the collection of snivelling cowards who lurked in the staffroom? His nostrils flared with disgust. As word spread about the incident with the student, how many of those colleagues had supported him? None. Not one, despite the amount of time they spent in that precious room, moaning about how students were always using their phones in lessons.

He raised his right foot and stamped down on the cake.

It hadn't taken long before footage of what had happened appeared online.

His stamped down again.

Something needed to be done. Respect was an alien concept to the vain, self-important preeners. It shouldn't have been a surprise to learn there was a video of him striking the student. How often would phones chirrup and buzz as he was trying to make himself clear? Always checking their bloody screens, tapping and swiping and tilting them to their neighbours and rolling their eyes when he demanded they turn the cursed things off.

The foil was now like a silver pancake fringed by a halo of crumbs. He stepped away from it and waited for his breathing to slow. His set of ladders lay beneath the workbench that ran the length of the garage. He lifted his gaze to the uppermost shelf.

The jars formed an orderly row. Most of what filled his garage had been fashioned from metal. Tools and implements with straight edges or hard, flat surfaces. The row of four glass jars stood in contrast. Their delicately curving exteriors allowed the passage of light. The liquid that filled each one glowed a faint, honeyed yellow. The butchered tongues suspended in that liquid resembled sea creatures. Once living things that had been torn from shells or ripped off rocks.

'Julie, it's Linds. You not ignoring me, are you? Listen, it's Sunday, almost lunchtime – well, you know that. Maybe you got an extra shift? Can't remember if you said you were due in today. Head's pounding, Julie. You missed a good one. Faye came out and was fucking on one. Did I ring you? My phone says I rang you at half eleven. We were trollied! Call us – you and me need a catch-up. OK, later, yeah? Bye.'

The phone that jutted from the dead woman's lips lit up and emitted a single beep.

New voicemail.

The red circle on the screen now displayed the number six.

On the other side of the living room wall came the muffled sounds of a man coughing.

TWENTY

Sean kept a surreptitious eye on Ransford as he stepped out of his office. There was a frown on his face; still no break-through with Cahill. It was almost three o'clock.

He was accompanied by a DI from a different team. Sean gathered that she had notched up a few successes with getting locked-down suspects to speak. Unlike Ransford, her face had yet to carry the corrosive effects of repeated exposure to lies and deceit. The exhausting effect of dealing with those who committed dark acts and then denied it.

The woman was not much over five feet tall and in her mid-thirties. When she spoke, Sean detected traces of a soft Scottish accent. 'I had him put in number two.'

'OK,' Ransford replied. 'Let's give it twenty with your approach. But if nothing significant comes up, I lay out the murder stuff.'

'Clear.'

Sean rose from his seat and set off towards them. He had no

idea of what he was going to say; the urge had materialized too suddenly for any planning. By almost breaking into a jog, he managed to intercept them by the doors. 'Sir?'

Ransford glanced to his side, but didn't slow down. 'Not now, Detective.'

He pursued them out into the corridor. 'Sir, I only want permission to observe.'

Ransford looked back. 'Observe what?'

Sean scrabbled for a coherent response. Something to justify what he'd found himself doing. 'The interview, sir. I've been spending a lot of time going over the three victims' final twenty-four hours. Hearing Cahill's responses first hand, I think that – maybe – I could pick up on . . .'

Ransford slowed to a stop. He turned round and raised the manila folders in his hand. 'You mean, you're party to information I don't have? Is that what you're saying?'

Sean shook his head. 'Of course not, sir. But . . . but I've been—' he gestured to the doors – 'I've been in there . . .'

Ransford's expression was growing more disdainful by the second. 'Since the incident with DC Wheeler, I've been in there and I've spent a lot of time—'

'It's Blake, isn't it? Your surname?' Ransford's voice was light with impatience as he began backing away. 'What planet are you from, DC Blake, that makes you think—'

'Let me see him, sir.' His voice was too loud. He looked down for a split-second and tried again. 'I just want to look at his face.'

Ransford's gaze raked him.

Sean nodded. *This*, he realized abruptly, *is why I'm standing here. Everyone thinks I bottled it, that I was frightened of him.* 'He was as far as you are now, sir. Spattered with blood. Ready to jump at me with that spike of metal. I want to see him, sat there in cuffs, and I—' the surge of emotion was drying up faster than it had appeared – '. . . I need to see him, that's all. He didn't scare me, sir. He did not scare me.'

No one said anything.

Then the female DI turned to DCI Ransford. 'This is the other detective, from when Cahill—'

Ransford nodded.

She stepped forward and, to Sean's horror, began to scrutinize him. 'Lift your chin, can you? And look at me.'

Sean felt like he was at the doctor's. Like he was some kind of specimen. 'You what?' Anger prickled him and he tried to look away.

'No, look at me.'

At the edge of his vision, he could make out Ransford's perplexed expression. He stared back at her, defiant now. *Go on then, have your fun.*

Finally, she blinked. 'You pack a heck of a lot into that stare, don't you?' A smile appeared. 'It's intense.'

'Sorry, Penny, but what's this about?' Ransford asked.

Her eyes had narrowed in thought. 'The kind of man Cahill is? He won't enjoy being stared at like DC Blake was just staring at me. He really bloody won't.'

As a uniformed officer began to open the interview room's door, Sean kept DI Penny McMillan's instructions in his head. *Take the left hand seat. Don't speak. Don't adopt a confrontational posture. Just look at him. That's all, just look at him. And as soon as you hear a knock on the door, get up and leave the room.* The woman's voice had been gentle, almost soothing.

Cahill had both elbows on the table, head down as a thumb made circles in his palm.

Sitting next to him was a wispy-haired solicitor with a long nose and slightly bulbous eyes. The man watched carefully as they crossed to the table and took their seats.

DI McMillan started the recorder and stated who was present. At the mention of DC Blake's name, Cahill raised his head, a look of boredom on his face. The moment he saw Sean, he glanced at his solicitor then at McMillan.

Sean kept his eyes on Cahill, expression neutral. When Cahill came off the trampoline, his mouth had been open. He'd been panting like a wild animal. Sean could remember the man had a crooked front tooth. It slightly overlapped its neighbour. That tooth was now missing, along with the ones to either side. Cahill's lips were still swollen. A series of tiny stitches ran from his bottom lip to halfway down his chin.

Just before the TAU officer had shouted from the first-floor window, Cahill had run his tongue across his lower lip. The flecks of Mark Wheeler's blood that were peppering it had all vanished.

'Mr Cahill.' DI McMillan sounded like she was addressing a

valued customer. 'I'd like to run through, one more time, the reasons you gave for fleeing from your house.'

Cahill had sat up in his seat. His eyes kept cutting to Sean.

'Mr Cahill, could we do that?' DI McMillan's voice was like water flowing across pebbles. She didn't wait for his agreement. 'You stated that, when you heard officers entering the property you—'

'My client didn't know for sure they were police officers,' the solicitor interjected.

McMillan nodded. 'When you heard people entering the property, clearly identifying themselves as police officers, you panicked. Is that right?'

'Yeah, that's right.' The words came out clumsily. His lack of teeth had left him with a lisp.

His voice, Sean thought, wasn't as rough as he'd expected. No drawn-out nasal twang. No sandpaper rasp.

'So you immediately made for the window, terrified that members of a criminal gang were racing up the stairs to attack you?'

'Yeah.'

'And everything was a blur? You don't recall grabbing the sharpened implement from the sill as you manoeuvred yourself out of the window?'

'Yeah.' He glanced at Sean yet again.

Sean kept staring back, trying to keep all emotion from his face.

McMillan placed a finger on the printed statement. 'And in your state of panic and fear—'

'What the fuck's this?' Cahill rubbed a hand along his jaw and gestured at Sean.

McMillan made a show of looking confused. 'I'm sorry?'

'Why's he here?'

'DC Blake is part of the investigating team,' McMillan replied. 'Now, Mr Cahill, if we can return to the incident. You stated that you dropped from the window onto the trampoline below, and, before you—'

Cahill leaned forward to better address Sean. 'Keep sitting there, like a big man. Stare all you fucking want.'

Sean inclined his head the tiniest fraction in reply. *Thanks, I will.*

Cahill sat back in the chair, and as he did so, the short chain attached to the cuff around his wrist made a slinking sound.

McMillan suddenly seemed to be engrossed by the sheet of paper before her. The solicitor was frowning. As the silence stretched out, Sean willed himself to not look at the man's hand. At the fingers that had gripped the sharpened screwdriver. The droplets of Mark Wheeler's blood that had slewed off.

Cahill made a snorting noise, eyes drawn back to Sean's.

Sean felt blood rising to his face. *Do not look away. Keep eye contact.*

'I seen you, dickhead,' Cahill sneered. 'You weren't the big man back there, were you? You little fucking—'

'Ian?' His solicitor placed a hand on Cahill's forearm. 'Stop speaking, Ian. DI McMillan, who is this colleague?'

She didn't appear to hear the solicitor's question. 'Ah, yes. You were grappled to the ground by an unknown assailant and so struck out blindly in self-defence.'

Ignoring McMillan, Cahill shook the chain connecting him to the table, 'You wouldn't be fucking looking at me like that, if this was off.'

'DI McMillan,' the solicitor warned.

'As soon as you were able,' McMillan's voice was growing louder, 'you got to your feet and, in fear of your life, ran for the gate.'

The solicitor sat forward. 'I asked you who this officer—'

'You are nothing.' Cahill spat. 'You are fucking nothing!'

'Mr Cahill,' McMillan said, 'you stated that you had no opportunity to identify anyone as being a police officer. Isn't that right?'

'Do not answer that question,' the solicitor cut in.

'However,' McMillan glanced at Sean, 'my colleague – who you have obviously recognized – was wearing items that clearly identified him as a—'

The solicitor started waving his hands above the table. 'No, no, no, no, no – my client will not be answering any—'

The door banged loudly and Ransford stepped inside. Sean saw the solicitor's head turn and used the opportunity to seek out Cahill's eyes. He gave the other man the hint of a smile as he stood. *Got you, you bastard.*

As he passed his senior officer, Ransford gave a cough. 'Mr Cahill, now we've established that what you've told us so far is a pack of lies, I have some photos I'd like you to look at.'

*   *   *

By the time Sean had let himself into the adjoining observation galley, DCI Ransford had laid out photographs of all three murder victims. At least six other officers were already in the narrow half-lit space.

'Nice going, Detective,' someone murmured.

'You play poker?' another voice asked. 'Because you bloody should.'

On the other side of the glass, Ransford continued to speak. '. . . found dead in her home on Hurst Walk, Gorton.' His hand moved to the next image. 'Francesca Pinto, a twenty-nine-year-old solicitor who once acted on your behalf. Found dead in her home off Napier Court, Deansgate.' His fingers tapped the final image. 'And Victoria Walker, age twenty-one, of Urmston. She was found dead in her home on Pinner Street.'

Cahill's head was jerking about now. His face shone with sweat.

'DCI Ransford,' the solicitor's voice wobbled. 'What is the relevance to my client—'

'The last two women had been murdered in exactly the same way as Pamela Flood.' Ransford was speaking directly at Cahill. 'Both of them had willingly let someone into their home, as had Pamela. Someone all of them most likely knew.'

Cahill twisted towards his solicitor. 'This is pure shite. I tell you, there is no fucking—'

'Say nothing else!' The solicitor pointed weakly at the photos. 'My client has nothing further to say. I want this interview terminated and I want to know exactly what he's being charged with!'

Ransford suddenly smiled. 'Well, let's not rush this. A magistrate has granted me an extension for questioning your client. Plenty of time to uncover what's really been going on here. Right now, Mr Cahill, I have dozens of detectives combing every aspect of these three women's lives. And deaths.'

'I've never seen them two,' Cahill spluttered. 'And I didn't kill Pam. This is pure fucking—'

His solicitor raised a hand. 'Enough!'

In the observation room, Sean realized his face was nearly touching the glass. Remembering he wasn't alone, he turned self-consciously to the shadowy audience beside him. 'Good to see the piece of shit finally crack.'

TWENTY-ONE

He decided to chance it and drive Heather Knight's BMW into Kersal Mews' parking area. The gamble paid off: whoever owned the white Range Rover had now moved it. As he pulled into her space, he imagined what might have been said if she'd caught the owner. Another thought occurred. What if that person had been staying in Heather Knight's flat? Maybe they were both going at it when he'd tried calling earlier. Yeah, she was probably into all sorts of stuff. Martin said she was a ball-breaker. Probably a dominatrix. What if she answered the door in black leather and fishnet tights? Invited him in for so kindly bringing her car back . . .

As he crossed the courtyard, he let the fantasy play out. By the time he pressed the doorbell, he was spread-eagled on black satin sheets, looking up at her as she slowly . . . still no answer. *Fucking bitch.*

Martin had tried her phone a couple more times either side of lunch. He'd said that, if she still didn't answer her door, he was to just post the key through her letterbox with a note saying where the vehicle was.

He rang the bell again, just to be sure. A minute ticked slowly by. *Right, that's it then.* He extracted a biro and note pad from the side pocket of his cargo trousers and wrote a message to say the car was in her slot. Dropping to one knee, he raised the flap of her letterbox.

Everything appeared exactly as it had earlier: all the doors were shut except the one to the right. By angling his head at the far end of the rectangular opening, he was able to partly see into what must be her front room.

She was bloody in there!

He could just make out the ends of her feet. She must be sitting down, in an armchair or on a sofa. He could even see the fingers of one hand draped over an armrest. What the fuck was her problem? Was she deaf?

'Hello? It's Gleesons – I've got your car. Miss Knight, can you hear me?'

She stayed perfectly still. Too still. For the first time, he felt a trace of uneasiness. Something wasn't right. Straightening up, he reached for his phone. 'Martin? Yeah, I'm here. Thing is, I can see her. Well, I can see her feet. Sitting in the front room. She could be wearing headphones. I thought if you try her phone again, it'll cut off any track she's listening to. OK, will do.'

He crouched down, phone still held to his ear. A few seconds later, the now familiar ringtone started to repeat. 'Yeah, I can hear it. No, she's not moving. I think something's wrong with her.'

Ransford looked at his watch. Ten to four. Tina Small – Head of Media Relations – was leaning against the doorjamb of his office. As usual, her attention was on her phone. He watched her for a moment, marvelling at how fast her fingers worked. Then he checked the statement another time. 'Right. Being questioned in connection with their murders, it will have to be. And, as it's an on-going investigation, I can't elaborate further.' He sighed. Out in the incident room, nothing much was happening. No hand shooting up, no cry of triumph. Nothing.

Preliminary forensics had failed to find anything to suggest Cahill had been in Victoria Walker's flat. Same story for Francesca Pinto, and a team had spent two days in her home, going over it properly. No doubt the bloke was forensically aware – he'd been arrested enough times to have built up an understanding of how to avoid leaving any incriminating evidence. But to not leave a single trace of anything? Ransford tried to push the doubts from his mind.

'Shall we head down?' Tina said, glancing up from her screen.

He reached for the statement, fingers hovering above it. If only they'd found a phone call or text. Under section 18 of PACE, all other properties connected to Cahill had been entered and searched. Even residences he was known to only occasionally visit. Plenty had been found on his on-going crash-for-cash scam, but nothing to do with Pinto or Walker.

'DCI Ransford?'

He blinked. 'Sorry. Yes, let's get going.'

*   *   *

'Miss Heather Knight?' The police constable waited a moment, then lowered the flap of the letterbox. He looked up at an older, larger colleague and shook his head.

Now standing a few metres back, the garage delivery driver's eyes gleamed with interest.

The older officer put his hands on his hips and regarded the window of the front room. 'What do you reckon? This or the door?'

His colleague shrugged. 'Less mess if it's the door?'

'Yeah, you're right. And I'm not climbing through a window frame of broken glass. Have a check, then.'

The younger officer grasped the door knob and gave it a shake. Then he held a palm to the upper part of the door and tested it. Pressing the toe of one boot against the lower corner, he repeated the move. 'Just one lock engaged at the midpoint, here.'

'No bolts drawn?'

'Nope.'

'And that's a Yale?'

'It is.'

'Want to do the honours?'

He glanced over to the patrol car parked on the road. 'We're not using a hooly bar?'

'No need. Not for a single Yale.'

'You've done it before.'

'Come on. Good a time as any to break your duck.'

'OK.' He flexed his knees a couple of times. 'Here, then? On the keyhole?'

'That's right. But before you enter the property, it would be a good idea to do something else.'

The younger officer frowned. 'Something else?'

His colleague lifted a hand and waggled his fingers.

'Oh. Gloves.'

'Correct.'

They both pulled on pale blue latex gloves.

'Use your heel. It's all in the heel.'

The younger officer took a step back and drew in a breath. Then he lifted a knee and kicked out, both elbows jabbing back with the effort.

The door flew open.

'Ten out of ten,' the older officer announced. 'After you.'

The younger one stepped cautiously into the hallway. 'Miss Knight? Police. Can you hear me?'

The older officer held a finger to the garage employee. 'Come nowhere near this door, understood?'

He nodded.

The older officer spoke to his colleague's back as he stepped inside. 'Let's see what we've got.'

'Oh Jesus, oh—'

The younger officer was retreating from the doorway of the front room, a forearm pressed against his mouth. His cheeks bulged out then in.

'If you're going to spew, do it outside!' The older officer pulled him out the way and peered into the room beyond. 'Fuck's sake.'

Ransford stepped up to the lectern. The whiteboard behind him was illuminated by the logo of Greater Manchester Police. Before him stood a group of ten or so journalists. Tina Small watched from the side of the room, eyes checking the feeds of her phone every few seconds.

'I have a statement,' Ransford announced, 'in relation to the attack on a detective constable last Thursday and in relation to the murders of three women in the Manchester area. I can take questions at the end, but this investigation is on-going, so my responses will be limited in light of that fact.'

He placed a hand on either side of the lectern. During his recent training course with Tina, she'd encouraged him to do this. According to her, it imparted an impression of authority and confidence.

Someone's phone went off. In the periphery of his vision, he registered Tina turning away as she took the call. He scanned the printed statement, trying to refind his place.

'Late yesterday morning, a thirty-seven-year-old man was arrested in the Middleton area of Manchester. This man was being sought for the attack on a detective constable that is now being treated as attempted murder. The officer in question is still in a critical condition as a result of the injuries he sustained. In addition to—'

His speech ground to a halt as Tina stepped up onto the small dais.

The first thing she did was turn the microphone off. She then ushered him a couple of steps towards the back wall and whispered into his ear. 'Do not give any reaction to what I'm about to say, other than to nod. Another body has just been found.'

Ransford said nothing for a second. 'Where?'

'In Didsbury. She was killed very recently.'

'How recently?'

'After the arrest of Ian Cahill.'

TWENTY-TWO

He removed his shoes while standing on the rubber mat just inside his front door.

His slippers were aligned neatly on the carpet just beyond it. After stepping into them, he turned round, picked up his shoes and placed them on the wooden rack behind the door. Further in the house, a clock ticked.

On the lower shelf were his Karrimor hiking shoes. He had visited a massive sports outlet on the edge of the city centre the previous year. Once there, tempted by the loudly marked special offers, he had purchased a pair of Hi-Tec ones. It was a decision he immediately regretted. The level of workmanship was, in his opinion, shoddy. It had been the impulsiveness of the purchase that riled him most as he'd dropped them into the collection container for a charity. He'd then driven to the specialist hiking shop on a side road in the unfashionable town of Hyde that he'd frequented for years. There, he'd invested in a proper pair.

A single black-and-white photo dominated the hall area. It was of his grandfather, Frederick. He was in his army uniform, and it had been taken two days before he'd set off for France. Two months later, he was dead. Pulverized into the Passchendaele mud.

The dining room table doubled as his study. His computer and printer were located on a desk in the same corner. A filing cabinet was positioned beside it and above that was a small shelving unit. Most of it was taken up by instruction manuals and technical guides.

The dining room table was never actually used for meals. Not since Mother had passed. Since then, no one had been invited into the house. The large expanse of wood made a good area for marking assignments. Plenty of room to arrange the students' papers into a production line with himself – green biro in hand – at the midpoint.

Above the computer was a magnetic noticeboard. As he sat down, he studied the timetable at its centre. It was for the previous academic year, but experience had taught him dates for training days rarely varied.

Last year, Monday the nineteenth had been allocated. In previous years, that had entailed toe-curling away-days. Team exercises to build rapport among the college's beleaguered teaching resource. Forced cheer and manufactured camaraderie. Fortunately, budgetary restrictions had put a stop to such nonsense. More recently, staff members were encouraged to arrange their own Continued Professional Development activities. He bet that, for most, it consisted of a day at home, lounging about and doing nothing.

He brought the computer to life. His employment had been officially terminated several weeks ago. He wondered if the IT department had already disabled his access to the system. Logic and prudence dictated that they should have. But he knew the department to be so slow, he suspected them of recalcitrance.

Opening the staff area resulted in the usual login screen. He tried his username and password.

Invalid. Please see your administrator.

Well, well, they had actually performed their duties with a degree of efficiency. He opened the college's main site. From the tabs that ran along the top of the screen, he selected academic calendar. At the side of the page, he selected the year view.

A spreadsheet design appeared, days and weeks colour coded into squares and strips. As he thought, the third Monday of the month had been set aside for staff training. He knew that Katherine – or Kat as she liked to call herself when dealing with students – was an ardent believer in the power of social media. The college corridors were festooned with posters so brightly coloured, they smacked of desperation.

Would students please like this or follow that?

No wonder they were always stuck to their bloody phones. He selected the *Principal's Message* from the home page. There were her banal words telling prospective students that, if they believed in themselves and reached higher, they could be the best.

At the bottom of her message was a series of icons. The blue bird thing would, he guessed, be where her latest witterings could be viewed. He clicked on it.

There was her thumbnail photo, grinning inanely out at him. He studied the clumsy frames of her retro glasses. Her splayed fringe that hung so low her eyebrows were obscured. The ridiculous bun arrangement on the top of her head and the long tresses of hair that fringed her chubby face.

He scanned through her latest comments. There was bound to be something; she was unable to maintain any kind of silence for long, in the real world or the virtual. To do so required a degree of dignity. A measure of sagacity. Qualities she didn't possess.

Three things about the abuse that followed the incident in his classroom surprised him.

First, was how fast it began. That, he came to learn, was the power of social media. Messages to the academy's Facebook page, comments to its Twitter account, emails to his work address. The flood of vitriol was beyond belief.

Second was how many people joined in. It was nothing more than a mob: students, their friends, family members. People from around the country – and further.

Third was how Katherine Harpham had failed to support him. In a way, that hurt the most.

He continued scanning the screen and found what he was looking for five comments back.

Can't wait to spend Monday on CPD: you never stop learning! Take care and see you all Tues!!!

His focus shifted back to her photo and he conjured their coming doorstep exchange.

'Brian? Erm . . . what are you doing here?'

'I have a delivery for you.'

'Yes, of course. I can see that, silly me. So . . . so, you've already found a new job? Courier driver. That's really great, Brian, really great. It really is.'

'Yes, it's not bad.'

'You must . . . um . . . you must get to see all sorts of interesting places round Manchester. Places you'd have never thought to visit, normally.'

'That is very true. My schedule, as a matter of fact, is rather tight.'

'Of course! What am I like, keeping you here, chatting? Do you need a signature?'

'I do. On this screen. Here, you can use this.'

He broke from the reverie to look at her message again. *Take care and see you all Tues!!! No, Kat, you won't. The college will open its doors and, at some point, people will begin to wonder why your office is empty. Why you're not answering the phone. Tongues will start to wag, Kat. But not yours. Yours will have finally stopped wagging.*

He thought about the jars in his garage. *Your tongue will belong to me.*

TWENTY-THREE

The instant the search team from Heather Knight's flat came through the incident room's doors, Ransford called the briefing. Chairs were wheeled away from desks as they congregated before the noticeboards.

Sean found a gap beside Magda and they both watched as a new photo was pinned up. That made four of them. Four victims in eight days. And, it now seemed, murdered by someone other than Cahill.

'This is going to keep us very busy,' Magda said from the corner of her mouth.

Sean nodded. Cahill formed the foundation of the entire investigation. Remove him and the whole thing would collapse – leaving them sifting through the debris, looking for something. Anything.

'Listen carefully,' Ransford said. The man's voice was full of energy that sounded forced. He gestured at the latest photo. 'The Home Office pathologist has now confirmed Heather Knight died between eleven a.m. and three p.m. yesterday. Cahill was in the A&E at the Manchester Royal Infirmary for most of that time. Allow for the fact Heather Knight's flat is in Didsbury and Cahill was picked up all the way over in Middleton, and it makes it even more certain he didn't kill her.'

'That time of death is beyond all doubt?' The officer who'd asked the question didn't sound optimistic.

Ransford eased his head forward in a regretful nod. 'The pathologist was able to go off lines of hypostasis and the extent of rigor
mortis. She also took the victim's internal temperature at the scene
to provide us with more certainty. So,' he clapped his hands, 'other
possibilities?'

'He's not working alone.'

'Good,' Ransford replied. 'He's not working alone. Given the
theory that all the victims were killed in order to silence them,
this could have legs. If the style of the actual murders is serving
as a warning to others, it suggests a criminal enterprise of some
sort. Something large. But,' he held up a cautionary finger, 'we
have yet to obtain any evidence – forensic or otherwise – that
links Cahill to Francesca Pinto, Victoria Walker or – so far –
Heather Knight. So, we need other options.'

'This latest one is a copycat?'

Sean recognized the voice and looked across.

DS Fuller's eyebrows were still hopefully raised. 'That way,
Cahill is still our man. For the first three, at least.'

Yes, Sean thought. *If you're happy to overlook pretty much every
other aspect of the investigation so far.* He couldn't believe the
man could have blurted something like that out.

'Interesting,' Ransford said. 'Talk me through your reasoning.'

'Well,' Fuller shrugged. 'A third party picks up on the attacks
so far and thinks, yeah, I'll have some of that.'

'Cahill having confided in this person how he has been carrying
out the murders?'

'Not necessarily,' Fuller said. 'Just someone with a grudge
against Heather Knight.'

'But if they're not learning the specifics of the killings from
Cahill, how have they got that information in order to copy it?'

'Oh,' Fuller grunted. 'You mean, because we've not yet made
that . . .'

Ransford had stepped over to a new portion of the whiteboard.
He plucked a marker pen from the ledge at its base. 'Which leads
us to this.'

He wrote out two words. Sean glanced about, sensing what
everyone else in the room was thinking: they were faced with the
nightmare scenario.

'Random victims,' Ransford declared slowly and deliberately. He surveyed the room. 'We must now treat this as a working possibility. Which means everything we've done so far must be reviewed in that light. House-to-house enquiries, crime-scene evidence gathered, checks on the victims' final movements. The lot.'

He let that sink in for a few seconds before continuing.

'Samantha Greenhalgh is a psychological profiler who has provided advice on a number of high-profile cases where the victims had no prior contact with their murderer.'

Serial killer, Sean thought. *He's talking about a serial killer.*

'She's already been given access to our records and has started an assessment. Mrs Greenhalgh is currently at a conference in Brussels, but will be with us via a video link tomorrow to share her initial thoughts. Anyone have any questions?'

An officer at the front immediately raised her hand. 'What's the official angle? I mean, are we now acknowledging that there might be—'

'Absolutely not,' Ransford cut in. 'We still have Ian Cahill. We can still claim he's being questioned in connection to the women's deaths. And he will be charged with the attempted murder of Mark Wheeler. By the way, for those who haven't heard, Mark was brought out of sedation a few hours ago. He can't yet speak, but he was able to confirm that he has some sensation in both arms and both legs.'

Applause, slow at first, but quickly gathering strength, broke out. Sean exchanged a tentative smile with Magda. Behind her, he caught sight of DS Fuller. The man was methodically bringing his palms together. A slow clap, directed straight at Sean.

'OK, OK.' Ransford raised both hands. 'Firstly, a magistrate has given permission for us to detain Cahill for another sixty hours. Until that period expires, our line is that he is being questioned in connection to all four murders.'

'So, publically, we're still treating him as our prime suspect?' the same female officer asked. 'Even though we now think—'

'That's correct, DC Williams. We've got him as a shield, but only until late on Tuesday. Two and a half days, people. I don't need to emphasize to you all how fucking vital it is we have something before then.'

TWENTY-FOUR

'**R**ight, DC Blake?' The printed sheet the allocator carried was so long it had folded itself over the man's hands. He looked like a waiter, approaching a table with an oversized napkin.

For the last twenty minutes, Sean had tracked the man as he'd worked his way through where the main bulk of detectives were seated. Team after team had then risen from their seats and headed out to pursue the line of enquiry they'd been tasked with.

'I need you to contact the council to confirm any refuse collections scheduled in the area of Heather Knight's house for tomorrow have been suspended. Same goes for drain cleaning. We've got a team to do those searches, but it won't be until first thing in the morning. Understood?'

'No problem.'

'After that, go over the inventory of the contents of Heather Knight's house to ensure everything's been catalogued correctly.'

Filler, Sean thought. Not real work – just going over other people's. He felt more keenly how he was being kept at the periphery. Tossed jobs that were of no consequence. Remembering the conversation he'd had with his mum in the kitchen, he sat up. 'Who's doing the mobile phone analysis?'

The allocator paused in the act of walking away. 'Which victim's?'

'All of them. I wanted to check the transcripts . . .' He caught the man's expression. 'After I've completed what you've just given me, of course.'

He nodded. 'You need to see Maggie about that.' He pointed over to the coordinator of the Civilian Support Workers. 'That's her shout.'

'OK, thanks.'

Within an hour, the allocator had returned. 'Change of plan, DC Blake. How far through that are you?'

'Council have suspended all their operations in that post code. I've just started on the inventory.'

'OK, a CSW can finish that off. You're needed to assist with the house-to-house enquiries around Heather Knight's residence. Seven thirty on a Sunday night: most people should be in by now.'

Sean was already on his feet. *At last, I get out of this bloody office.* 'Who do I report to?'

'DI Heys is coordinator at the scene, rendezvous point is on the grass verge before the property. You know where you're going?'

Sean didn't need to check the sheet on his desk. 'Sixteen, Kersal Mews.'

Knowing things would be busy close to Heather Knight's flat, Sean parked on an adjacent street. As he strode round, he pulled cool air deep into his lungs. Above him, the evening sky was dull tangerine. It felt good to be outside.

The clang of a gate to his right. A man stepped out onto the pavement, phone held to his ear. 'Says it should be raining. Seriously, my weather app says *Manchester: light showers.* Right now!' He briefly regarded the sky. 'How mad is that?'

When, Sean wondered, did people start trusting apps over what was in front of their face? He thought about people who drove their cars into lakes or off cliffs because that's where the satnav was directing them.

A uniform in a high-vis jacket was standing before a *Road Closed* sign positioned at the end of the Darlington Avenue. *That was me not long ago*, Sean thought. *Doing grunt work.*

'Are you a resident here?' The constable's hand was raised. 'Only there's no access.'

Sean took his ID out. Second time he'd needed it. 'DC Blake, Serious Crimes Unit.'

The officer stepped back. 'OK. You'll see where to report in.'

Ahead, the road had been blocked by a couple of liveried patrol cars, a Crime Scene Investigation van and a couple of Volvos he knew to be unmarked police vehicles.

Crime scene tape formed a perimeter that started thirty metres away from the turning into Kersal Mews. Sean approached the access point, badge ready. 'DC Blake.'

The uniform signed him in and Sean proceeded towards the grass verge where several officers were gathered. The inner cordon started at the turning itself; anyone going beyond that point would have to be wearing a forensic suit. Sean glanced towards the entrance to the inner courtyard. A couple of white figures lingered like ghosts in the archway's shadow.

'DC Blake, here to assist with house-to-house—'

'Right.' DI Heys had short hair that had been overloaded with gel. Thick shiny spikes stood proud of his head. Flab had accumulated around his lower jaw, the weight of it forcing his bottom lip out. 'I need you to take the top half of Seymour Road. Annie will sort you out.' He turned his back to continue his discussion and another officer with a clipboard stepped forward.

'Seymour Road is—'

'The next one over. I'm parked on it.'

'Very good. Retrace your steps. Last house on the right side is forty-eight. Work your way back to the mid-point. By that time, you should encounter DC Morris, who started at the other end about ten minutes ago.'

Morris, Sean thought. *DS Fuller's sidekick.* Part of that thing in the canteen with the newspaper. He realized he never did work out what that was about.

'Victim's estimated time of death is late yesterday morning,' the other officer continued. 'A resident saw someone stepping into the victim's property around noon.'

'Male or female?' Sean asked.

'He couldn't say. He was in his car and the archway was in shadow. Dark shoes and trousers is all he could report. Probably male. So, the window we're interested in is around that time. Clear?'

'I'll get started.'

'And DC Blake? Word's started to spread. At this stage, it's a suspicious death. And that's all you know.'

'But what is it?' The woman kept glancing down uneasily at the young boy standing beside her. One hand rested protectively on his head.

'At the moment, all we can say is that it's suspicious.'

The boy craned his head back. 'What's suspicious?'

'Nothing to do with you. In fact, back in the telly room, please.'

He didn't move. 'Have you got a proper badge?'

Fourth time! Sean thought, immediately producing it. He kept the leather holder closed. 'Are you thinking of becoming a policeman?'

'No. Vlogger.'

Sean was left struggling. 'Well . . . if I show you this, you go back in the telly room like your mum asked. Deal?'

'OK.'

He flipped it open and let the youngster have a good look. 'That's your lot.'

The kid stalked off, mum watching over her shoulder until the telly room door closed. She turned back to Sean, now not bothering to hide her concern. 'But it was a female. Am I right? The person who died, she was female?'

'That's correct.'

'Jesus.'

'Were you in yesterday, around noon?'

'No. Sam plays football on a Saturday morning. We're out the house by ten fifteen.'

'And that's everyone? The house was empty after that?'

'Yes.'

'And you returned . . .'

'Not until one o'clock.'

'OK. Nothing caught your attention as you left? Unusual vehicle or anyone hanging around?'

'Sorry, no. When will we be told what's actually going on?'

'Local radio is a good bet. They receive updates same time as me. Sometimes before. But, really, we'll be in the area for a long time yet; there's no need to worry.'

'OK.'

He made his way to the next house, noticing the icy glow of a TV beyond the curtains as he began to knock. It wasn't until the eighth house that Sean felt a flicker of excitement. The portly man spoke with a strong Italian accent.

'Late morning, you say?' His eyes had narrowed. 'Lou-lou? When did you say to me about that van?'

He was soon joined in the doorway by a birdlike woman, who was busily drying her hands with a dishcloth.

'Yesterday morning, Lou-lou, you spotted that van parked at the front.'

'Yes.' She lowered her voice. 'The family at sixty-eight, they don't like when people park too close to their drive.'

'And this van had done that?' Sean asked.

She cocked her head. 'Close enough for them to come out and tell the driver to move it.'

'Did they do that?'

'No.'

'They couldn't have spotted it,' the husband interjected. 'Or they would have come out and started shouting.'

'They can be very aggressive,' Lou-lou concurred. 'But they were probably all asleep.' She motioned daintily with a forefinger and thumb. Sipping from a tiny glass. 'That's what they normally do on a Friday night.'

Doubt it's thimbles of sherry though, Sean thought. 'Did you see who was in the van?'

The couple looked at one another. Some kind of communication, evolved through decades of marriage, flitted between them.

'We didn't see,' the man said. 'It was there at about eleven and it was gone when I went for a paper. That would have been . . .'

'Twelve thirty,' Lou-lou stated.

Sean noted everything down. 'What kind of van was it?'

'White.' This from the husband.

'A transit van? Large, with a high roof?'

'No. One of those little ones you see all over the place. The size of a car.'

'Did it have windows in the rear?'

'Yes, it—'

'Ettre!' The woman batted his arm with the damp dishcloth. 'It didn't have windows!'

'Yes. A window at the back.'

She looked at Sean while shaking her head. 'Don't listen: there wasn't a window. It had the outline of a window, but no window actually there.'

'You mean like a panel?' Sean asked. 'A window-shaped depression in the bodywork?'

'Yes.'

'I think it was a window,' Ettre muttered.

'*Tsss!*' She shot back.

Sean suppressed a smile. 'Any writing or markings on the van?'

'No.' They spoke in unison.

'And could you say which make of van it was?'

Ettre checked his wife's face. Lou-lou lowered her eyelids to indicate she couldn't say. 'Just a van,' Ettre stated. 'A little van. The ones that are everywhere.'

'OK, thanks. We might call back with some images to see if any stand out. Would that be all right with you?'

The next houses drew a blank. By the time the numbers were into the eighties, he could see DC Morris further down the street. Twenty-five minutes later, they met.

'How's it gone?' Sean asked, readying himself to describe the van sighting when asked.

DC Morris walked straight by.

Sean found himself staring at a patch of empty pavement. It felt like he'd been slapped. He turned to look at the other officer's back. 'Problem?'

Still walking, Morris spoke over his shoulder. 'No problem. Keep well away from me, Blake, and we've got no problem at all.'

Sean set off after him. 'Hey.'

Morris turned round, slowly and deliberately.

'Were you in that back garden?' Sean demanded.

'Didn't need to be.'

Sean halted an arm distance away. 'You don't know what happened.'

'Yeah?' Morris stepped closer. 'I know enough.'

Sean glanced down and saw the man had clenched his fists. He lifted his eyebrows in question. 'Really? You want to try and punch me?'

'Try?'

Sean lifted his hands and put his weight on his front foot. A fighter's stance. 'Go on, then.'

Their eyes stayed locked together. Sean discerned a minute shift in Morris's pupils. Instantly, he knew the other man wasn't going to do anything. Not on his own.

Morris breathed out noisily through his nose, as if what Sean had suggested was ridiculous. 'Yeah, right. Here in the street? Get to fuck, Blake.'

Sean partly lowered his hands. 'If you ever grow a pair, Morris, come and find me.'

TWENTY-FIVE

He turned into the car park of a DIY superstore and backed his van into a slot on the far side. As the dashboard clock edged closer to nine, he watched the various work vehicles pulling up by the entrance for trade customers. Plumbers, electricians, painters and decorators, landscape gardeners: all collecting materials and supplies whose costs would be marked up by a good thirty per cent for the customer's bill.

He knew how it worked. Before getting his job at the college, he'd spent years working for himself. The erratic income was a problem, but not a crippling one. He lived at home, with his mum. Tea on the table each evening and a packed lunch if he was out on a job. Overalls washed and ironed every Sunday.

The reason he couldn't go on had been the customers. Female customers. Most of the time, if a woman needed an electrician, they'd accept his recommendations without question. Often, they were gushingly grateful for the fact he was able to fix the problem. Things went smoothly and without incident.

But, as time went by, he noticed a growing tendency among certain females to challenge. Even disagree. They'd demand explanations, even though they clearly didn't understand his responses. Or they'd make him justify each bit of the final bill, suspiciously poring over the amounts, as if he was a charlatan or a cheat. He found their attitudes offensive. The outrage built in him and often he'd accept a lesser amount because he knew, if he stayed in their property any longer, he might do something he'd regret.

It was similar to when he went back to the academy. Returning there wasn't something he was supposed to do, not while suspended. But Harpham wasn't answering his calls and his work email had been frozen.

He hadn't even got to see her. While walking to the main entrance, two female students had called him things. After a brief exchange in the foyer, security staff had escorted him back to the gates. Then, while waiting for his bus, Shelley's mother had pulled up in a car and jumped out. Ignoring her had been almost impossible. The woman had marched up, ranting and screeching. She'd been so close, her words created little puffs of air against his face. Threats to have his legs broken, dares to hit her.

He had to stand there like a statue.

By the time the 419 appeared, her fury had given way to mockery. *You pathetic little man*: her phrase was a scrap of litter snagged in the branches of his brain. It could not be freed.

As he stepped round her and climbed on board, he heard her spit at him and, as he turned to find a seat, he spotted several phones being hastily lowered.

He took a long breath in and looked at the time: almost quarter past. He restarted the van and continued towards where she lived. Minutes later, he rolled to a stop outside her cottage. The country lane was free of traffic.

Before getting out, he sat with both hands on the wheel, head tipped forward. He completed a mental checklist knowing that, with this visit, there could be no room for error: Katherine Harpham was the first female he'd targeted who knew him.

Several times now, he'd contemplated the prospect of getting caught. He knew that with each attack, the chances of it happening increased. Simple probability dictated that it was only a matter of time. Saturday's visit had been especially risky. He nodded. One might even have classed it as reckless.

But, he had to admit, the satisfaction of it succeeding was intensely sweet. In fact, he hadn't experienced emotion like that in . . . how long? Since racing down a snow-covered hill on a wooden sledge?

He still remembered that Sunday morning. Trudging reluctantly up the slope, gently encouraged by mother. Every child he could think of already there having fun. The creak of snow as the sledge's metal runners began to edge forward. Then the whisper of cold air turning into a rush.

But his exhilaration had been replaced by revulsion when he realized that it was his mother's voice he could hear shrieking behind him. Her delight that, for once, he was like all the other children.

As soon as he was able to stop, he'd got off and stared back up the hill at her. She was alongside all the other mothers, still shouting. He'd dropped to his knees and clapped his mittens over his ears.

He wrestled his focus back to the present. Just as he understood the simple probability of his eventual capture, he also was learning how to mitigate its likelihood. For a start, he had no criminal record. His DNA wasn't present on any database. Leaving behind evidence of a forensic nature was of no consequence.

He also appreciated the threat posed by CCTV. He knew it was time for him to change vehicles. Another type of van with a different colour and registration. He'd probably get a new courier suit, too. Simple preparation and adequate precautions, that's all it took for long-term success.

Checking no cars were coming, he opened the van's door. As he climbed out, he wondered if – one day – his collection of jars might stretch from one end of the shelf to the other.

There was a little red Mercedes on her drive. That, if he remembered rightly, was new. Yes, definitely new. She used to drive a pale blue Fiat 500 with a collection of furry toys arranged across the dashboard. Not actual animals: absurd brightly coloured caricatures of cuteness. Massive eyes and miniscule noses. He could see himself faintly reflected in the Mercedes' glossy surface as he passed it. The trappings of success, something she wouldn't be enjoying for much longer.

Her rose bushes were doing well. Come the summer, they'd be laden with blooms. The strip of lawn to either side of the path was also well tended. To be fair, the entire property was in a superb state of repair. *Well done, Katherine.*

Now at her front door, he allowed himself a moment. This was it. This was when the bitch got what she so richly deserved. Clamping the fake package under one arm, he lifted the brass knocker and let it fall back. A solid honest sound.

Within seconds, he heard her approach. After announcing he had a package for her, he'd decided to keep quiet and let her speak. His silence, he felt sure, would further unsettle her. When she finally had the stylus in her hand, those nerves would ensure she was gripping it tightly.

A key turned in the lock and the door swung inwards. The woman who stood there was and wasn't Katherine Harpham. He knew he was frowning as he examined the woman's face.

Had Katherine managed to lose a couple of stone? This woman's face had the same rounded features, but her nose wasn't so squashed. No glasses. And her hair . . . it was all tied back. No

fringe at all. Katherine clung to that fringe so fiercely, he sometimes suspected she'd let it cover her entire face, if only she could.
'Is that a package?'

She sounded like Katherine, though less squeaky. 'Sorry?'

Now starting to smile, the woman looked purposefully at
his side. 'You're holding a package, so I'm guessing it's for this
address?'

He looked down at the brick-sized cardboard box in his hand.
The label was in plain view.

Katherine Harpham, Russet Cottage, Oldbrook Fold.

'Ah, yes,' she continued. 'It's for my sister.'

He looked back at her. 'Your sister?'

'Yes.' She drew out the word, as if he was hard of hearing.
Now her hand was moving toward him. 'I'll take it; she's nipped
out.'

'Out?'

Her bauble earrings rocked as she nodded. Katherine never
wore earrings. This woman was, he could now tell, slightly older.
It showed in the wrinkles of her eyes as her smile widened. 'Thank
you. Do you need me to sign that?'

Before he could stop her, she was sliding the package from his
fingers. She placed it inside the door, out of sight and looked back
at him expectantly.

He really needed to speak.

'I can give you a signature.' She flexed her fingers.

'Signed for, yes.' He swallowed. This . . . he needed to think.
This was not good. The package contained nothing but—

'Is it working?'

He looked at her again.

'Your little machine there. Is it working?'

She had slowed her words, he realized, to the speed you would
use for a foreigner. He contemplated the device in his hands. Of
course it wasn't working. The LED screen was backlit, but that was
all. It wasn't touch sensitive. It could not record any information.
'No,' he murmured.

'Sorry?'

He tapped a knuckle against the casing. Gave it a small shake.
'The battery . . .' He stepped back and made his words falter. A
comical compression of his vowels. 'It is not working. It sometimes
does this.'

She sighed. 'Well, can we do without one? Unless you
have . . .' her eyes shifted to the lane behind him, 'a spare?'

'No.' He began to turn. He needed to get away. She thought he
was foreign. 'You have it now. That is fine, thank you.'

She crossed her arms and watched him with a bemused expression. Her eyes flicked momentarily to his uniform. He felt like the
flimsiness of its stitching must be visible from outer space.

'Very well, then,' she stated. 'Thank you.'

TWENTY-SIX

Sean had submitted his report for the house-to-house enquiries
by half past nine. The morning briefing had been delayed
until ten because the psychological profiler had asked for
a bit more time.

He turned to the sheaf of printouts that Katie May had dropped
off at his desk an hour earlier. Phone record summaries and
call transcripts for all the victims. The smile she'd given him
had been tentative and brief – but it had been a smile. He realized his eyes had tracked her as she'd made her way back across
the room. There was something about her that he found . . .
intriguing.

The top sheet was marked with Pamela Flood's name. As the
first victim, he wasn't sure what could be gained from studying
her phone's history. The analyst had already run a cross match for
any of the other victims' numbers: none had shown up.

He placed her summary aside. Next was Francesca Pinto's.
Three times the number of sheets as Pamela Flood. A quick scan
confirmed his suspicion: the vast majority had taken place during
office hours.

He went to the day Pamela Flood's body had been discovered.
Estimated time of death was in the morning. Between eight and
noon, Francesca had made fifteen calls and received eight.

Sean turned to the actual call transcripts. Words like *beneficiary*,
ancillary relief, *third party*, *proviso*, *litigation* and *disbursements*
cropped up repeatedly. Work-related. He checked the location
of her phone at the time; it had been triangulated to the same

point on Bride Street. She must have been at her desk in Woodhall's offices.

He drew the fingertips of one hand slowly along his jaw. If this was his mum sitting here, what would she be searching for? He placed Francesca's paperwork aside to reveal Victoria Walker's. He checked her phone records at the estimated time of Pamela Flood's death. No activity. Same as for the time at which Francesca was believed to have been killed. Victoria Walker worked in a call centre: personal use of mobiles was, no doubt, strictly prohibited. Triangulation analysis showed she had been in her office both mornings.

Last report was Heather Knight's. She also spent the mornings of Pamela's and Francesca's deaths in her office. The morning Victoria Walker had died, she'd been driving around. First to Princess Street in the city centre, then to Bengal Street in Ancoats and, finally, the James Brindley Basin, Piccadilly. All locations were where the firm she worked for had apartments for rent. Her appointments diary confirmed that she had been showing prospective tenants around.

Sean flicked forward to the day of her death. Same thing: morning appointments out at Salford Quays, each one tallying with her diary. He turned to the transcripts. The day before her death, she'd had what looked like quite a fiery conversation with a rep at a BMW garage.

Sean scanned her words. Yes, the bloke at the garage her car had been leased from had come in for some stick. Immediately after, another call had come in. The boyfriend, from overseas. It was mandatory to verify the whereabouts of all partners and family members around the time of the victim's death. The analyst had traced back the call's origin: Budapest. Alibis didn't get any better, Sean thought.

Next call, her opinions on their competence had been relayed to a colleague at the estate agent's. Then she'd phoned the firm's cab company for a car to get her back to the office. Twenty-two minutes later, she'd received another call from the BMW garage. Clearly well pissed-off by then. Sean winced at some of what she'd said. The cab driver, he guessed, must have enjoyed being party to that conversation.

He went back to Heather Knight's timeline. She'd swung briefly back into the office, was home by noon and dead shortly after that.

'Everyone!' Ransford's voice rang out. 'Let's get this done.'

Sean raised his head. The projector screen had been lowered from the ceiling at the far end of the room. People were on their feet, pushing chairs in its direction. Following suit, Sean found himself a gap towards the rear. Notepad and pen ready on his lap, he sat back to observe proceedings.

Among the gaggle of detectives to his left were Detective Constables Morris and Moor. His eyes touched with those of Morris and the other man immediately looked away, mumbling something as he did. Moor began to turn his head but Sean directed his gaze to the front. *No way,* he thought, *I'm getting into pathetic death-stare games.*

Ransford was seated at a side table with an open laptop before him. Someone from IT was fiddling about with his keyboard. The DCI looked uncomfortable, but was trying his best not to show it. 'Are we nearly there?' he asked quietly.

Behind them, the projector lit up. The view was of Ransford's laptop screen. A variety of icons were spread across it and Sean just had time to glimpse a folder labelled *DC Blake* before a new window began to open. It finished loading and a woman stared out at them with a patient expression. Her face was framed by long strands of light brown hair and her eyes looked like she spent a lot of time laughing.

'Guv?' someone said. 'I can see her.'

Ransford twisted his neck to look up at the screen. 'Oh.' He leaned towards his laptop. 'Mrs Greenhalgh, can you hear me?'

Her voice emerged from the ceiling speakers. 'Perfectly.'

The IT bloke stepped back. 'If you need to bring any other stuff up, that icon will get you back to the webcam.'

'Great, thanks.' Ransford positioned himself directly before the laptop. 'Mrs Greenhalgh? We have you linked up to our AV system here so everyone can hear your thoughts.'

'So I gathered.' Her eyes moved from the screen to, Sean guessed, the materials she'd prepared. 'How large is my audience down there?'

Ransford fluttered a hand. 'Twenty, or thereabouts.'

It was the first time Sean had seen his senior officer acting in a deferential manner. It was odd. After all, she wasn't of a senior rank. She wasn't even in the police. Clearly, he had pinned a lot on whatever she came up with.

'I've explained your time has been very limited on this,' Ransford continued. 'And we're very grateful you agreed to get involved. Any impressions you've been able to form will be . . . all the team will be interested to hear them.'

He definitely sees her as a life ring, Sean thought. The man was floundering.

Mrs Greenhalgh's face had grown more serious. 'As you pointed out, I haven't had much time. These are just preliminary impressions. I will continue on this later today, at which point I can hopefully qualify some of what I'm about to say.'

'Absolutely.' Ransford's head bobbed up and down.

She reached for something. The side of the screen hazed white as she examined a sheet of paper. 'OK. So far, we have four victims. At least, four of which we're aware.'

Sean looked down from the screen. Ransford's face had changed to match the pale wall behind him.

'The first thing is to consider the killer's geographical domain. With cases like this, a good place to start is with the circle hypothesis, which I'm sure some of you will be familiar with. Taking the two attacks furthest from each other, a circle is drawn with these two points on its perimeter. Statistically, it's likely the killer lives inside – or very close to – this circle. DCI Ransford? I emailed that map?'

'Yes, one moment.' He sent a beseeching look at Sergeant Troughton. 'That attachment, Colin. The one you . . .'

The office manager scooted across. A moment later, he was edging the pointer towards a .png file on Ransford's desktop. On the row below it, Blake could see the yellow folder bearing his name. He cringed, wondering how many others in the room had spotted it.

A view of Manchester marred by a heavy black circle appeared. It encompassed the entire city centre and, at times, curved beyond the meandering blue line that marked the M60 motorway that ringed the city.

Mrs Greenhalgh's disembodied voice emanated from the ceiling. 'Despite the killings being in a relatively tight cluster, it's an area that contains a very large number of people. Somewhere in the region of 2.8 million. How, then, do we focus the search? Hopefully, in several ways.'

Troughton reached out and the view of the psychological profiler returned.

'All the victims are female, but you won't find the attacker on any database for sexual offenders. I'm almost certain of that. None had been assaulted in that way, despite there being ample opportunity. They had, however, had their phones forced into their mouths. Really forced: tongues have been severed to achieve this.'

'Except in the case of the first victim,' Ransford interjected.

'And this, in itself, is significant. Initial theories centred on the assumption these crimes were being committed by Ian Cahill, the sometime partner of the first victim, Pamela Flood. We now know he couldn't have killed the fourth victim, Heather Knight. With that knowledge, the theory that victims are being silenced for something they might have said – or were planning to say – is discredited. What, then, is the motive behind the tongue removal and phone insertion?'

She looked aside for a moment, gathering her thoughts.

'For the second victim, it appeared unplanned. The removal was clumsy and only necessitated by the size of the phone. That wasn't the case with three and four; he's now taken to doing it voluntarily.'

'Trophies,' someone stated flatly.

She nodded. 'He's making a collection, unfortunately. And he's now coming to his victims' houses with the means of doing it efficiently.'

'What are your thoughts on why he's doing this?' Ransford asked.

'For the moment, I'd prefer to not concentrate on that. I believe what will be most useful in actually stopping him is to consider how he is gaining entry to his victims' homes.'

Ransford looked cowed as he sat back. 'Of course. Please, carry on.'

TWENTY-SEVEN

The key trembled in his hand. He couldn't get it into the van's ignition. Like a blast wave from a bomb, the implications of what had just happened kept expanding. She'd seen him. Clearly seen his face. She'd heard his voice, too. Would the accent he adopted have worked? Maybe. But what about when they opened the package? Scrunched-up balls of newspaper and a piece of wood. Oh God. Might they think it was a mistake? Some kind of joke?

Don't be so bloody ridiculous.

He looked at his eyes framed in the rear-view mirror. They shone with panic. The sisters would do what any reasonable adults would do: call the police. An unknown male, making a fake delivery of a dummy package. No return address or barcode or contact details. At the very least, they'd suspect Katherine's house was being lined up for a burglary.

His eyes widened.

When the police came, they would ask for a description. What if Katherine recognized him from what the sister said? He could hear the woman's thin reedy voice. *That sounds just like a teacher I had to remove from his position. There were a number of incidents. Students made complaints. He actually struck one.*

The police would come to his house. He'd be driven to the station and questioned. They'd take his fingerprints, swab his inner cheek for DNA. The instant he went on the database, they'd know. He was the one who'd been in all the murdered women's houses. He would be stopped before he'd even started. No. No!

The van shook on its chassis as he pounded his palms against the dashboard, the steering wheel and the seat beside him. This wasn't fair. It couldn't all be over. It couldn't.

He looked into the rear-view mirror at the road behind. What had the sister said? Katherine had nipped out. There was still time to rescue this! He could go back and knock on the door. Say the machine was now working. Could he have a signature? It would save so much trouble with his manager. *Two seconds just to sign your name . . .*

He didn't know if it was relief making him shiver. He needed to hurry. Katherine had only nipped out. He might only have minutes, but minutes would be enough. He could finish the sister and be ready for Katherine when she came home. Two tongues, not one. How could he have thought all was lost? It was only just beginning.

He leaned to the side and reached into the passenger footwell.

As the fingers of his left hand clamped on the rubber casing, he heard the sound of a vehicle.

It was getting closer.

He kept his head down and listened. The tone of the motor shifted as it changed into a lower gear. The hum of the tyres grew louder as it passed his van.

Once he was certain the vehicle was behind him, he straightened up.

There, in the rear-view mirror, was a pale blue Fiat 500. Its left indicator was flashing as it turned into the cottage's driveway.

She was home.

And that wasn't all. She'd have seen his van, as well. A van, but no driver, parked right outside her house . . .

As he accelerated off down the lane, his lips kept touching against each other in an anguished mumble.

TWENTY-EIGHT

Samantha Greenhalgh consulted her notes for a few seconds. Like everyone else in the room, Sean couldn't take his eyes off her image on the projector's screen.

'OK,' she said. 'We know he's not using force to get into their homes. He's arriving at their properties in broad daylight – mostly during the morning, it seems.'

Her choice of the word arriving snagged in Sean's mind. She didn't say calling or visiting.

'I would expect our man to be dressed in a way that doesn't give the victims any cause for concern. That could indicate smart dress, possibly a uniform. These women – who are alone in their homes – are willingly opening their doors. What sort of a person arrives at a private residence during the day, without arousing any suspicion? Come on, let's throw this open: suggestions, please.'

A voice immediately called. 'Police officer.'

Nervous laughter.

Ransford sent a fiery look across the room and it went silent once more.

'It's possible,' she said. 'But before we go down that route, who else?'

'A tradesman,' someone else said. 'Like a window cleaner. Or those types who offer to do your drive.'

'He's getting into their homes – it appears he's being invited in—'

'Gas meter reading!' It was Magda who'd called out. Sean looked across at her. One hand straight up, as if in class. 'These men, sometimes they just work for an agency. They don't even have a thingy round their necks. The last one to call at my house didn't. He said it was in his car, so I told him to bugger off and get it.'

Sean found himself smiling at the way she said things. No messing.

'Good,' Mrs Greenhalgh was nodding. 'Who else?'

'Engineers: internet connection or phone line,' someone else volunteered.

'Without a prior appointment? Possible, I suppose.'

'Council staff? Maybe checking water supply or something similar.'

'OK.'

'Door-to-door salesman, possibly?'

'Keep them coming. This is good.'

'Pizza delivery.'

'In the morning?'

'Not pizza, then. But something like—'

'What if he's familiar to the victims?' Ransford cut in. 'We're assuming he's a stranger. What if he's already met them in some other scenario, and that's why they opened the door? He's a familiar face.'

'What kind of a scenario?' Greenhalgh responded.

'Perhaps he's been into their respective workplaces. A photocopier repairman, vending machine bloke, the person who drops off the containers for the water cooler.'

She considered this. 'So, they're on vaguely friendly terms and he uses this to his advantage?'

Ransford gave a cautious nod.

'Interesting. That fits with another consideration. He's moving around during the day. From the geographical spread of attacks, I believe he has his own transport. If we assume he's in employment, has he got a company vehicle? Is he self-employed? A sole trader?'

Sean half stood. 'Sir?'

Ransford looked over.

'The house-to-house enquiries I carried out in the street near to Heather Knight's address. There was a mention of a white van parked up around the time of her death. It didn't stay long.'

'You logged that?'

'In the report I just submitted.'

'Good work.' He then addressed the room. 'Anything similar from any other murder scene?'

No one said anything.

'Colin? Let's run a check for that.' He turned back to the laptop. 'Mrs Greenhalgh, you were saying?'

'If he's not using his own vehicle, is a supervisor keeping an eye on what he's up to? Most company vehicles are now fitted with tracking devices. Telemetrics, I believe is the term they use. I don't think where he goes is an issue for him; he's got leeway to do what he wants. Freedom to roam, if you will.'

'Maybe he still has access to a company car when he's not on shift?' someone near the front said.

'That is worth considering,' she replied. 'As is everything that's just been suggested. Now, the crime scenes themselves tell us a bit more about him. He's clean and he's efficient. These aren't disorganized crime scenes. If anything, they're amazingly orderly. Have we considered how he's subduing his victims prior to killing them? I believe there's no sign of any struggle, so far.'

Ransford nodded. 'That has been puzzling us. We were thinking that, if it was Cahill, he could have caught them off guard and then suffocated them—'

'That's been the cause of death in each case?'

'Correct. The pathologist thinks they've had a bag of some description put over their heads. There are light abrasions on each victim's throat, like from a drawstring. And there are signs of them being restrained; bruising to the upper arms.'

'That is interesting. This organization: he clearly takes pride in what he does. I think he's skilled in a professional sense, whether as some kind of tradesman or engineer or similar, I'm not sure. But I imagine he'll be the type of person who removes his shoes in the porch before entering a house, certainly if it's his own. I think he'll be well-groomed. Short hair, kept neat. No stubble. It's even possible he has a certain appeal, maybe in a fatherly sort of way. I would be very surprised if he looks at all intimidating; heavily built or shaved head – none of that stuff.'

'Any thoughts on his age?' Ransford asked.

'Over forty, if he fits with the majority of people who kill in this way.'

Sean noted she had still to use the words serial killer.

'Most likely Caucasian, also.' She moved a strand of hair away from her face. 'So, in summary, we're looking for someone who's able to move freely around during the day. He's probably white, middle-aged and of a respectable appearance. Possibly in work clothes or a uniform, certainly with some kind of plausible reason for arriving at the victims' houses. He isn't on the sexual offenders database, but he may well have a history of incidents with women, though none so serious he has ever been arrested.'

Ransford nodded. 'So, for starters, we'll need to find out if the victims are all customers of a particular company – broadband, gas and so forth.'

'Yes. Plus shops visited, cinemas, anything like that. I think someone mentioned pizza – do they all order from Domino's?'

'Same for their workplaces,' Ransford added. 'Who services the photocopier, cleans the toilets, comes round with sandwiches.'

'Maybe they've all had some kind of work recently done on their homes – new windows or whatever. I assume you have access to all their financial records?'

'We do.'

'Good. They've all crossed paths with this person somehow. Later, I'll spend some time on what's fuelling him. Clearly, he has a problem with women. All women? The victims are very diverse: age, appearance, socio-economic group. But something has acted as a trigger.'

'That's been incredibly useful. Thank you.' Ransford started getting to his feet. 'All detective inspectors? My office. We need to decide on next steps.'

'That's weird, Linds: I was thinking of ringing you.'

'How's it going. You all right?'

'Yeah, I'm all right. You?'

'Yeah. Listen, Danny, where are you?'

'Up near Newcastle.'

'That shop fitting?'

'Yeah.'

'When's it finish?'

'We're done. I'm heading back tomorrow.'

'Tomorrow?'

'Yeah.'

'Have you spoken to Julie?'

'Nope. Left her a couple of messages. Why I nearly rang you. You spoken to her?'

'No. Same thing. She's not rung me back.'

Neither said anything for a few seconds.

'When did you last speak to her, Linds?'

'Thursday.'

'Thursday?'

'Yeah.'

'I thought you two were going out over the weekend?'

'She never rang me back. I called round earlier. She's not there.'

'You knocked on?'

'Yeah.'

'No answer?'

'Yeah.'

'When was that?'

'Elevenish.'

'Probably at work.'

'Yeah, probably.'

'Have you got her work number?'

'No. You?'

'No.'

'I know the bloke in charge is called Steve. Right knob head, though.'

'Yeah, she said.'

'I don't want to ring in. Might drop her in the shit.'

'Yeah. I'll be back by the afternoon. Work out what she's up to then, the dozy bitch.'

'I know. Bet she got larruped. Still asleep, probably.'

'That's our Julie.'

'Get her to call me, yeah?'

'Will do. Cheers, Lindsay.'

'Yeah. Bye, then.'

TWENTY-NINE

The top of his cul-de-sac appeared from nowhere. He searched his mind for any detail of the previous thirty minutes. Nothing. Not a shred. The entire drive had been done on autopilot, his mind entirely focused on what had just occurred. There was only one way to describe it: catastrophic.

He was out of his van and hurrying towards his front door before he realized he was still wearing his courier uniform. *Stupid, stupid, stupid!* Knowing he would be visible from Edith's house, he hesitated. Turn back and get changed in the garage? No, too late. He wanted to punch himself in the face.

Once inside the house, he kicked his shoes off but didn't place them on the rack. Instead, he took the stairs two at a time and, at the top, headed straight for the closed door on his right.

Mother's room.

The door swung open and he strode across the pale pink carpet in his socks. He passed a wardrobe that was still full of her dresses and, as he knelt before the bedside table, he let out a little whimper.

In the top drawer, a wooden handled hairbrush lay beside a white enamel jar and a leather spectacles case. He'd carefully stripped the brush of every single strand many years ago: the clump was safely stored elsewhere. His fingers reached for the small jar. It had a metallic pink lid and small green leaves formed a circle round the letters at its centre.

Yardley of London. Hand cream. Smooths and softens to help keep skin young and lovely.

He was still twisting with trembling fingers as the pot neared his face. At the last moment, he got the lid off and thrust his nose towards the cracked and yellowed remains inside. It took all of his self control not to snatch the air into his lungs with one violent sniff. Gradually, he let his nostrils fill, eking out every particle of faint scent inside. He half rose and let himself sink onto the eiderdown. His head toppled towards the pillow, the pot still clutched to his face. One more breath. Just one.

Reluctantly, he allowed it: exposing the contents of the jar to the outside air was damaging. His sense of anguish still wouldn't subside. He had to have more of the smell. He needed it on his skin so it could seep into his system.

He moved the jar away from his face to bring it into focus. The surface of the meagre contents bore shallow gouges. Impressions left by her fingers. Actual places where she'd touched it. Meticulously avoiding them, he scratched at the base and transferred a miniscule amount of cream to beneath his nail.

He closed his eyes and, careful not to use that finger, screwed the lid back on. He could feel how its rotation was impeded by the rime that crusted the thread of the jar's neck. Once the lid was tightly in place, he rubbed his oily fingertip back and forth across the skin beneath his nose.

Memories of her floated across the canopy of his mind. The way her hair would softly frame her face when she looked down at him. The soothing feel of her fingers on his cheek, then the delicate waft of her hand when she waved him off to school. Walking along subdued streets. Seconds of long silence between each passing car. A sense of calm began to take hold. He traced his finger across his lips and recalled the tickle of a drinking straw in his classroom. The milk in the stubby bottles was so creamy. He remembered entering the playground one snowy morning to see the red crates stacked beside the front doors. The contents of all the bottles had frozen. From the necks, white columns had forced their way up, each topped by a silver foil cap. He brought his knees to his chest and smiled.

Everything had been so much quieter. Silence that was respected, not scorned. The wonderful lack of noise: queuing in shops, sitting on buses, even lounging at the beach. Trips to Lytham and the taste of freshly dipped toffee apples carrying on the breeze, strong as smoke. Waiting at the kitchen table for homemade bread-and-butter pudding.

At her funeral, he remembered two things that the vicar said. *She'd graced us with her presence. She was a woman of dignity and poise.* An elderly stranger had approached him and used a particular word to describe her. *Fragrant.*

He lay on her bed and rubbed at his lips, willing more of her to appear. That smile, so kind. But measured, too. Like it was a commodity that had to be rationed. Like she couldn't manufacture happiness at will. But she could, for him.

He began to breathe more deeply and, when his eyes opened, he wasn't sure how long he'd been asleep. He sat up and placed the jar of hand cream back where it belonged. Staring at the wall, he realized his feelings of panic and despair were gone. In their place was a sense of peace. He felt serene.

His fate, he realized, belonged to him no longer. If it ever had. Forces which he had no chance of influencing were controlling his future. His destiny.

To his astonishment, he wanted to laugh. The knowledge was liberating. Harpham could go to the police. Of course she would. She'd report what had happened and the cogs – slowly and inevitably – would begin to rotate.

On the way down the stairs, he spotted Mrs Fowler. She was in her slippers, opening her side gate. Behind it, he could see her blue and green wheelie bins lined up. He checked his watch: not even lunchtime, bless her.

A minute later, he stepped outside in a pair of grey trousers and a plain navy jumper. 'Edith,' he called out, striding down the abrupt slope of his drive. 'Allow me do that.'

The act of looking over her shoulder weakened her grip and the wheelie bins corners made a hollow thud. 'Oh, these silly things.'

Why, he wondered yet again, didn't she ask the council for a smaller food caddy? She hardly ate anything, after all. 'Not the friendliest of designs,' he replied, grasping its handle and tipping it back onto the two front wheels. The thing rumbled emptily as he manoeuvred it closer to the pavement. 'Blue as well?' he asked, brushing his hands together.

'Yes, blue. Has college finished early?'

'Coll— oh, yes. Actually, it's a reading day, today. I only went in to collect some marking.'

'Did they like the cake?'

'The cake?'

'In the staffroom? Did they like the ginger cake?'

'Of course, Edith. There was only a handful of us in, but it was soon finished off. They sent their thanks.'

Smiling scored her face with even deeper wrinkles. 'That's good.'

He positioned the blue bin alongside the green. Nice and neat. 'Back to my marking, then.'

Once in his kitchen, he sat down. How long before the police came round? It could be days. Or it could be hours. He looked at the clock on the kitchen wall. The endless sweep of the second hand. Time was so precious. He got back to his feet and checked his Weekly Wayfarer ticket was in his jacket pocket. It was valid for three more days.

THIRTY

I t took the senior team until late morning to finalize how the investigation would now move forward. As the allocator made his way closer to Sean, the phone on his desk rang. 'DC Blake speaking.'

'This is a good one,' Troughton announced quietly. 'Don't let me down.' The line went dead.

'DC Blake?'

Sean replaced the receiver to see the allocator scanning his printout.

'It's highly likely there are some non-council sources of CCTV footage yet to be recovered from the vicinity of the first victim's residence. It's now vital we have it for comparison with footage from the surroundings of the other victims' homes.'

Sean nodded. 'Have we the locations of any cameras?'

'No. You'll need to get on Street View and complete a visual audit of shops and businesses close to where she lived. Get on the phone to each one. If any have street-facing cameras, tell them to not record over the tapes and pass the information in Inspector Troughton's direction.'

Sean turned to his monitor and clicked on the web browser.

Just before lunch, an officer who sat on the far side of the incident room made his way over. 'DC Blake? I'm DI Levine.'

He perched himself on the edge of Sean's desk. The man was somewhere in his forties, shortish brown hair swept to the side.

'Talk me through the couple who saw this white van, can you? I'm due to question them in more detail.'

'Lou-lou and Ettre,' Sean replied. 'They're quite a double-act. Italian, I'm pretty sure.'

'You'd say they were on the ball?'

'Definitely. If you're going back, I'd take some images of vans' side views. They might be able to narrow it down to a make or model.'

He tapped his notebook against his thigh. 'Good thinking, cheers.'

The rest of the day was spent ploughing on with the CCTV survey. When it got to six o'clock, most commercial premises had reverted to out-of-hours answerphone messages.

He reached for the ceiling, feeling the tendons in his forearms stretch. After rotating his shoulders, he stood. His hips felt stiff. He looked down at his chair. *How many hours have I spent welded to it?* Too many. He had the urge to be out running. The local park or even a pavement. Something to get his blood flowing properly.

Officers who'd been on outside enquiries were beginning to drift back in. Sean looked on enviously as they retook their seats. Magda wandered through the doors and slumped in her seat. He caught her eye and mouthed a word. *Coffee?*

She nodded her thanks.

When he got to her desk, she'd removed her shoes. One ankle rested across a knee as she kneaded her foot with both thumbs. The nylon of her tights crested and flattened with each circular movement. 'My poor plates of meat.'

Aching feet, Sean thought. *That would be nice.* He noticed how muscled her lower legs were. Images of a weightlifter appeared that he quickly banished as unfair. 'No luck, then?'

Her head shook. 'You?'

'Same. Hours on the internet and phone.'

She let her foot drop to the floor and started flexing her toes back and forth. 'Anything on what's in the six thirty briefing?'

'Nope – apart from the psychological profiler. I think she has more to say.'

'That should be good.'

He saw DI Levine come through the doors, so he plonked her coffee down. 'See you in a bit.'

The other officer was taking his jacket off when Sean got to his desk.

'DC Blake! The Italian couple came through.'

'Really? What did they say?'

'Couldn't give me any of its registration, but they agreed on it being a Peugeot. So, better than a kick in the bollocks, wouldn't you say?'

'Yeah, nice.'

'I'll instruct a CCTV analyst to look for white Peugeot vans in the vicinity of the other murders. You never know. Clever idea about taking a photo selection, by the way. Saved me a lot of time that did, cheers.'

'Glad it helped.' Sean allowed himself a small smile as he walked back to his desk. For the first time since arriving, he felt justified in even being in the room.

A woman, sounding harassed: 'Could you move down a bit?'

A few people glanced up from their screens, but no one in the packed train carriage replied.

'Please, can you move down!'

A few of the people standing closest to the doors tried edging forward. Those standing in the aisle only looked to either side, unwilling to deprive themselves of any precious space.

'Move down!' A male voice, on the verge of real anger. 'There's room towards the middle!'

He was pressed against the bike rack at the end of the carriage. Inches from his face was the word Superdry, the orange letters stitched into purple fabric. A hand reached over his shoulder. Black hairy fingers tugged a narrow window open as the train began to move. Cool air started washing against his face.

'It's an absolute disgrace,' the woman who'd originally spoken stated irritably. 'It should be a four-carriage service, this. How can they just chop it in half?'

'I know.' Another female, her voice older. 'Didn't help them cancelling the Sheffield train.'

'They didn't?'

'Says here. On my phone.'

'That explains a lot.'

'It does.'

'United are playing at home this evening,' a male voice added. 'That has an effect, as well. Makes it busier, like.'

Other phones had started to buzz and ping. Conversations gradually began to build. He closed his eyes to better focus on their words.

'Yeah, I'm on. Just. It's packed. Saw it last night, bruv. Netflix. Nah – too similar to *Prison Break*.'

'Hiya, it's me. I was saying, he says it's come back again. Two weeks, but that's just for starters. Last time, he was off nearer two months.'

'Weevils, apparently. In the soil. Neil, he said to plant strawberries. They love strawberries, he said. No! Wild ones spread like billy-o. Normal ones.'

He kept listening, hoping for a raised female voice. Any kind of argument. An aggressive tone. Someone behaving inconsiderately. He'd purposefully chosen the most crowded platform at Piccadilly station because the chances of conflict seemed better.

Instead, he was getting this . . . cheerful stoicism. This resigned acceptance. It was pathetic. The train pulled into a station. Bodies pressed and slid and shuffled as several passengers squeezed to the doors and got off. When the train moved on, some space had opened up. He could now see around.

The two women who'd been chatting were by the doors. One was black, with braids in her hair. The older one's hair was silver. The man who'd joined their conversation was seated. He had a can of beer in his hand.

Still the quiet peaceful murmur of voices. His frustration mounted.

More people flooded off the train at the next stop. A young woman with two blonde pigtails was out on the platform, an empty buggy in front of her. A foul-faced toddler of about four stood next to it. The woman's exasperated voice filled the carriage, even though she had yet to get on.

'You're going to Nana's, and that's it. Now, get on, Harrison. Now!'

The kid stomped aboard. 'Minstrels.'

'In a minute! Jesus. Give me a bastard chance!' The woman lifted the empty buggy up the step. 'Danielle, you still there? Christ: kids!'

He spotted the wire hanging across her throat. She was on the phone to someone. Unbelievable. The pair who'd been chatting edged to the side and she backed into the space they'd created. The heel of her foot came down on his toe. She didn't appear to notice. 'I'll be back at mine in a half hour. It's only Ryder Brow. Half hour to get ready; meeting at eight will be fine.'

The man with the can was hauling himself to his feet. 'Sit here, love. The little one can sit here.'

'Ah, cheers. Harrison – sit there!' As she pushed the buggy forward, a folded five-pound note dropped to the floor.

He was about to say something, but placed his foot over it and kept quiet instead.

The door to the driver's cabin opened and a ticket collector stepped out. The boy leapt onto the seat, dirty shoes and all. 'Minstrels?'

'Minstrels,' she parroted. 'I said wait, fuck's sake! Danielle? His nana's dropping him at school tomorrow. I know. So we can just see where we end up.' She cackled loudly.

The sight of the ticket collector had prompted people to start reaching into pockets. He stooped down, quickly slipped the note from beneath his shoe and put it in his pocket. The ticket collector stopped at the woman, who'd produced a family-size bag of Minstrels from her handbag. She dumped it in the child's raised palms.

'Tickets?'

'Yeah, adult return to Ryder Brow.'

'Three pounds ten, please.'

She peered into her bag, frowning. A hand went to her pocket and came back out. 'Harrison? Did I give you that money?'

He gave her a blank look, cheeks now like lumpy balloons.

'Fucking money's gone.' She craned her neck to check near the doors. 'I had it just now.'

'I'll come back,' the ticket collector sighed, moving on down the carriage.

She was dumping the boy with his grandma, he thought. She was then getting a train back. He could jump off at the next stop and be outside Belle Vue station for when she returned. After that, it was only a case of following her home.

'No, it was the ticket collector. Lost my money for it,' she announced to the air in front of her. 'He can try. Good luck to him.'

When the ticket collector returned, something told the man the woman's behaviour would grow considerably worse. And she'd already said more than enough to warrant him taking her tongue.

THIRTY-ONE

'That was lovely; the whole weekend's been lovely. Really, Katherine, it's . . .' She sent an admiring glance around the cottage's lounge. 'I always forget what a lovely place you have here. So cosy.' She started to gather in the plates.

Katherine lifted a hand. 'I'll do those, don't worry.'

'You certainly will not.' She shooed away her younger sister's outstretched fingers, then proceeded to place the cutlery on one plate. 'And it sounds like the job's going so well, too. You deserve this, Katherine. You really do.'

'I wouldn't say it's going well. Sometimes, it feels like I'm just rushing from one incident to the next.'

'I mean results are improving.' She scraped the woody ends of asparagus stalks into a shallow bowl that still contained shreds of rocket and shavings of parmesan. 'No job just runs like clockwork; not from a leadership perspective.'

Katherine's smile was strained. She asked herself if her older sister was even conscious of doing it. Conversations never advanced far before Amanda's comments grew patronizing.

'When I got that first big promotion at Glaxo, it was such a shock – to begin with. But, you adapt.' She lifted the plates and carried them through to the kitchen.

Katherine took up her half-finished glass of Merlot and followed. 'Twenty past seven. The roads will be quiet.'

'Yes. I'll risk the M56 past the airport.' She set the plates down beside the sink and moved towards the back door, where her coat was hanging. On the windowsill beside it was the album of her holiday photos that she'd brought to show Katherine: two weeks with Jeremy, trekking in Myanmar. Before the hordes arrive en masse and ruined it.

'Oh, Katherine. I completely forgot.' She moved the album aside. Hidden below it was a small cardboard package. 'A courier came by this morning.'

Katherine put her glass down and crossed the narrow kitchen. 'Really? When?'

'When you popped out for the fresh bread. Sorry. I was in the middle of doing the eggs . . .'

Katherine picked it up and waggled it slightly, gauging the contents. 'Something's in there.'

'Yes. I imagine there is.'

'I mean something solid. I wonder who it's from.' She was already reaching for the thinnest knife on the magnetic rack. 'That horrible brown tape, it's impossible to tear off.'

'He said it was signed for, the courier man. But his machine was playing up. Something from the college?'

Katherine ran the blade along the top. 'No label. In fact, no return details at all. He didn't leave a form or anything?'

'No.'

She folded the flaps back. Balled-up bits of newspaper. They covered what looked like a small block of wood. She raised a frown to her sister. 'What is it?'

'Is there no letter? A delivery slip? Check at the bottom.'

Delicately, like she was scooping up baby birds, Katherine gathered the uppermost balls of newspaper in both hands. They were placed to one side. Then she lifted out the block. It was nothing more than a piece of timber, edges splintered by a saw.

'How very odd,' Amanda murmured.

Katherine set it down then used a forefinger to stir the scrunches of paper that remained in the box. 'No documentation at all. What did he say, the man who called?'

Amanda glanced in the direction of the front door. 'Just that . . . it was a package. He had a package and that . . .' Her eyes narrowed. 'He actually seemed a bit lost. I assumed he was new to the job. But, thinking about it, he couldn't have been; he said the machine often played up . . .'

Katherine's head shook. 'And was he definitely a courier? I mean, he had a uniform—'

'Yes, of course. The one for that American company. Is it K something? Three letters.'

'UPS?'

'That's it.'

'So he was wearing a brown UPS uniform?'

'No, it was blue.'

'But UPS is all brown. Even the trucks they drive.'

'I didn't see any vehicle. You might have; you were home within a minute of him leaving.'

'All I saw was a white van parked out on the lane. But no one was in it.'

'I think you should call the police.'

'The . . . why?'

'Katherine, it was clearly a ruse. I don't think he was genuine. What if . . .' She glanced uneasily at the window. Darkness now lay beyond. 'They case properties out, in rural areas. Ones they're looking to rob.'

'But why this package business?'

'As an excuse! He didn't actually think anyone was at home.'

Katherine folded one of the flaps of the box down. The label was printed with her name and address. 'That doesn't make sense. He can't have packages addressed to every property he's got in mind.'

'They can get anything from the internet. It's not hard. I read, with a lot of rural burglaries, they go on Google Earth. Take a good look first and work out the best way in.'

Katherine smiled. Amanda had always been critical of her moving to the country. Silly little sister with her dreams of a rose-gardened cottage. 'There'll be a far more rational explanation. Student prank, probably.'

'Katherine, if you really believe that—'

'In fact, you've far more chance – statistically – of being burgled while living in a high value urban property like yours.'

'Really?'

That flutter of the eyelashes. Always a sign of irritation, not quite suppressed.

'You don't think this merits ringing the police?'

'I didn't say that,' Katherine replied. 'But I'm not phoning now. I'll drop it in tomorrow. There's a station just along from the college.'

Amanda put her coat on. As she retrieved the photo album, she sent a wary glance towards the box. 'If you can sleep soundly tonight, I take my hat off to you.'

'Amanda!' She chided her sister in a light-hearted voice. It was so rare she had the chance to turn the tables like this. 'I do have security lights and alarms. I don't think you need worry.'

'Well . . . I'd better be going. They'll come on, won't they? The ones for the drive? How you manage out here without street lighting.'

Out here, thought Katherine. *Like it was the middle of nowhere.* 'They'll come on and I'll see you out.'

The gravel of Katherine's drive seemed to have been bleached by the floodlight's glare. They embraced briefly while standing beside Amanda's car.

'You promise to take it to the police tomorrow?'

'I promise,' Katherine said, stressing each syllable. 'And you drive safely.'

She watched as Amanda backed out on to the deserted lane. Pale fingers waved from behind the glass, then the Mercedes moved off.

With a single click, the security light died. Katherine immediately turned, not allowing herself to look around as she hurried towards her kitchen's warm glow. As soon as she was inside, she bolted the door.

THIRTY-TWO

'I thought you wouldn't get home until later.' Janet took the plate out of the microwave and set it down before her son.

'They said not to stick around if you didn't need to; tomorrow will be busy enough.'

'And how was it today?'

'Better, actually.' He used the edge of his fork to start dividing the omelette up. 'A DI went back to get a more detailed statement about the white van. He said my suggestion to take a load of photos off the internet worked really well.'

Janet beamed. 'So, what else?'

Oh, yesterday, he thought, *I had to challenge another detective to a fight. But the other bloke backed down.* 'The psychological profiler fed back for a second time.'

'What did she say first time round?'

Sean filled her in on the morning report as he wolfed mouthfuls of food down.

'Very considered,' Janet said, approvingly. 'Especially him having his own means of transport. I like that.'

'Not because it makes the white van thing significant, by any chance?' Sean asked, head cocked to the side.

Janet gave him an innocent look. 'What was the follow-up analysis?'

'More theory, less actual stuff.'

'That happens. What was the gist of it?'

'She said it's likely he's had a traumatic experience at the hands of a female. Treated unjustly, victimized, slighted: that kind of thing. That, in itself, suggests some kind of power relationship where he was lower in the pecking order. Could be a boss, but could be a bank manager, a doctor, a planning officer, an MP, even. Someone pointed out Greater Manchester has loads of female MPs and councillors.'

'If it is a boss,' Janet mused, 'what kind of a workplace has females in charge? Not many in the building trade. More among utility companies, I imagine. Telecoms suppliers, gas, electric.'

'She also reckoned it could have been a personal, not professional, incident that set him off. His mother dying or his wife leaving him, for example.'

Janet screwed her nose up. 'Bit wishy-washy now, if you ask me. What else?'

'She was going on that the something that's tipped him into killing will have happened recently. There have been multiple attacks in a very short space of time. Normally, the pattern is long spaces between attacks, but gradually lessening. Usually years to begin with, sometimes decades.'

'What about him already having a history of violence?'

'Yeah – she said we should be looking for minor stuff that might have only resulted in a written notice.'

'Stalking? If the complaint was made a few years back.'

'Yes, or just using threatening language. Perhaps low-level harassment. Things could have been logged somewhere, but no further action taken.'

Janet's attention had moved to the bag Sean had brought into the kitchen. 'Did you manage to take any copies?'

He moved his empty plate aside. 'I did, but only Pamela Flood's transcripts.'

'Not all the victims'?'

He shook his head. 'I felt paranoid enough copying just hers. Data protection, Mum. I could lose my job over this. So, the shredder, yes? As soon as you've had a look.'

'Of course.'

When he came back downstairs from the shower, the kitchen table was hidden beneath a layer of white. He looked in from the corridor. His mum was utterly engrossed, bent over the documents, oblivious to his presence. 'What do you reckon?' he asked, stepping through the doors.

She spoke without looking up. 'I tell you what's bugging me. How does he know they're alone?'

Sean took a chair. 'How do you mean?'

'Each victim was alone in their home when they died – correct?'

'Yes.'

'The others – some have got boyfriends or partners – but none of them were there. How did the killer know that?'

'Maybe he didn't.'

'Mmm. In which case, he's calling at a lot of houses, trying his luck.'

'This could relate to what Ransford said: the victims and the killer aren't complete strangers. He knows them from some prior context. Photocopier repair man, that type of thing.'

'And he then shows up at their home address and they're all right with that?'

'They don't need to be all right with that. They just need to be caught off guard.'

She looked down at the table, eyes roving the pieces of paper. He hadn't seen her this energized in years.

'It would be so good to see the transcripts for all the victims' calls. Not just Pamela Flood's.'

'Because?'

'Whatever links these women.' She tapped a printout. 'I reckon it's somewhere here.'

'Despite there being no common factors? People, places, topics in texts – nothing.'

An elbow went down on the table and she jammed her fist against a cheek. 'I don't know . . .'

Sean smiled. It was like when she got stuck on a crossword clue. 'How's your back been?'

Her head lifted. 'My back?' A row of red knuckle marks now ran across her face. 'Hadn't even thought about it until you just said.'

'Is it giving you any grief?'

'Not really. The doctor gave me a new load of pills. I just pop one of them.'

'How many have you got?'

'Enough for now.'

'OK.' He got to his feet. 'I'm heading up. Don't leave that lot lying around, will you?'

'I'm not shredding them now. I've hardly got started.'

'I bet you haven't.' He went round the table and bent to kiss her cheek.

Up in his room, he logged on to the Facebook group. As expected, everyone else had now added a reply to Guy's news about his dad. Sympathy and warm wishes for the future. Light-hearted comments about feeling jealous over his trip. Stern commands with a trail of smiley faces about staying in touch.

Sean knew as well as them that it wouldn't happen.

Alice had replied to say the mould trick seemed to be working.

His eyes moved to an alert for a new email and he brought up the screen. It was from Jay at the Snowdonia Wolf Sanctuary. As Senior Keeper, Jay had monitored both of Yurok's litters. Frowning, Sean clicked on the message.

Hi Sean, I have some news about Kaska, the three-year-old female you sponsor here.

Recently, there's been some tension in the enclosure that will be linked to the new pups. Being part of Yurok and Cree's first litter, Kaska and the others have been busy adjusting. Poor Haida remains the Omega at the bottom of the pack, but recently Makah (he's the Beta male) has been targeting her with some quite vicious treatment.

Earlier today, Kaska moved in to defend Haida and there was quite a stand off! Kaska wouldn't back down and it only ended when Cree appeared. I've never seen a Gamma female like Kaska challenge the Beta male in this way and I don't know how things will develop – but it could be a case of moving Kaska from the enclosure if things between her and Makah escalate. I'll keep you informed, thanks, Jay.

Sean immediately clicked on the web cam. Most of the pack was motionless in the sleeping area. He searched for Kaska's dark ears but couldn't pick them out. This time, he went straight to the camera that overlooked the pool. There was the slightly built Haida licking at what looked like a laceration on her hind leg. In the shadows behind was Kaska, wide awake and watching over her sister. Something – perhaps an owl calling from the nearby forest – caused both animals' ears to pick up. Kaska rose to her feet and stared towards the edge of the enclosure. Her entire body was tensed. Sean's face moved closer to the screen. *You would, wouldn't you? If that fence wasn't so high, you'd leap over it and run right through the night.*

THIRTY-THREE

'Sure this'll do? No worries carrying on round.'

'No, mate. This is perfect.' Danny pointed briefly through the stationary van's windscreen. 'After those lights, it sends you all round the houses. I can just cut down there. Quicker for us both.'

The driver reached across. 'Safe.'

They clasped hands. 'Appreciate this, Andy. Call you in the morning?'

The driver broke their grip to check his watch. 'Just gone eleven. Not too early, mate. Gonna head home and have me a nice fat doobie.'

'Sounds good.' He reached for the door handle. 'And I'm going to see why that dopey tart I call a girlfriend can't even pick up her phone.'

'When the cat's away . . .'

He lifted a middle finger over his shoulder as he stepped down onto the tarmac. 'Passed out in a puddle of her own piss, more like.'

He banged the van door shut, and before he could start circling round to its rear, the vehicle pulled away. He looked at the back doors. *Mr Masters. Retail Interiors.*

It had been good of the boss to let him get a lift back with Andy. The agreement was for six days' work, but it was only tidying up the next morning. No point all of them spending another night in Newcastle. Especially not in that dire bed and breakfast. Double rooms above a pub were never a good idea, however cheap. He thought about eating breakfast on a table that was still sticky with drink spillages from the night before. The fruit machine flashing away beside the bar. Flat-screen tellies with Sky logos silently ricocheting their way round dead grey screens. Shithole.

The road that connected to the side street where Julie lived was deserted. He turned the corner onto Aden Avenue. A cat froze halfway across the narrow street, eyes wide and assessing. When he continued in its direction, the animal doubled back, paws silently dabbing. It vanished beneath a parked car.

TV sounds leaked from windows as he walked along, holdall bumping against his back with each step. He had a Simon and Garfunkel song going round in his head. 'Home, where my love lies waiting.' It reminded him of his time in the army, arriving back on leave, wondering if anything had changed, realizing that nothing had. Weird how, despite that, he always found it faintly exciting.

The big house where Julie lived came into view. A couple of lights were on in windows at the top. She had a ground-floor flat on the corner. Best thing about it was not having to share the main entrance with the other tenants.

He stopped at the side door, dumped his bag down then leaned across to the nearby window. Lights were off. If she was in bed by now, she'd really been hammering it over the weekend. As he reached for his key, he imagined the state of the place. Would there be burned bits of foil among the empty cans and bottles? He hated it when she went on the skag. There'd be no milk or bread in for a start.

The door opened and he decided not to call her name. The flat was so quiet, she must have crashed out already. *If she's even here*, a bit of him said. He scrubbed the thought: Julie liked to get off her head, but she was always faithful. Quite conservative in that sense. Traditional.

He turned a light on, put the bag down gently and paced carefully along the short corridor. The bedroom door was half open. Odd. She always liked to sleep with it shut. He poked his head in, waiting for his eyes to adjust. One pillow on a diagonal. A rumpled duvet. Was she under there, all curled up? He entered the room properly and stood over the bed. Silence. The air was cold;

free of the smell of sleep. He patted the crests, lightly at first, then with more force. The duvet flattened beneath his palm. Nope.

He backed out, frowning now as he headed back towards the front door. Bathroom was dark and empty. Same as the miniscule kitchen. She definitely wasn't watching TV, so where the hell was she? She hadn't answered her phone since Friday. That was, what? Three days?

The switch for the living room light was just inside the door. His fingers searched it out and he turned it on, shoulder simultaneously pushing the door fully open.

Yeah, three days and not a— Legs. Pink dressing gown. She was sitting in the armchair. His mouth actually started to open, words beginning to form. 'Fuck's sake, Ju—'

Mottled grey skin and milky eyes. Blackened blood coating her chin and neck. Lips stretched too wide, like a letter box. An edge of hard grey jutted out from her mouth. Head bent back, she looked like a failed sword swallower. A red light blinked. Voicemail messages, waiting. *My messages. Trying to call you.*

Why had she gone and done this? He turned his head, saw the wine, the cans, the ashtray. *What sort of a crazy state did you get yourself into that you'd try and eat your own . . .*

Another thought smashed into his mind. It wasn't her. Someone else had done this. Had someone been in here? His eyes roved the room, searching for any sign of a visitor. Nothing. He slid his own phone from his pocket, taking slow steps backwards.

The option came up, saving him the trouble of keying his code in. *Are you sure you want to make an emergency call?*

THIRTY-FOUR

The moment Sean stepped through the doors, he knew something was wrong. The incident room felt ragged: people speaking too fast, voices tense, movements jerky. Eye contact was brief and flickery, until he saw Magda.

She waved him over. 'Another has been found.'

'A body? Jesus.' He looked sharply about, feeling the atmosphere infecting him. 'When?'

'Late last night. By the boyfriend who'd been away with his work.'

Another absent partner, Sean thought. *Just like Mum had pointed out.* 'Whereabouts?'

'I'm not sure. He works for a company that—'

'No, I mean the victim.'

'Ah – Failsworth.'

'That's not far from me. Where in Failsworth?'

'The street is Aden Avenue. You know it?'

'No. We're on the edge of Hollinwood, really. But still, it's the next bit in as you head into the city.'

'She was in the front room, propped in an armchair.'

'Was her phone . . .?'

'Yes. Definitely him again.'

'Any idea when she was killed?'

'Not in the last twenty-four hours, that's for sure. The body's already been taken for autopsy.'

Sean glanced across to Ransford's office. He was in there, three other officers at his desk. One of them was chopping at the air with the edge of a hand. Ransford looked exhausted. 'Have they called a briefing?'

'Not yet. I heard Troughton talking to Maggie James. They want to move the CSWs to an adjacent room. That will free up more space in here for other detectives.'

'Where from? Aren't we already running at capacity?'

'They'll rustle up more, don't worry. Borrow from Liverpool and Yorkshire, if necessary. Anyway, until the briefing's called, just press on with whatever you were doing.'

'Right. I'll see you later.' He hurried across to his desk, mind spinning. That made five victims in as many days. Could there be more? This was totally out of control. And when it got to later that afternoon and they didn't charge Cahill with the murders, everyone else would know it, too.

He sat down and looked to the end of the room. They'd need another bloody noticeboard for the latest victim. Pamela Flood, Francesca Pinto, Victoria Walker, Heather Knight. And now the one from last night. He studied the women's faces, as he did several times each day. How had the profiler described them? Diverse, that was it. Pamela, late thirties. Victoria, barely twenty. Francesca, fine featured with long black hair. Heather, short and choppy blonde strands, too-perfect eyebrows. Why were they being selected? What had they all done?

Troughton's voice startled him. 'Where are you with that CCTV survey, DC Blake?'

He lifted his head clear of the chair. 'Sorry, sir. Trying to work out—'

Troughton had clocked the direction of his gaze. 'Don't. Just get on with what you've been tasked with.'

Sean reached for a folder. 'Eighty per cent there.' The uppermost sheet was a screen grab of the streets surrounding where Pamela Flood had lived. 'There were three places I couldn't get through to last night. Another four have yet to ring me back.'

Troughton nodded. 'It's quarter past eight. If they're not already open, they will be soon. See what you can get before nine. Still no joy after that, call in on them.'

'In person?'

Troughton was already making his way to the next desk. 'Yes, DC Blake, in person. We haven't the time to be fucking around.'

Katherine Harpham kept her eyes on the row of etched letters that spelled her name. When they were no longer visible beyond the bonnet of her Fiat, she knew the vehicle was sufficiently far into its parking space.

Being the principal might have meant a constant struggle – with students, with staff and with bureaucracy – but at least she got a decent parking space. Less than ten feet from the glass canopy of the walkway that led to the college's main entrance.

She reflected on her days as a newly qualified Sociology teacher. Trekking in from the outer reaches of the car park, trying to protect whatever she was carrying from the wind and rain. Yes, it was nice to think those days were gone. Especially considering the amount of stuff she had to ferry about nowadays.

She examined the assorted objects spread across the back seat. When she carried this lot in, no one could possibly suspect she'd spent the previous day catching up with her sister.

She wondered if all older siblings acted as Amanda did. The passive plays of power. Subtle assertions of a hierarchy established in childhood. She smiled, amused by how Amanda had tried to belittle where she lived. The alarm she'd feigned at the risks of living out in the country. Alone. Katherine knew it was all just a way to press home the fact Amanda lived in a hideously expensive house right in the middle of Wilmslow. With her very successful husband.

And the business with that strange delivery. Yes, it was . . . disturbing. It would certainly be interesting to hear what the police made of it. Perhaps they'd be aware of burglaries where a bogus delivery driver first called at the house.

She opened the driver's door, but had to place a hand on the seat to lever herself out. Her knees didn't like it and she told herself, yet again, that she really needed to lose a little weight. A brisk stroll to the police station at lunchtime would be good. Fresh air, too. She opened the rear door and a snapshot image appeared in her head. The suspicious package, each piece of scrunched-up newspaper back in, flaps folded down, neatly packed away in a plastic shopping bag on the floor by the back door.

She'd left the bloody thing at home.

THIRTY-FIVE

The van drew to a stop at the end of her street. Yesterday's preparation had worked perfectly. He'd stood for less than half an hour outside Belle Vue station before a train arrived from the direction of Ryder Brow. He spotted her dyed yellow hair through the railings as she stepped down from the carriage, the toddler and buggy both gone.

She bowled along like a weight had been lifted from her shoulders, which – he supposed – it had. Halfway along the platform, she paused to light a cigarette, even though signs clearly stated it was a no-smoking area.

She didn't care. Only one thing mattered to her at that moment: herself. When she emerged onto the street, he was twenty metres away, loitering by a parked car, waiting to see which way she turned. Left or right. *Come on*, he thought. *We haven't got all day.*

The phone was in her hand and she made a call before starting to walk. That was good. Jabbering on the thing only made her less aware of what was around her. She'd never notice someone following her.

Her voice carried back to him as she strode happily along.

'Sorry about earlier: I was well stressed. I love the little man, 'course I do. But, you know, he can be a pain in the arse. No, fuck knows where the money went. A fiver. Let me off when I acted like the tears were coming. Anyway, how long since us two went out? Jesus, it must be. Too right, loads of lost time.'Course there are. Castlefield Locks is always busy. Yeah, yeah. Easily. Before then. Yeah, eight o'clock. Nearly home already.'

The cigarette was tossed to the side. It was still burning brightly when he reached it. With only a slight shortening of his stride, he was able to bring his foot down on it. A quick twist of his ankle as his foot left the pavement. He glanced back. There it was, crushed and lifeless. He fixed his stare on the cheap shade of her hair.

She opened her eyes but before her vision could focus, a slow pounding filled her head. Drumbeat ominous. Her eyes reclosed. When had she got in? No idea. Not a clue. They'd been in Sahara, then Piccolo's. Danielle caught a bloke's interest, as per. Drinks off him, easy. They left when he went to the toilet. She remembered tottering along Deansgate, their arms interlinked. Laughing.

She got them in at the Sky Bar! That was Danielle: outrageous. Up in the lift, giggling like mad. Looking down at the city, she'd said they could have been in LA. So many twinkling lights, some moving, some fixed, distant ones seeming to shimmer.

He lifted the package and checked the label. Leanne Kessler, 17 Crossfield Court, Taylor Road. He didn't know why he felt so calm. It was like a higher force was in control, shepherding him along a predetermined course.

Calling on Katherine Harpham had been wrong. That had been him – arrogant and presumptuous – trying to exert control. He now realized how mistaken he had been: the ones who would die had been chosen for him. He had no influence in what happened. Calling on Katherine Harpham hadn't just been foolish: it had been futile. Like a hot-air balloonist thinking it possible to navigate a stormy sky. All he could do was ride the currents and be ready for when another was presented to him.

Now he understood that, surely he could be forgiven his error? It made no sense if Katherine was allowed to ruin everything. Perhaps the whole thing had been merely intended as a warning. A way of making him realize how things should be done. That was it! The incident had been a test. Now was his chance to demonstrate he had learned. And he would keep learning. Keep getting better for as long as he possibly could. The van door thudded shut. Baseball cap pulled low, he set off for her house.

But the Sky Bar hadn't been buzzing. They'd plonked themselves down on high stools at the bar. Quick look about as they waited for their wines. Monday night and just a few business types sipping drinks. She'd wanted to move on, but Danielle shook her head. These were the best types. These were the types where you could really cash in. Men away from home, with expense accounts. She'd turned to face her, shifted forward on her seat so their legs were touching. 'Remember our old trick? Flies around shit?'

'No! In here? No.' But Leanne hadn't been able to keep the smile off her face.

'Trust me, Leanne. It will so work. Come on! Us two, again. Are you up for it?'

She looked down at their knees. An interlocking expanse of denim. 'We're not even wearing dresses.'

Danielle was already leaning in. Provocatively, she slid the tip of her tongue across her upper lip, leaving it shiny. 'Pucker up, babe, I'm coming in.'

Leanne swallowed. They were really doing this. They were really bloody doing this. Holy shit. And then Danielle's lips brushed hers. Her tongue started to probe. Gentle. Sensuous. Just like lesbians were meant to be.

Leanne had one eye on the mirrors that lined the shelves behind the bar. Reflections of men's faces were turning in their direction. Three, four. Now five. The barman did a double take then quickly looked away.

'Any of them biting yet?' Danielle murmured.

Leanne place a hand delicately on Danielle's upper thigh. 'Oh yes.'

The scrape of a front gate. A postal worker appeared on the pavement, directly ahead. Mailbag's shoulder straps digging into the fleecy surface of her red gilet. Head bowed, she was busy making a fan of the letters in her hands.

There was time to dart across the road. They didn't need to pass. But he carried on. Why shouldn't he? The woman was, in a loose sort of way, a colleague. Less than ten feet apart, she looked up, but only long enough to ensure they weren't on a collision course.

'Morning,' he announced cheerfully.

She didn't reply.

He felt a pang of irritation. Had she slighted him? Did she regard herself as superior, somehow? Her, part of the respected Royal Mail. Him, a mere delivery man for God-knew-who. Was that how she saw things? He almost stopped and called after her. Fucking bitch.

Then he remembered why he was there. What his purpose was. He walked on.

The line of properties beside him changed from a decrepit terrace to modern-looking flats. It screamed social housing. With that kid, she would have gone straight to the top of the waiting list. He knew how it worked: he'd had to try and teach enough of the little tarts. Disinterested, haughty little cows. Once they realized the course took some effort – that life itself took some effort – they spread their legs and got themselves pregnant.

He reached a side path and cut down it, not slowing. Number seventeen was on the left. To one side of her door was a brick bay that contained a row of wheelie bins. To the other was the side wall of the adjoining flat's kitchen. Only one window: long, thin and set high. Unless the occupant was in the room and standing on a chair, he couldn't be seen.

Everything was going so smoothly. Like clockwork.

Two flutes of champagne had been placed on the bar before them. They'd acted surprised. Taken aback.

'From who?' Danielle asked.

The barman had tipped his head. Looking behind them, they saw a giant of a man. He lifted a paw-like hand. Charcoal grey suit and dark purple tie. Thick curls of black hair. He was, Leanne thought, bloody gorgeous.

His hand turned palm up. A speculative wave to the empty seats beside him.

As she slipped off her stool, Danielle spoke through her smile. 'We're in.'

Leanne half-opened her eyes. The skull-thudding pain wasn't going away. She tried to dredge up what had happened after they'd joined him. The rest of the champagne was in a silver bucket beside him: that lasted about two minutes.

Her mind lurched with a new memory. Dancing on a circular window set into the floor. Toy people walking the thin band of pavement far, far below.

'Jeez, I better get myself together.'

Her eyes snapped fully open. The voice had come from behind her. That accent. His accent. Canadian, not American. What the fuck?

He rang the bell and transferred the console back to his right hand. An answer, he guessed, would be some time coming, judging by what she'd been saying on the phone. Nothing to worry about until the school pick-up is what she'd said.

He rang again, keeping his finger pressed down for much longer. *You need to get yourself out of that bed. I have something for you.*

'Can I bring you a glass of water? I have some ibuprofen somewhere.'

Leanne lifted her head from the pillow.

She tried to focus, not sure if she was seeing right. Before her was a massive cloud-filled sky. Below that, tweed-coloured hills, then the crowded roofs of Manchester. There was no wall, just a huge sheet of glass. The bottom of it connected with plush carpet.

Looking over her shoulder made her wince. He was sitting up in a huge bed. Thick hair covered the twin slabs of muscle that formed his chest. 'Where's Danielle?'

'Your friend?' He rolled his eyes. Bloodshot whites. 'She did the sensible thing: bailed just after midnight. You had your heart set on ordering some brandy.'

Christ, she thought. *That explains this bastard of a headache.*

'Listen,' he continued. 'Stay as long as you want, but I really need to hit the shower . . .'

'Cheers,' Leanne said, head falling back against the pillow. She couldn't face going home. Not yet.

* * *

He didn't dare ring for a fourth time. If any neighbour had noticed him, they'd be wondering why he hadn't posted a note through her door. Worse, they might come out and offer to take the package on her behalf. He took a reluctant step back. How dare she not come to the door? He wanted to swing a foot, kick the thing off its hinges, barge into her room and shake her by the throat. And when her mouth opened for air, he'd jam the stylus into her mouth and start shocking her. Keep her flipping about for a while, like a fish on the end of a line. Instead, he turned on his heel and marched back towards the main road.

THIRTY-SIX

S ean looked through the front window of the shoe shop where Pamela Flood had worked. Poorly lit, with crowded racks and tired carpets. Definitely a bottom-of-the-price-range sort of place. Three staff were gathered by the till chatting, while a few pensioners browsed.

He knew the employees who'd been in on Pamela's last day had all been questioned. None had noticed anything unusual. Pamela had said her goodbyes and left work at five forty-one.

Sean traced a finger down the timeline. She'd popped into the Spar, which was a couple of shops further along, at a quarter to six, where she'd purchased a tin of oxtail soup and a packet of white pitta breads. That was tea sorted. The shop's CCTV had been looked over; footage of Pamela paying for the items had been copied. The staff member who'd been behind the till didn't recall Pamela speaking to anyone else.

There was only one place that he hadn't received a reply from. A travel agent's called Crystal Tours. He could see the sign a little further up the road, almost next to the bus stop. As he got closer, he could also make out the camera mounted above its entrance. Window posters of sun-drenched locations obscured the view inside. A notice on the door said to press the buzzer for entry.

The door clicked and he stepped into a room that, apart from a few shelves of brochures, was completely bare of decor. Built into the corner was a glass booth. *Foreign currency exchange*, Sean thought. *Hence the door lock.*

For a brief moment, he wondered if the premises were a front for something else. It didn't seem quite right, that was for sure. A man was in the booth, patiently waiting. He was completely bald, apart from an impressively bushy, jet black moustache.

Sean produced his badge and laid it on the counter. 'Morning. How are you today?'

His eyes were the colour of horse chestnuts, lashes surprisingly long. 'I'm very well. And you?'

'Fine, thanks. You have CCTV coverage of the pavement outside.'

'And also in here.' The man directed a thumb over his shoulder. A small camera was attached to the ceiling.

'Could I ask if you have the recordings for the Saturday before last?'

'Ten days back? Sorry. One week only.'

Sean suspected as much: the places he'd got through to on the phone had been the same. Too much time had elapsed since Pamela's death. 'OK, thanks anyway.'

As he continued towards where she caught the bus, Sean had to step aside as a group of teenagers swept by. All had book bags slung over their shoulders, but none was wearing a uniform. More voices. Another two walked past, laughing about something on the screen of one of their phones. Then the tinny hiss of music. A single lad this time, ears clamped by wireless headphones.

Where were they all going?

He looked at the large building that now flanked the road. The downstairs windows let him see into what appeared to be science labs. A class was going on, a single teacher at the front. Sole performer to a disinterested crowd. Sean could see CCTV cameras mounted on the building's exterior. Must be the Lightwater Academy. It was much bigger than he'd expected. The sheet showed its CCTV footage had all been recovered.

Sean approached the bus stop. Alongside it was the main entrance into the college. A large sign dominated the turning in. *Principal: Katherine Harpham.*

A ticket recovered from Pamela Flood's purse showed she had caught the seven five-seven towards her home in Gorton.

As he retraced his steps back to his car, he thought about the call she'd received from Cahill at one minute to six. Sean had studied the transcript as, no doubt, half the investigating team had. The gist of it had been that Cahill wasn't supposed to be calling her number and no, she wasn't interested in taking him back and, no, she certainly wasn't interested in making any money: it was too much hassle and only a matter of time before the insurance company sniffed something was up. The exchange had steadily got more heated. Cahill had tried to say she owed it to him. She'd responded along the lines of not owing him a thing: he'd lived rent-free in her flat for months.

Sean slowly drove the route the bus had taken. When he saw a fried chicken place called Dixie's, he pulled over to consult the sheet again. CCTV from the shop had showed Pamela walking past it at six minutes past six.

Her phone had still been held to her face. Sean knew the call with Cahill was connected for another few minutes. In that time, Cahill's level of aggression had quickly escalated. The threats to slice her throat open had followed. Pamela had finally had enough; after telling the bloke to piss off, the call had cut.

Sean pulled out and drove to the turn off for Hurst Walk, where Pamela lived. He parked in the first space he could find and walked the last hundred metres to her house. She'd probably ended the call right here, while taking her key out. Getting a good look at her front door was tricky: ugly panels of plastic fencing formed a screen from the road. Sean paused at the narrow gate. Her door was still sealed over with police tape.

He glanced to his left and right. Similar houses stretched away in either direction. The killer would have stood on this very spot. Why, Sean asked himself, did he go for this particular house? What had Pamela Flood done to become his first victim?

THIRTY-SEVEN

Assistant Chief Constable Tony Shipton drummed the fingers of his right hand up and down. DCI Ransford and Tina Small looked on in nervous silence, waiting for his verdict. Finally, he sat back and regarded them both. 'I agree,' he sighed. 'We have no other option.'

It was Tina Small's idea to call another press conference. Not only was the deadline for charging Cahill rapidly approaching, she'd got wind of the fact the *Manchester Evening Chronicle* knew about Julie Roe's death. Now, it was a case of acting first. Damage limitation.

As a result, DCI Ransford would confirm to reporters that another victim had been found. The total was now five. Cahill would be charged with a variety of offences, including threatening to kill Pamela and breaking the conditions of a restraining order that banned him from going within a kilometre of her house and workplace and from contacting her in any way, electronically or otherwise.

However, for the time being, the charges against him would not include the murders of Pamela Flood, Francesca Pinto, Victoria Walker, Heather Knight or Julie Roe.

They all knew full well this would be when the reporters pounced. It didn't matter about Cahill's history with Flood or his previous criminal activity: he wasn't the killer.

All Ransford could do was fall back on the time-honoured response of multiple lines of enquiry, a fast-moving investigation, and a vastly experienced team with every resource being made available.

It would do nothing to relieve the pressure.

'We need someone,' Shipton announced. 'God, we need someone.'

Tina's eyes cut to Ransford. She gave him a tiny nod of encouragement.

'We cannot have five murders in the same city,' he continued quietly. 'Some sick bastard is chopping off tongues and we have no one – not in custody, not even for questioning.' He shook his head in despair.

Ransford placed his elbows on the armrests of his chair, fingers interlinking. 'There is a person who's been recently released. He was in for a sexual assault that involved the use of a knife on his victim. Not stabbing: slash wounds. One was to the facial area.'

'You said victim? Singular?' Shipton asked.

'His ex-wife,' Ransford responded.

'Not a stranger?'

'No.'

'And where is he currently?'

'In the Sheffield area. Bail hostel.'

'But the assault was sexual?'

'It was.'

'But these aren't.'

'No,' Ransford conceded. 'But he cut the face of his victim. He's one hour away by train. That's not too far.'

'His movements in and out of the bail hostel will have all been tracked, will they not?'

'Yes: but they're encouraged to be out of the building by nine each morning. Apart from Heather Knight, these murders have all taken place before lunch. I know it's not ideal, sir, but it's enough to bring him in for questioning.'

Shipton weighed up the proposal.

'I can arrange for his details to reach a reporter,' Tina added. 'Anonymously.'

The assistant chief constable brushed at the sheets on his desk. Dirt that only he could see. 'You've done this kind of thing before?'

'The poisonings at Stepping Hill hospital, sir. I was media advisor on that. Initially, a nurse who had a prior history for some minor misdemeanours was arrested.'

'I remember. She was innocent and her career was ruined. Did she not sue us for a substantial amount a few years later?'

Tina nodded. 'But it was a name, sir. That was what was needed at the time. Something to give the impression we were – that the investigation was—'

'No.' Shipton looked flustered. He got up, walked to the window and opened it a crack. 'We're not quite that desperate. Not yet.' He turned round and looked at Ransford. 'And we really have nothing else to go off?'

'A white Peugeot van. We think it's been in the vicinity of two, possibly three, of the murders. So far we've only got a partial registration from CCTV.'

'And?'

'DVLA say there are over one hundred and sixty vehicles in the Greater Manchester area with registrations that could match.'

'How is that being actioned?'

'We're flat out, so I've handed it across to local patrols. They'll check the address for each vehicle and talk to each owner.'

'Hardly going to crack the case anytime soon.'

Ransford looked down at his notes.

'OK,' Shipton said. 'Give the bloody press conference, as agreed. And then find someone – a genuine suspect – and not a sodding scapegoat.'

He sat in his front room. On his lap was a plate with broken pieces of digestives and a wedge of Wensleydale cheese.

He disliked eating while in front of the television, but when the radio had said a statement about the string of murders was imminent, he knew he had to watch.

They'd found the first ones, then. All five. A series of photos had appeared on the screen: he'd barely recognized them. They looked relaxed. Happy. Their mouths hadn't been smiling when he'd finished with them. Not at all.

The man doing the talking had said a dedicated team of detectives were working round the clock. They were all trying to track him down! He stared at the screen, slowly chewing. Nothing about the need for women to be careful when receiving unexpected courier deliveries. They couldn't have made the connection with Katherine Harpham, then. Perhaps she hadn't even reported the incident.

He shaved off a slice of cheese, put it on a fragment of biscuit and popped it into his mouth. Perhaps Katherine didn't intend to make a report. Perhaps it really had been meant as merely a lesson for him. A warning. He turned the knife over in his hand. But if that was the case, why then deny him the one from that morning? He looked at the package on the floor beside him. Leanne Kessler, 17 Crossfield Court. Why hadn't she answered her door? He recalled crushing her smouldering cigarette beneath his shoe. Why hadn't she been presented to him? It didn't make sense.

There was a fault somewhere. If it was a circuit board, he could do tests. Isolate components. Measure current. This wasn't like that and it infuriated him.

A dedicated team. He imagined them all at their desks, furrowed brows and hunched shoulders. The knife glinted in his hand as he turned it over. Maybe, he should go through to his garage. Open up his jars and take off a few slithers. Send them to the station in envelopes. Then they would know they were dealing with someone special. A person with the power to change the world.

Tempting, but unwise. If anything, he needed to be even more meticulous with his approach. That was the best way to ensure his project could continue. That included changing his van; if the police really were studying CCTV, it was the sort of thing they might notice.

THIRTY-EIGHT

J anet accessed the phone book of her mobile and scrolled down to Tony Shipton's private number. Busy. She should have known that: assistant chief constable, what else would he be?

But Sean's comment about the newspaper article was like a piece of gravel in her shoe. Had the officer who'd left the newspaper been making a very unsubtle hint? And if he had, how did he know? The consequences for manipulating any kind of recruitment process within the police were severe. Of course, that didn't stop it from happening. But it did ensure that, when strings were pulled, they were pulled extremely discreetly.

She was aware that Tony knew the DCI leading the team Sean was now part of. The two men spent time away together outside of work. Time when they could chat about things with complete freedom. It was the only reason Janet had decided to cash in on Tony's offer. So how on earth could Tony's quiet word with the DCI have gone any further?

The television was playing quietly in the corner. She was circling the pad of her thumb over her phone's call button when the news announcer mentioned the words *Manchester murders*.

Immediately, she placed her phone aside and reached for the remote. As the volume increased, the scene cut to a press conference. It was Sean's case! His boss – DCI Ransford – was preparing to give a statement.

Janet watched closely, hanging on every detail as the officer took to the stage. The man was doing his best to appear concerned, but in control. Sombre, yet sharp. It wasn't easy.

The victims' faces started to appear on the screen. Below them was a phone number. Ransford was requesting that any member of the public who had anything suspicious to report should ring the number in complete confidence. His officers were waiting.

Janet gazed at the poor women's faces, trying to gauge something about them from just a single image. The fact they all looked so different made it even more disturbing.

The victim found most recently had dyed her hair a washed-out maroon. Thin-faced. Mean-looking. Janet felt herself frown. Ransford was now talking about a man being held in custody. Charges, at this stage of the enquiry, didn't include murder.

The reporters started going ballistic and he had to wave both hands to restore some kind of order. Once it had quietened down, he gripped each side of the lectern. That was good, Janet thought. He looked like he was in control, even though she recognized the usual phrases for when the opposite was true.

He fought his way to the end of the statement then swiftly headed to a door in the corner. A woman with wavy hair and thickly framed glasses already had it open. As they vanished into the corridor beyond, the number returned to the screen.

Janet paused the footage. The face of the victim who'd been found most recently was still on the screen. Julie Something-or-other. Why did she seem familiar? Julie Roe, aged thirty-three. Lived in the Fairfield area of the city. That wasn't far up the road.

Janet closed her eyes, trying to think more clearly. Maroon hair. Sharp features and darting eyes. Skinny – yes. Stick thin, judging by her face. Janet thought she could remember seeing the woman. In real life. She could even remember thinking that she looked like an alcoholic. And an aggressive one, at that. *Where on earth*, she wondered, *did I see her?*

A vague recollection of the woman being on her feet. But before that, she'd been sitting. Now Janet could recall hearing the woman's voice. She'd been complaining about something. Had it been in a shop? No – a bus. Was that it? Had the woman been on the same bus?

Over the past two weeks, Janet had spent hour after hour sitting on buses, handing out customer survey forms to passengers as they'd climbed aboard. She sifted back, trying to isolate the image. The woman's odd-coloured hair. Her sharp nasal tones, voice filling the entire vehicle. A scrap of another image: she'd been on the phone. That was it. But why the impression she was aggressive? Something else had happened to create that impression.

Then it clicked.

There'd been a man sitting across the aisle from her! He'd

complained. Asked her to keep it down. Janet felt her scalp start to tingle. The woman had turned on him, laid into him for earwigging, told him to get another bus. He'd told her to watch her mouth. Her mouth. The victims' phones had been shoved into their mouths! The woman had mocked him, too. As she'd left the bus, she'd mocked his stammer.

Janet opened her eyes. Was it the same woman now on the TV screen? The memory of the journey was clearer in her mind: a short-haired man with the broad shoulders and kindly face, sitting in a bus utterly humiliated.

At the very next stop, he'd disembarked.

She realized that, if he'd hurried, he could have caught the woman up. He could have followed her right back to her own front door.

THIRTY-NINE

A s he wheeled his chair back to his desk, Sean went over Ransford's latest briefing.

The autopsies for Heather Knight and Julie Roe had been prioritized and, when compared to those of the other three victims, several similarities had emerged.

Cause of death for all had been suffocation. However, they hadn't been strangled. Alongside the previously identified bruising to the upper arms that was consistent with being forcibly restrained, they had other bruises to the backs of the heels and lower legs. Scuff marks on the hallway floors and carpets suggested the women had died just inside their front doors. They'd kicked and thrashed, but to no effect.

Light abrasions to the latest victims' windpipes also mirrored those on the earlier women to have died. The pathologist had surmised the killer had used the type of shopping bag that had a drawstring incorporated into it. By placing it over the women's heads and drawing the string tight while pinning them down, he had caused them to gradually lose consciousness. Death would have soon followed.

Toxicology reports had revealed nothing conclusive. Pamela

Flood had tested positive for cocaine. Francesca Pinto and Julie Roe had very high readings of blood-alcohol. Julie had also tested positive for heroin and cannabis, though the drugs had been in her system for a few days prior to death. Both Victoria Walker and Heather Knight were clean. And no victim's readings, with the exception of Julie Roe's, were so high as to seriously incapacitate them.

How each had ended up on the floor, unable to prevent their own suffocation remained a mystery. Not a single neighbour had heard any sounds of a struggle.

Fingerprint analysis had also now been rushed through for all five crime scenes. The only house Cahill's prints had been found in was Pamela Flood's. There were, however, traces of the same person having been in Victoria Walker's, Heather Knight's and Pamela Flood's homes. The prints were mostly partials, but with enough common characteristics – including a distinctive ulnar loop on what was probably the right forefinger – for the examiner to say they were from the same person.

Hairs not belonging to the victim had also been recovered from each crime scene. In Pamela Flood's and Francesca Pinto's homes, a single strand from the same person had been recovered from the armchair the victim had been propped in. Both hairs were just under two inches long, one white and one light brown, suggesting that the person was turning grey. Unfortunately, neither hair had enough of a root to enable DNA analysis: all the forensic biologist could venture was that both had come from a Caucasian, aged around thirty-five or above.

Sean was still a couple of metres away from his desk when his phone started to ring. Seeing whose name was displayed on the screen, he sat down and turned towards the wall. 'Everything OK, Mum?' he asked quietly.

'Sean, you need to listen. Where are you?'

She was fighting to keep her voice under control, but she didn't sound distressed or in pain. If anything, she sounded elated. 'At my desk. What's going on?'

'I just saw it on the telly, Sean. The statement from your boss along with all the victims' photos. Now, you need to be very careful how you play this, Sean. It needs to be you it comes from—'

'Mum, can you slow down? I have no idea what you're—'

'I think she was on the bus, Sean! The victim they just found. Julie Roe. I think I was on the same bus as her.'

Sean rubbed at the back of his neck with his free hand. 'You saw her on the bus. OK. When?'

'That's the point. I worked it out: last Thursday. I know because I'd just come off the phone to you. It was your very first day in the new job.'

Sean abruptly became aware of Mark Wheeler's empty chair facing him. He swung his focus back to what his mum was saying. Julie Roe had died at some point during the morning after he'd started.

'She had an argument on the bus, Sean. I was handing out surveys in the east part of the city that day. One of the routes goes quite close to our house. She lived in Fairfield, right?'

'She did.'

'There was this man who asked her to shut up. She was on the phone speaking really loudly to a mate. She turned on this bloke. Gobby, she was. Well-practiced, too. He said she should *watch her mouth*: those were his actual words. Then she got really nasty – took him apart because he had a slight stammer. I can remember actually feeling sorry for him. She got off and then – at the very next stop – he did, too. What if he doubled back? To find her?'

Sean swivelled his seat and picked up a pen to take notes. 'What did he look like?'

'Heavy set. Somewhere in his forties. Light brown hair, straight and cut fairly short. And he was wearing work clothes, Sean. Bits of paint on them, I think.'

Sean jotted it all down. The hair matched the psychological profiler's prediction, that was for sure. And the age.

'There was something else, Sean. Apart from how furious he looked when he got off, that is. He was carrying an equipment box. You know, like the ones fishermen have? You open it and the top folds out with little compartments. Black, with red handles, I think.'

'You're saying it looked like he had this for his work?'

'Precisely. A handyman, a plumber: someone who calls at people's houses.'

Sean underlined the words *carrying a toolbox*. This was . . . if his mum had remembered correctly, this could be . . .

'Listen Sean: have Julie Roe's phone records come in yet?'

'I think so.'

'And CCTV coverage of her last twenty-four hours?'

'People will be working on it.'

'OK. You've been tasked with reviewing some of the victims' timelines, haven't you? No one will think it odd if you access Julie Roe's phone transcripts. It was about nine twenty on that Thursday morning. You'll see she had a verbal altercation – she was relaying it all to the person on the other end of the phone. You need to get hold of the CCTV footage from the bus at that time.'

Sean was thinking about Pamela Flood. She'd caught a bus, too. She'd been arguing with Cahill for the entire journey. 'OK – that's easy enough.'

'Then you'll be able to see him. The camera on the back of the driver's cab points at the rows of seats. He'll be on film, Sean.'

'Won't you be, too?'

'Me? No – the wheelchair bay is up by the front doors. It's not covered by CCTV. Sean, find that footage. If it's her, take it to Ransford along with the call transcript. But make a note on the system, first. If this turns out to be significant, you want the record to show it came from you.'

FORTY

'**N**o: it should definitely be me who buys,' Magda said, leading the way into the canteen. 'You have earned coffees for the rest of the month!'

'Don't be silly,' Sean said, shaking his head. 'It was a bit of luck. Anyone could have stumbled across it.'

She wagged her finger. 'No, no, no. Plenty of people had the chance, but none did. You are the early bird.'

'The early . . .?'

'You did the hard work – and now you get your reward.'

Jesus, he thought. *I really have to get her an up-to-date book on British sayings.*

'Watching DCI Ransford's face go from thunder to sunshine,' she added. 'That is also worth lots of drinks.'

It hadn't been easy getting his boss to listen. When he'd first knocked on Ransford's door, Sean had been greeted by a raised palm.

'DC Blake, you really need to—'

'I think we need to find this man, sir.'

His DCI squinted at the sheets Sean was holding up. 'Explain.'

By the time Sean had reached the image of the man waiting to get off the bus, toolbox in his hand, excitement was making Ransford's eyes glitter. 'Get Inspector Troughton in here,' he barked at Sean as he grabbed his phone and punched in a number. 'Tina? I need you in my office, now. I think, at fucking last, we have a face!'

It had been agreed that the man's image should be immediately released to the press, along with an appeal for information from the public.

Images of his face hit online news sites at eleven forty-six. By one o'clock, they'd received dozens of calls naming a variety of people. Five different people had all identified a man known around the area to the east of the city centre as Dutch Pete.

Detectives were sent to interview each caller face-to-face and, by two thirty they were looking for a man believed to be based in, or near to, Droylsden. No one seemed to know exactly how he earned a living: three of the callers were under the impression he did odd jobs, probably for cash. Another thought he might be a gardener. The last caller often saw him in a local convenience store, but had never actually spoken to him.

The owner of the convenience store was then visited. He confirmed that Dutch Pete often called in to buy items such as bread, milk and – every now and again – cans of Polish beer called Tyskie. A panic button had been attached to the side of his till: all the shop owner had to do was press it the next time Dutch Pete appeared.

A surveillance van with four officers had been parked at the rear of the building. Two would enter through the shop's back door, two from the front.

Meanwhile, arrangements were being made for every scrap of CCTV to be rechecked to see if he cropped up in the vicinity of any other victim shortly before their deaths. The lead CCTV analyst estimated there was dozens of hours of footage, from a total of sixty-seven different cameras, including those on public transport. The job was huge.

'So,' Magda held up her coffee. 'To you, DC Blake.'

Sean tapped the rim of his wax cup against hers. 'Cheers.'

'It now feels you're part of this team?'

He looked around the canteen. Empty. 'Getting there.'

She grinned. 'This is a big plus for you, Sean.'

'Maybe. But not everyone looked pleased back in there. I didn't see DS Fuller smiling.'

'DS Fuller is little more than an ape. He just happens to have a police badge.'

Sean checked the doors; Magda hadn't even bothered to lower her voice. They were still alone.

'You need to not be pushed around, Sean, with people like him.'

If he'd been gliding pleasantly along, her comment was like a stick through his spokes. 'Thanks.'

She frowned. 'It's nothing.'

'That was sarcastic.' His head was shaking as he started to lift his drink.

'You do not actually agree?'

He put his cup back down. 'It's not that easy.'

'Why not?'

'He's a detective sergeant, for a start.'

'And?'

'And I'm a detective constable. That makes him senior to me.'

'No reason to be letting him—'

He raised a finger. It was like getting a lecture off his mum. 'You're not the one who's new. I haven't been here two minutes.'

'That's why you have to be firm! It must be from the very start.'

'Yeah, right.' He crossed his arms and looked towards the corridor. It was very tempting to just walk away. Leave her to lecture an empty room. 'You talk to me like I don't know how to handle bullies.'

'Do you?'

For a moment, he pondered whether to tell her about his school years. Or about the recent face-off with DC Morris. 'I've never met anyone like me who doesn't.'

'What do you mean, like me?'

'People who – as kids or teenagers – had a parent to care for. We're different. Anything different at school and you get bullied.'

She frowned. 'But why—'

'The other night, in the Oddfellow's Arms, you asked me if it was the sort of place I go to with my friends. Magda, I don't have that type of friend. I've been to a pub, perhaps, a dozen times? I can't stand the places, if I'm honest. I hate watching people getting pissed. Being so . . . not giving a shit. Why would I ever do that? I've got Mum to look out for.'

'It is like you are the parent. For her!'

He nodded. 'That's about right. Not so much now, but until I was sixteen or so, it definitely was. I'd hurry straight home from school, sort out tea, clean up, do my homework, help her to bed, then go to sleep myself. I didn't do what my classmates did. I didn't hang around outside the local shops. Or in the park. I didn't spend hours playing computer games or uploading selfies. The times I did get to myself, I mostly spent at the police cadets. That makes you very sensible, or very boring. Either way, you're a target.'

'I get it. The ones who'd pick on you. How . . .?'

'I couldn't do much. Not until . . .' He flexed his shoulders. 'Once I'd filled out, then I could.'

'How?'

'I learned to box. As the poster at the gym said, kids who box don't get bullied. Simple.'

She smiled. 'Will you thump Fuller?'

'Yeah, and get kicked back into uniform. When it's right, I'll sort things out with him.'

She leaned back, the traces of her smile still on her face. 'You are like that cowboy with the mask. The Lone Ranger.'

'More Romanian kids' telly?'

'What?' She laughed. 'You didn't watch the *Lone Ranger*?'

'Sorry,' he grinned, shaking his head. 'My parents might have. Were you here when Fuller first arrived?'

'He was here first. I was the one who was new. Add to that, I'm female and – to people like him – foreign. That makes me a ticked box on a quota form.'

Guiltily, he recalled his first impressions of her. The curious hairstyle and stout build. Her accent. When she'd appeared at his desk, he'd hoped she would say her welcome and move on. Like an idiot, he had prejudged her. 'Did you have any kind of confrontation with him?'

'He made a couple of comments, testing the water. I did not bow to him. Now . . .' She shrugged.

Sean studied her. No one gave her any shit. She obviously wasn't part of the main group of – mostly male – detectives, but he got the impression that was as much her choice as theirs. 'The situation with Mark Wheeler. I know that's why Fuller's going for me; the two of them obviously got on.'

'And Mark will get better. And when he does, the truth of what happened in that garden will come out.'

'You believe that I tried to help him? That I didn't freeze?'

'Yes. Even more so now.'

'Thanks.' He ran a finger across the cup's ridged surface, composing his words as he did. 'And I will, you know, push back. Next time Fuller says anything snide.'

'It's important.' She gestured toward the modest pile of free newspapers at the counter. 'Now you are showing yourself to be good, he cannot play his tricks.'

Sean sat forward. 'What was that with the paper? I didn't get it.'

Magda shifted uncomfortably. 'Just silly rumours.'

'What rumours?'

'The connection to your mother, I think.'

'My mother?'

'Sean, there are many officers whose mum or dad were also in the police. When those officers move up – get a position like this – there are always whispers.'

Fuller's words were coming back. *It wasn't what you knew.* 'That's why they'd left the paper open on the story about the cabinet minister? He reckons I got this job through my mum?'

'Whispers: that's what people like him feed on.'

He felt like marching straight into the incident room and up to Fuller's desk. *All the work I did on my aidship. The years I spent before that in the cadets. All that effort.* 'The prick.'

'He is insecure, Sean. That's why he jumps at the chance to attack others.'

But Sean was now thinking about his application to join the team. Who had so eagerly cajoled him every step of the process? *Mum.*

FORTY-ONE

t was weird to be getting home at a normal time. He was still pushing the front door open when she called from the telly room. 'How exciting is this?'

He smiled at her choice of words. The thrill of the chase once the quarry had been sighted. 'You saw the later press conference, then?'

'Of course. Been glued to the telly since you rang.'

He was loosening his tie as he entered the front room.

'Here. I got it with the zapper.' She directed the remote at the screen, brought up the list of recordings and selected the news. The suspect's image from the bus' CCTV footage filled the screen. 'That's definitely who I saw.'

'Seems he's an EU national, possibly over here doing casual labour.'

'Don't say it: Polish plumber?'

'Dutch. Or that's his nickname. Dutch Pete.'

'And they think he lives in the Droylsden area?'

'That's what a couple of callers reckoned.'

She turned to look briefly at the curtains. 'Not that far away.'

'No.'

She shivered her shoulders. 'So, come on then, spill! How did it play out?'

He kicked off his shoes and jumped sideways onto the sofa, ankles over one armrest, back of his head on the other.

'Sean! How many times . . . you'll break the bloody thing doing that. Well?'

Gazing up at the ceiling, he said, 'It was all fine. I'd already been reviewing what we had on Pamela Flood.'

'Has he been spotted in any other footage?'

'Not yet. But there's tons of it to be checked. The CCTV analysts will be working through the night.'

'Pity: I was half expecting you'd have found him. It would fit with my theory.'

'Which theory is that?'

She removed a TV listings magazine from the coffee table beside her armchair. He noticed it was open on the crossword page. Beneath it were her photocopies of Pamela Flood's phone transcripts.

'I said to shred those! Mum – bloody hell.'

'I will. Soon as you've seen this. The bit everyone focused on was Cahill's threat to kill her, yes?'

'Yes.'

She ran a finger down to the bottom of the transcript. 'But that occurs late in the call. She hung up on him almost immediately.'

'Yeah. I followed her route, today. She was probably right outside her house by that point.'

'Go back earlier in the call, when she would have been still on the bus. Look at what she said; the actual words. She practically tells everyone in earshot that she lives alone.'

He beckoned. 'Let's have a look.'

She reached over to hand him the sheets. Certain parts of her conversation had been highlighted in yellow.

> *Yeah, and it's my fucking flat! Who paid the rent? Who*
> *paid for the gas and electric? Bollocks. You never did.*
> *Quite happy there without you, cheers.*
> *Quite happy.*
> *I'm not like you, I can handle being on my own.*

'See what I mean?' Janet asked. 'If this Dutch Pete person is hearing all that, he only had to then follow her home. Once he knew where she lives, he creeps back when it suits him.'

Sean sat up. He considered what he knew about the other victims. They had certainly all been using their phones. Exactly what had they talked about? If Dutch Pete had also been on the bus, or tram, or train, sitting close by . . .

His mounting sense of excitement was suddenly snuffed out.

'I just realized something. Heather Knight didn't use public transport; she drove a company vehicle.'

'But didn't it break down?'

'Yes, but she called a cab on the firm's account. She was picked up and taken back to the office.'

'And her journey home after that?'

'A lift home with a colleague.'

'Really?'

'Yup, I went over her timeline, looking for anything odd. I can have another check tomorrow, but . . .'

Janet looked despondent. 'I had such a good feeling about that, too.'

'Anyway,' Sean said, lying back. 'Julie Roe. I took the stills from the footage of her and showed them to Ransford. You should have seen how eager he was to call a press conference. Shows how much pressure he was under.'

'Oh, it's hideous. And so much bloody information is coming in that needs to be sifted through.'

Sean's eyes settled on the man's face that filled their TV screen. 'Huge number of calls, but five quickly named that one bloke.'

'I'm so pleased for you, Sean. This is the start you deserved. Not what happened in that back garden.'

He sighed. 'It was your spot, not mine.'

She flicked her fingers.

'And I got to the bottom of this thing with the hostile detective.'

'Mmm?'

'The one who's been having a go at me. He made a hint using a newspaper story.'

'Good for you. Though I doubt it matters much now.' She pointed the remote at the telly and it switched back to the evening's schedule. 'There's that documentary about Judi Dench, later. I love Judi Dench.'

Sean watched her with a bemused expression. How come she was acting so odd? 'The newspaper story I mentioned. In the canteen?'

'Oh yes, that. You weren't quite sure why they'd left the paper open on a certain page. I think I'll record it since it doesn't finish until midnight. No way I'll last that late.'

He watched her fiddling with the buttons. The sudden switch in enthusiasm: from him to some programme on the telly. 'DS Fuller,' he continued, 'that's the name of the detective with the attitude. He reckons I only got on the team because of you.'

'Me! How ridiculous. This stupid remote. I don't want a series link!'

'Obviously, there are loads of officers with family members who also served.'

'Quite right. Don't react. Ignore him. It's your best option.'

He tilted his head back to study the ceiling once more. Magda had said Fuller jumped at any opportunity to belittle others. But she hadn't said he'd manufactured the chance. It had presented itself and he'd taken it. He looked back at his mum. 'You didn't put a word in for me anywhere, did you?'

When she didn't look at him, he knew. Perhaps it was something he knew already. But this was confirmation.

She couldn't meet his eyes. 'No, I did not.'

'Mum.' He doubled over to place his head in his hands. No wonder Fuller and his sidekicks had it in for him. He dug his fingernails into his scalp. What she had done meant he could never be properly accepted by people like Fuller. All he'd ever receive was their scorn. 'Mum.'

'What are you trying to imply here? That I—'

'Don't.' He looked up. She shimmered beyond his tears of rage. 'Don't lie! Jesus Christ. No wonder. No wonder! That's why they've been treating me like a fucking leper.'

'Sean, you just said, if every appointment was judged on family history, no one would—'

He waved a hand. Everything made sense: even Inspector Troughton's knowing smirk on their initial meeting, when he'd asked if it was Sean's first stint since making detective constable. 'How did you do it? You must have called someone. Or was it face-to-face? A quiet word, off the record.' He wiped at his eyes. 'Someone senior enough: the one you worked with years back. Was it him? Was it that fucking assistant chief constable?'

She placed the remote on the armrest. 'We had a brief chat, that was all.'

'A brief chat!' He rose to his feet and glared down at her. 'A brief chat!' He wanted to topple her armchair over, leave her sprawling there on the floor. 'It's always you, isn't it? Fucking meddling. You said I should do the aidship as soon as I could. When did you have your brief chat with that ACC? Before I'd even finished it? Could you wait that long?'

She kept her eyes at the level of his knees. 'No one just goes off the formal application. Not in any job. They always make other enquiries.'

'That's not the same!' He retook his seat to force eye contact.

'Ransford had his hands tied. Because of you, he didn't get to pick the new detectives for his own team. No, actually, he did get to pick one. Someone with the right qualities, the experience, the ability to fit in. He got one of his choices. And then he also got me.'

'Now you're being ridiculous, Sean. You have every necessary qualification and more. You've been in the cadets since you were—'

'Another of your suggestions. Fuck, it's always been you pulling the strings.' He lifted his elbows and jiggled his arms up and down. 'Off I fucking go again.'

'I will not have this discussion if you're going to be stupid. I will not.'

'You know, I couldn't figure how I got the nod. I know of three other constables who finished their aidships way before me. Yet none of them were offered a place in the SCU. Now I know why.'

'Candidates are chosen on all sorts of considerations. It's not a simple queue system, Sean.'

'Really? So none of those guys will feel like they were leap-frogged?'

She struggled to sit up. 'Do you know how often I was passed over for positions that were tailor-made for me? You think I wanted to never make it past a uniformed sergeant for my career? Do you? It's a competition, Sean. And you use whatever edge you can—'

'I've had enough. I am sick of this.' He got back to his feet.

She leaned to the side, trying to search out his face. 'What do you mean?'

He looked around the room as if he'd never seen it before. Not properly. 'You were right the other night.' His words were calm and cold.

'Pardon?'

'You do hobble me.' He walked towards the door.

'Sean! What are you doing? Sean?'

'I'm going.'

'What do you mean?'

Her voice carried after him as he started up the stairs.

'Sean, where are you going?'

'Should have done this years ago.'

*   *   *

He knew that she'd come up the stairs. That she'd use every single thing she could to dissuade him. Including, if necessary, her disability. Or was it, he wondered, really his? To live an independent life. She might be physically incapable. What was his excuse?

He'd rammed enough clothes into a holdall by the time he heard her at the bottom of the stairs. He didn't want to set eyes on her. As soon as her mouth opened, he'd be tempted to punch it. And for the first time in his life, he didn't know if he'd want to stop himself.

By the time the whirr of the stair lift started, he had put some music on a low setting and slipped quietly out of his room, leaving the door almost closed.

He stood in the spare bedroom. The one they used as a storage area. His sleeping bag, like a giant stubby sausage. The silver roll mat next to it. A black pull-up bar he hadn't used in months. Lying across a cardboard box was the tweed coat she'd bought on impulse. As he waited, he fiddled with one of its giant tortoise-shell buttons. Eventually, he saw her through the crack in the door. She looked panicked and a bit ill as she shuffled along the corridor toward his room.

'Sean? Can we please talk? This is silly. Can I come in?'

His bed was positioned behind the door; she would only see he wasn't lying on it when she had fully entered the room.

He heard her tentative knock.

'Sean?'

As soon as he heard the hinge creak, he stepped onto the landing and silently descended the stairs.

FORTY-TWO

'**N**o, I fully agree. As does Sascha. We just spoke. It's ridiculous, well – actually – it's so arrogant of him. I know! Doesn't even realize he's doing it. Never. Not with a male colleague. But us? Every single time. OK, honey. Not tomorrow. I've got the day off, remember? The tram's stopping, hang on.'

He trailed her onto the platform, hanging back as she transferred her handbag to her other shoulder.

'Where were we? Oh yes. A lie-in? I wish! I'll get up at eight thirty: I have a class for nine forty. Pilates. It's a new studio, just round the corner. Introductory offer. Aah, thanks, sweetie. You too. We will. Definitely. You take care and let's talk later in the week. Bye!'

They had walked down the platform ramp and onto the pavement as she tucked the phone back in her pocket. He immediately crossed to the other side of the street; experience had shown him that, when a call ended, awareness of surroundings increased. And people were definitely getting more nervous. Women, especially. If she glanced over her shoulder now, he'd be sufficiently far away so as not to be a worry. With each clock of her shoes on the pavement, a tremor went through her blonde ponytail.

This was a problem: to stay behind her meant moving from a casual stroll to something that resembled a pursuit. She'd soon realize all wasn't as it should be.

On the tram, her conversation had been so obnoxious. The male colleague they were plotting against had been scathingly described. Even mocked. His coffee breath. His poorly trimmed eyebrows and chewed nails. It was her derisive tone that made him decide she would be the one to die. Up until that point, he'd been more tempted by an obese woman loudly complaining about the shit service she'd just received in a restaurant.

The rhythm of the woman's footsteps altered. She was slowing down. He looked across the road. Is this it? A shoulder-high brick wall ran along the front of the property. There was a thick metal gate set into it. He scanned for any CCTV, saw none. Perfect. Back on the tram, she'd received a call from someone called Clive. It was raining in Boston. She missed him. Being alone in their place wasn't her idea of fun. His return at the weekend seemed like a lifetime away.

He was making a mental note of her house number when he realized she wasn't actually stopping. Just retrieving a set of keys from her pocket. The next property was as large as its neighbours, but it had an open area at the front for parking.

He checked the houses directly behind him. The view across was uninterrupted. That was bad, as was the fact there were three cars on the drive of the property she was approaching. Worse was what he could see in the two spaces that lacked a vehicle: white numbers painted on the tarmac. That meant the house had been divided into flats. He slowed to a stop.

Disaster.

Once she'd let herself through the front door, he crossed over. There was a camera directly above the front entrance. He kept his face averted as he strode up the drive. He didn't know her name. Beside the front door was an intercom. The neat labels beside each buzzer all spelled the same thing: failure.

Flat 1 – C. Reynard
Flat 2 – J. Cartwright
Flat 3 – B. MacArthur
Flat 4 – C. Sheldon
Flat 5 – J. Baxter

He squeezed his eyes shut and moaned. This didn't make sense. Why wasn't his project working? What was causing it to go so wrong? The pressure in his head was building. Like his brain was swelling and the plates of his skull were about to come apart. He dropped into a squatting position, pressed the heels of his hands against his temples and started to rock backwards and forwards on the balls of his feet. *Why? Why? Why?*

'Excuse me, are you OK?'

He hadn't heard the front door open. His eyes opened on a pair of white trainers and smooth shins.

'Are you . . . do you need help? An ambulance?'

He stood up too quickly and the world faded from view. A hollow crashing sound. His sight surged back: he'd staggered into a row of wheelie bins.

'Oh! Here, let me—'

Small hands gripped his upper arms. Twisting away, he swung an elbow at the voice. A bony impact jarred his arm. The woman who fell backwards on the front steps was wearing an orange T-shirt and grey leggings that ended just below her knees. Her head cracked against solid stone. It was like someone had opened a valve in the woman's nose: blood poured from both nostrils.

He saw that her hair was brown and curly. It wasn't the one from the tram, but it was still a woman. Without thinking, he leaped forward and swung a foot into her side. The impact jackknifed her body and she flipped over. A string of blood flew out, neck-lacing the cold stone by her cheek. He stepped over her and used his forearm to smash her raised hand aside.

The fingers of both hands sank into the soft mass of her curls. The step's stone lip jutted out a couple of inches. Clenching her hair in each fist, he had started to raise her head up when a man shouted out somewhere above him.

'Leave her! Hey! I said leave her!'

An open window? He didn't dare look. Releasing his grip, he whirled round and fled down the drive.

When he got home, he headed straight for the garage. His keys jangled as he unlocked the side door. Once inside, he stood perfectly still, soaking up the silence, breathing in the still air. After a minute, he felt able to turn on the lights.

A hum went through the plastic casings and the bulbs inside flickered and plinked before settling into steady brightness.

He took a moment to regard his collection. Puckered lumps hanging in honey-coloured liquid. The sight of them made him feel better.

From beneath his workbench, he slid out a high stool. He so rarely sat on it. Set against the wall was a rack of little drawers. Fuses, switches, resistors, transistors, diodes, crystals. He thought he'd established why his plan had ceased to work. Rather than simply accepting what destiny chose to present him with, he'd acted on his own, rashly attempting to silence Katherine Harpham. Evidently, that theory was wrong.

So where did the fault lie?

He reached across to the coat hanger bent into the shape of a hand and traced a finger up its wrist then along to the little finger. He hooked the end part of his own little finger into it.

Let me deduce what's going wrong and I'll work so hard. Promise.

When a circuit board failed, the reason usually fell into one of two categories. Manufacture problems included errors like misreading the schematic, mislabelling a component or installing it incorrectly. Poor soldering also resulted in failure. He found it inconceivable that he was responsible for the problem.

That left environmental problems. Exposure to variables such as moisture, heat or dirt. Factors that degraded or corroded.

He considered recent developments. The police had started to find the women he'd killed. They were asking for information on the television. Sharing images of the victims. All factors he had planned for. Stresses the circuit was built to withstand.

What else?

The police had made an appeal. They'd shown the face of a man they urgently wished to question. A man they said was known as Dutch Pete. He lifted his hand and ran a finger slowly along the coat hanger's cool wire.

How had they decided that man was the one who had to be found?

He slid off the stool and hurried out of the garage, locking it behind him. After he'd let himself into the house, he made straight for the television. Excitement was shallowing his breath. He had an idea.

Once he'd positioned his laptop alongside the television, he switched both devices on. Using the TV's remote, he went into the recording he'd made of the police appeal earlier that day. When footage reached the victim's photos, he pressed pause.

Next, he opened the laptop's browser and typed in 'suspect's photo Manchester killings'. The *Daily Mail*'s report topped the list of results. He scrolled down to the still of the suspect's face.

He pressed play on the TV remote. The photo of Pamela Flood stayed on the screen for a few more seconds. He could remember her; she'd been on the bus he sometimes caught outside the college. The 63. Not as good as the 148, but it ran far more frequently. Her image was replaced by a photo of the second victim, Francesca Pinto. She'd been on the free shuttle bus, number three, which ran a purple route around the city centre. She'd boarded at Deansgate, outside the big Waterstones. The third victim came up. Julie Roe. He remembered this one most fondly. The foul-mouthed harridan.

He paused the footage and stared at her face. Yes, this one felt right. He shuffled closer to the screen, close enough so her face began to break into pixels. Close enough to see his breath temporarily dull the glass surface. He continued to stare and, slowly, it came to him.

Where he'd seen Dutch Pete was on the same bus.

The man the police were now looking for had asked the woman

called Julie Roe to lower her voice. In a very reasonable manner, too. But her response had been the opposite. In fact, she'd subjected him to a whole barrage of disrespectful language.

He crawled back from the screen and thought about the bus journey. Which other variables were present on it? A few school-aged children on the back row of seats. And a woman – rather overweight – in some kind of mobility scooter at the front. When he'd originally got on, she'd pressed a form into his hand.

It was her, he realized. She'd called the police. He could remember her head tilting as she listened to every word of the argument.

He got up and walked over to the dresser. There was the form she'd handed him. He sighed with relief and smiled. He now knew the cause of the problem. Her. She was the dirt in the system. The disruptive element ruining his project. Remove her and everything would start flowing smoothly again.

He studied the form more carefully. *Customer Satisfaction Survey, Transport For Greater Manchester.* So that's who she worked for.

FORTY-THREE

Janet sat at the kitchen table and stared glumly at the walkie-talkies. It was their utter silence that announced most loudly to her that he'd gone. He'd really gone.

When she'd woken up, part of her had hoped that – somehow – he'd returned so quietly in the night she hadn't heard him. But his bedroom door was wide open when she emerged from her room.

She didn't need to look inside to know his bed was empty. She could sense it and the knowledge made her feel sick.

There were two eggs beside the frying pan and a pot of tea was cooling on the table. It was almost eight o'clock. He must have eaten breakfast somewhere else by now. He'd be at work, or travelling in. She hoped he'd been able to go in. To face his colleagues knowing that they all knew. How the hell had it got out? Who had Tony mentioned it to? Maybe it was DCI Ransford.

Yes, it was probably DCI Ransford. Who wouldn't resent being told who to recruit? She'd been so stupid. Sean would have been allocated a detective's position, eventually. He didn't need her interference.

She wasn't sure if it would ever be the same again. Something in him had changed. And it had changed because – this time – she'd really hurt him. He'd been close to crying and she'd never seen him like that before. Not since he was little. The memory made her eyes sting.

She bowed her head as a long shuddering sob fought its way up into her mouth. She dragged in a lungful of air, fighting to regain control. Using the backs of her fingers, she wiped at her lower eyelids. She wondered briefly if she might throw up.

The terrible lack of sound pressed down on her. She deliberately let her chair scrape across the tiles, relieved to shatter the silence, if only for a moment. Gripping her walking frame, she slowly made her way into the telly room and gathered up the sheets she'd promised to shred. It was the least she could do.

The machine was in the alcove beneath the stairs, computer on an L shaped desk next to it. As she fed the paper in, she pondered the latest developments in the case. The search was on for the person known as Dutch Pete. Officers would be handing out leaflets, speaking to anyone with knowledge of the comings and goings in their neighbourhood.

She thought back to when Cahill had been caught. Sitting in a McDonald's. Criminals, as she'd said to Sean, weren't generally the brightest bunch. Was anyone checking the bus route she'd seen him on? Because, if he was still in the area, that could be a good place to spot him.

All the man had to do was dye his hair, turn his collar up and keep his head down. People didn't make a habit of checking their fellow passengers. Eye contact was minimal. Non-existent when people could focus on a screen instead.

She closed her eyes and turned the thought over in her mind. *Are you just clutching at straws here? No*, she told herself. The chances were slim, but not non-existent. And certainly as good as any other avenues that were being pursued.

She let herself imagine catching sight of him. If that should happen, all she'd need do was call Sean. He could be there in minutes and appear to make the sighting himself. Then it would be his collar! And everyone – all the cynical bastards making his life a misery – would have to drop their sneers. They'd have to start showing him the respect he deserved.

Even better, though she hardly dared admit it, it might – just might – prompt him to forgive her. Things could go back to how they were.

After falling in the bath, her doctor had signed her off work until the following week. As an employee of Transport For Greater Manchester, she had a pass granting her unlimited travel. She also had a stack of customer survey forms in her bag. She nodded: *That's what I'll do. I'll do my best to put things right.* The queasy feeling in her stomach shrank slightly. *I'll travel that route all day, every day, if necessary. And I'll scan the face of every man who gets on until I find him.*

Gravel crunched under Katherine Harpham's feet as she hurried towards her Fiat. Balanced in her arms were three box files. The paperwork involved in being the principal of an academy! She'd worked on the feasibility study of the Health and Beauty students moving to a new purpose-built salon in the corner of the college grounds late into the evening.

The central locking pipped and she lifted the boot door to place the three files inside. As was often the case in the morning, the feeling that she'd forgotten something nibbled away at the back of her mind. Mobile phone. Handbag. She didn't need a brolly; the weather forecast was light cloud with sunny spells. Why, then, the feeling there was something she'd missed?

She started the engine and the radio came on. More about the on-going investigation into the spate of murders in Manchester. There was now one man in custody, and another they urgently wanted to locate. She stared at her cottage for a second. As she put the car into reverse, realization struck: the package! That's why the mention of police had made her pause. It was still on the kitchen floor. She cursed herself for coming so close to forgetting it, again.

FORTY-FOUR

The Transport For Greater Manchester office was in Piccadilly Gardens. It wasn't an area he found pleasant, not since the ugly grey wall had been erected. The thing acted as a barrier – visual and auditory – to the ranks of bus stops on the far side. But ragtag groupings of young men were always loitering at its base. What were they doing there the whole time? Nothing good, judging by their demeanour.

It didn't matter, though. The tram platform for Piccadilly Gardens faced the office's main door. The row of plastic seats beneath a rigid canopy meant he could just sit there and watch the entrance to the office without anyone giving him a second glance.

He checked his watch. Eight seventeen. That was good: he couldn't imagine her arriving for work earlier than nine. The intercom above his head let out a short crackle before a voice spoke. Next tram was an Altrincham service. Passengers wishing to travel to Eccles, MediaCity or East Didsbury should alight at Cornbrook.

Altrincham, he thought. *That would be a good route to go searching on.* There was a railway station out at Altrincham. If he found no one on the tram, he could hop on a train back to the city centre. Twenty minutes later, he'd be at Piccadilly. Once there, all he had to do was head down the escalators to the tram platform and he could repeat the journey.

He had to stop his mind from wandering. First, he needed to find the woman. Trail her home and silence her. Once he'd done that, his project could work again. Normal service, resumed.

The four CCTV analysts who'd worked through the night had a sunken-eyed appearance. Like box-set bingers who had blitzed an entire series in one sitting. Sean took in their slouching postures and subdued conversation. It wasn't the type of body language that signalled success.

I probably look similar, he thought. His room at the Ibis hotel by Piccadilly had been fine: cheap and cheerful, as his mum would have said. He couldn't stop thinking about her, his mind vacillating between anger and concern. But she had his mobile number. If she really needed him, she could call and leave a message. He'd have a listen and – if the problem was genuine – call her back.

That's the way it would have to be from now on. His life had to change. They needed to break free of each other.

The hotel booking was for five nights. As soon as he got the chance, he'd start looking for a flat or house-share near to her. Somewhere close enough to get to the house quickly if the need ever arose.

The canteen was busy, so rather than queue at the counter for a coffee, he went straight to the table of analysts. 'Morning.'

Greyish faces turned in his direction.

'Any sign of Dutch Pete in the footage?'

'Fuck all,' one of them muttered.

Sean was surprised; it had seemed so promising. 'Has it all been checked over?'

Another chuckled. 'We can't watch it speeded up. There's a good chunk of it still to go.'

'How much roughly?'

He sighed. 'About ten per cent. Should be done by about midday.'

'That's including what was sourced off the various forms of public transport?'

'Everything.'

'OK, cheers.' He turned away. No sign of Dutch Pete so far. The chances of him being in the remaining footage was looking flimsy. *Shit.*

He hovered near the counter, knowing he was only putting off the inevitable. It was time to face the main incident room.

Detectives were sitting at almost half the desks, which meant several teams were out there chasing down leads. He spotted Magda. She gave him a wave and he drifted across to her side of the office. 'Apparently, the CCTV footage isn't any use.'

'Yes,' she nodded. 'I heard that, too. But don't look like that, it's still got potential.'

'Maybe. It's just that . . .' He shrugged. 'I thought we'd nailed it.'

'There were more calls yesterday evening. The owner of a place where they sell plants and things for the garden . . .'

'A nursery?'

'Yes – that. The owner of it said Dutch Pete fixed a section of fencing for him less than a fortnight ago. He paid him in cash though – so no bank account we can go off.'

Handyman type, Sean thought. Another factor that fitted with the psychological profile. 'Any other interesting calls?'

'There was. A woman rang to say she'd been approached by him in a pub three weeks ago. They ended up going back to her place. But he made her feel uneasy and, when she asked him to leave, he became abusive and threatening.'

'Did he touch her?'

'No – but she'd been genuinely scared. He spat at her as he left.'

'So he also has issues with women. Seems that Mrs Greenhalgh's profile is on the money.'

'Except the physical description: this guy is big. Muscular.'

'True, but the jack-of-all-trades stuff. Travelling around with a toolbox. And this woman's report; I bet more calls like hers come in.' He glanced across to Ransford's office. 'Is the briefing still on for half eight?'

'It is. I hear there's something back from Interpol.'

When the briefing got underway, Sean spent the first part of it with his attention on the noticeboards. Most of what Ransford had to say was a repeat of what Magda had already told him. He looked up when his DCI lifted a new sheet of paper and announced: 'And now for the best news of the morning.'

Magda turned to him and lifted an eyebrow. *Told you so.*

'Interpol have now responded. Nothing came up on the database for Dutch nationals. However, they ran the facial image of our suspect across the entire system and got this match. Seems he isn't from Holland at all.'

He turned the sheet of paper round so everyone could view it.

'Petr Kadlec is from the Czech Republic, but no longer lives in that country. In 2011, he was convicted of criminal damage when he tried to kick down the front door of the matrimonial home. They're now divorced. Early 2012, he moved away from the town of Rakovnik. It is believed he headed to good old Blighty, looking for work.'

A question came in from the back. 'Nothing on our system for him?'

'No,' Ransford shot back. 'The PNC has been checked; he hasn't been arrested during his time so far in the UK. If he's working in the gig economy – cash-in-hand stuff – there won't be a huge amount on official systems we can go off. A request has gone into the Czech police to send us all they have—'

'Sir!'

Heads turned. Maggie James was almost jogging across the room. Ransford waved at the rearmost officers to move out of her way.

'A hit on his passport number. Petr Kadlec caught a ferry to Rotterdam on Saturday afternoon.'

Sean's eyes went to the timeline at the top of the noticeboard. That was shortly after the most recent victim's death.

Ransford obviously worked it out, too; he slammed a hand down on the table. 'You're saying he's out of the country?'

'Maybe not,' she replied. 'It's a return ticket. Foot passenger. The ferry he is due back on docks at Hull just after two o'clock. Petr Kadlec is on board.'

Ransford's entire body was tense. 'Two o'clock? Which two o'clock?'

'This afternoon, sir.'

FORTY-FIVE

Janet Blake snapped down the lid of her Tupperware container. Inside were a couple of ham sandwiches and a few sachets of dried fruit and nuts. Enough so she could stay on the buses all day.

She checked her phone. She couldn't stop checking her phone. Why didn't he call? Where had he stayed the previous night? She pictured him in a soulless hotel room. People thudding about on the ceiling, doors clicking open and shut, voices in the corridors at all hours. He wouldn't have slept well. She knew he wouldn't.

Perhaps she should ring him.

She was ready to apologize, if it would help. But he needed to understand she'd only done it for him. For his good. She thought about her own career. Ability and enthusiasm counted for a lot, of course. But they were both easily trumped by a quiet word from the right place. Something she'd never had the benefit of. How many of the officers she'd started out with had? How many had gone on to find positions far senior to hers? Most, if not all. It was how it worked and Sean needed to understand that.

Christ, Tony Shipton. Tony bloody Shipton! She could remember their first few weeks together on the job. He was so nervous. Nerves that manifested themselves in a heavy-handed approach when they'd been called to deal with a couple of teenage shop-lifters. He'd been embarrassing, they way he'd tried to intimidate them. As if that kind of approach would ever work. And now look how high he'd risen.

She checked her watch. Just after nine. If Sean hadn't called by lunch, she'd give him a ring.

Sean sat at his desk, staring at the checklist of the CCTV footage.

The briefing had been brought to a rapid close with news of the ferry booking. Ransford and a team of officers were heading straight to Hull. If Petr Kadlec really was on board, they'd make the arrest as he reached passport control.

Sean took a good look around; the sense of jubilation was palpable. The detectives nearest him were talking about how it would be a big night. One of them suggested starting a whip-round; he could do a booze run in Morrison's at lunch.

Sean turned back to his screen; his mum's theory was nagging at him. Check what they said, not who they spoke with. Could she have been onto something? If Kadlec hadn't eavesdropped on his victim's conversations, how else was he able to know so much about them?

Spyware on their computers? A hack of their voicemails?

He clicked on another tab; the transcripts from Pamela Flood's phone records. He started to go through them again. Most were bland conversations. The inconsequential crap people nattered about. He worked his way down the list to when Cahill had called her at 5.59 pm. The bickering went on for the next twelve minutes.

No. I said to you before, I'm not doing it.
You never fucking listen, Ian. You never fucking do.
I owe you nothing. Don't you even try that shit.
Yeah, and it's my fucking flat! Who paid the rent? Who paid for the gas and electric? Bollocks. You never did.
Quite happy there without you, cheers.
Quite happy.
I'm not like you, I can handle being on my own.

There it was: a clear statement where she said that no one else was living in the flat. He brought up the CCTV footage from the bus. An analyst had helpfully put a circle round Pamela's head as she spoke on her phone. The time stamp showed 6.03 pm.

He scrutinized the passengers around her for Petr Kadlec. No sign of him.

Letting the footage play on, he watched her disembark at 6.05, still talking to Cahill. Among the three people who got off at the same time as her was one man: but it wasn't Petr Kadlec.

This was so infuriating.

He minimized the screen and surveyed the other victims' files. Francesca Pinto had been next to die. In her CCTV folder, he searched out *Shuttle Bus Footage*.

The picture quality was far superior to that for Pamela Flood's final journey. New fleet of buses, Sean thought. Electric hybrids. Francesca made her way past the driver's cab at 7.11 pm. The bus was two-thirds full, mostly commuter types returning to Piccadilly Station. He paused the footage as she turned round. One hand grasped a ceiling strap, the other held a phone. He scanned the fellow passengers.

No sign of him, yet again.

A couple of clicks gave him a view of Francesca's call records. At 7.16 pm, she made a call to the offices of Wadden and Holden Property Management.

Sean sat back. Hadn't Heather Knight worked for some kind of letting agency? Surely it wasn't this one? That couldn't have been missed. He selected her file and opened up her Personal Details document. Employer: Mellor & Key. No panic, after all.

Returning to Francesca's transcripts, he searched for the call that coincided with her bus journey.

> *I was promised the issue would be resolved by now.*
>
> *Under the terms of my tenancy – I work as a solicitor, by the way – I am entitled to withhold the next rental payment.*
>
> *That's correct. No, number three. One bedroom, yes.*
>
> *I work normal office hours, so how am I supposed to be there at that time?*
>
> *No, it's just me.*

There it was again! An announcement that she lived alone. Surely it was significant.

He waited until ten o'clock. For the past thirty minutes, not a single staff member had gone through the doors. Either she was working a late shift or she had taken the day off.

He fixed the offices with baleful eyes.

Was there any way he could find out if she was due in? Not without drawing undue attention to himself. He thought about the bus trip where he'd seen her.

She'd been handing out the surveys – so there was a faint chance she could still be doing it. In which case, she could be anywhere on the city's bus network. Except, she was in a wheelchair.

That meant she could only travel on the newer types. The ones that had proper disabled facilities.

He left the platform and walked round to the Transport For Greater Manchester's office. It shouldn't be too difficult to get a list of all the wheelchair friendly routes.

The phone on Katherine Harpham's desk began to ring at 10.52. Rebecca, her secretary, was on the line.

'Hi, Becky.'

'Hi, Katherine. You had an eleven fifteen with the planning officer. About the Health and Beauty proposals?'

'Had? This is sounding ominous.'

'I just heard from her office. She's been called away unexpectedly and sends her apologies. We could reschedule for early next week? Monday at three works for her.'

'Monday it is, then. Thanks, Becky.'

That left her with a free hour. She looked down at the patches of sunlight moving across the college playing fields. The clouds were breaking up. It looked nice outside.

The plastic bag she'd placed the suspicious delivery in was next to her chair. *Why the hell not*, she thought. By foot, the police station on Brodick Street couldn't take more than ten minutes to reach. There'd be a form to complete, she was sure. But how complicated could it be? She gazed out the window, this time at the gently swaying fir trees that lined the perimeter fence. Fresh air, what a lovely prospect.

*   *   *

When she walked up to the front desk, the uniformed officer's response had been one of bemusement. 'Balls of newspaper and a block of wood?'

'Yes. Take a look inside – I'm not joking.'

He folded the top of the shopping bag down then picked up a pen and used it to lift up the flaps of the box. 'You're right. That is most strange. And this label? That's your name and address?'

'Yes. But there's no barcode. No return address. Nothing.'

'How about the underside? Anything there?'

'No.'

'Mmmm.'

He reached into the box, plucked out a single ball of scrunched-up newspaper and flattened it out on the counter. 'This has been torn out from a copy of the *Manchester Evening Chronicle*. Whoever's behind this lives around here, it would seem.'

'What's worrying me is what he was up to. Are there reports of any burglaries taking place after a fake package was delivered?'

'I'd have to check, but not that I know of. And this man: you say he was in a courier driver's uniform?'

'I only saw his van. But, according to my sister, he was.'

'Which company was he from?'

'She didn't know. The uniform was blue.'

'OK. Leave it with me. I'll need you to complete this form. And could you also include contact details for your sister?'

'With pleasure. I'll do it now, if that's OK.'

'Whatever is easiest. Apart from you and your sister, no one else has handled the package?'

'No – apart from the man who rang on the door.'

FORTY-SIX

The driver of the 419 bus waited until she'd backed her wheelchair into the bay beside the doors before he started to pull away.

'You all right, Janet?'

She lifted her chin. 'Mm?'

'Looking a bit down in the dumps today.'

'Oh, probably tired. I didn't sleep very well.' She did her best to inject some cheer into her voice. 'So, Arthur, you on until three?'

His eyes were on his right-hand mirror as he forced his way back out into the stream of traffic. 'That's the one. How long have they got you on this route? I thought it had been covered off last week.'

She started removing customer survey forms from her bag. 'All morning. Maybe the afternoon, too. Depends on how fast I can make this pile go down.'

'Well.' He looked briefly across. 'You could just dump the lot in the bin and have done.'

'Arthur!' She forced herself to smile. 'What a thing to suggest.'

'World's drowning in bloody paperwork. Why add to it?'

'You have a point.'

The lights in front turned to red and he started to slow. She used the opportunity to have a look at the passengers in the main part of the bus. No sign of the suspect. No matter, she said to herself. One thing a career in the police had taught her was patience.

He crossed the tram tracks and approached the long line of bus stops.

Lined up alongside them were royal blue Magic Buses with canary yellow lettering, lavender-and-turquoise single-decker Sapphires, Stagecoaches with red and orange ticks sweeping across the vehicles' rear wheels. Every time one moved away, another took its place. They tried to edge round each other, diesels rumbling, brakes phewing. A gigantic gyre, slowly churning all day long.

He examined the timetables he'd harvested from the visitor centre's racks. The number of wheelchair friendly routes was larger than he'd imagined. Much larger. In fact, there was hours of travelling involved, if he was to check each one.

He almost laughed. He was going about this all wrong. He clasped his hands together and raised them to the sky. 'You're testing me, aren't you?' he muttered. 'Well, that's fine.' *And I, in turn, have realized, there's no need for me to roam the city searching for her. Not if I just stand here, where the buses turn in from the main road. This is where she will be presented to me.*

*   *   *

Fifteen minutes after Ransford's team left for Hull, the ferry company came through with the full details of Petr Kadlec's booking, including an address in Chadderton.

Two detectives were immediately despatched to a magistrate to get a warrant signed to search the property. Another six set off for the house itself: the instant a signature was obtained, they'd crash the door in. The warrant itself could catch them up later. As Ransford had stressed via his car's phone, speed was everything.

Sean watched from his seat in the corner as the search team was led out by DI Levine. Apart from him, the only people now left in the incident room were Troughton and few specialist support workers.

He turned back to his screen and began mulling over the fact every victim, apart from Heather Knight, had talked freely on public transport – and by doing so had unwittingly revealed details about themselves.

Heather Knight had also been alone in her property when the killer called. The boyfriend was out of the country on a friend's stag do. How had the murderer known that? He retrieved the transcripts of her call to the BMW garage. This was the moment when, just like all the other victims, she let anyone in hearing know she was alone in the house.

> *You're going to deliver it to my house before Sunday evening.*
> *It's number sixteen, Kersal Mews, Didsbury.*
> *Yes, Knight with a K.*

Immediately after that call, she'd spoken to her boyfriend.

> *Silly boys and their stag-do rules.*
> *And you've got another two nights of this?*
> *A bath and season three of Crimson Rose.*
> *Lounge around in bed until at least eleven.*

Everything the killer needed had been in those two calls. The problem was, she'd been in a private car at the time. He went into the folder where the detailed account of each of the victim's last twenty-four hours were stored.

Inside Heather Knight's file, he skimmed through to VIP Cars.

The follow-up work had been carried out by DC Morris, Fuller's acolyte. The cab company had sent a driver called Khalid Khan to collect Heather at 9.55 on the Saturday morning. He searched for Khan's statement that confirmed that's what he'd done. No sign of it in the folder. Yet Heather was back in the office by 11.00 – she left again shortly after with a colleague, who dropped her off outside Kersal Mews. The colleague's statement to that effect had been filed.

So where was the cab driver's?

Sean looked over to where Morris normally sat. All the desks were empty. An internet search brought up the name for VIP Cars.

'Hello, it's DC Blake from Greater Manchester Police speaking. It's in relation to a driver of yours, Khalid Khan. Is it possible to speak with him, please?'

The woman's words were rapid. 'Out on a job. Finishes at – let me see – lunch.'

'Have you a mobile number I can reach him on?'

'No. Can't give them out.' A phone started to ring in the background. 'Hold please.'

He waited a full minute before she came back on. 'VIP Cars.'

'Yes, it's DC Blake. I need to speak with one of your drivers—'

'Oh, yeah. Lunch. OK?'

'No.' Another phone went off. She'd put him on hold again, if she could. 'This is urgent. You need to patch me through to him.'

A massive sigh. 'Hang on.' The line began to buzz slightly. 'Base to nine. Base to nine.'

'This is nine.'

'Got the police here, Khalid. He's on the other end of the line and can hear you. Can you speak to him?'

'Yes.'

'Go ahead.' The buzz vanished. They were alone. He jotted down the number that now showed on the landline's display.

'Mr Khan, DC Blake speaking. A colleague contacted you recently about a job. You picked up a female passenger, Heather Knight, from a location in Salford Quays to bring her back—'

'She wasn't there.'

'Sorry?'

'She wasn't there. I was running a bit late. I told this already. She'd already gone.'

'She'd gone? You didn't drive her back to her office in the city centre?'

'No.'

'But, according to the company she worked for, that's what happened. I have a copy of the booking from their records.'

'Oh, we'd have billed them for the job. But it was a wasted journey for me. She wasn't there.'

'Did you provide a statement with this information?'

'He never came to the office, the detective. I said when I could sit down to do it.'

Morris had forgotten, Sean thought.

'The man running the car park,' Khan continued, 'he said she got a tram.'

'What was that?'

'A tram. She caught a tram. He saw her get on. Told me when I showed up looking for her.'

Christ, thought Sean. 'Thanks for your help.' He cut the call and returned to Heather's transcripts.

> *Hello, this is Heather. You've just arrived? Even though you said you'd be there by 10:15? And it's now? That's right – 10:40. Bloody great, first the cab company, now you. Where am I? On the way back to my office.*

Sean reached for his keyboard. She hadn't been talking on her phone in the back of the cab. She'd been on a tram! He opened a new browser, typed in the postcode for the development in Salford Quays where she'd been waiting and selected Street View. Directly opposite the property was the Harbour City tram stop. Not only that, the tracks ran alongside the road. Phone mast analysis would never be able to distinguish between a car journey and a tram ride at that point.

He bowed his head. *Mum had been right.* The killer was listening in on conversations. Trains, buses, trams: he was using public transport. Had to be. The thought of how he'd left her all alone in the house made his teeth clench; he should ring and let her know.

But first he had to make sure. There was tram footage of Heather Knight they didn't know existed. If he could find Petr Kadlec in it, Janet's theory would be proved.

He walked over to where Maggie James sat. 'How fast can we get hold of tram footage?'

'If it's within—'

'I'm looking at this Saturday. Harbour City, going towards the city centre, 10.30 am.'

'Well,' she said, slightly taken aback. 'We could submit a—'

'It can't be their normal turnaround. This is highest priority.'

'I think,' she said, placing her pen down, 'that requires authority from someone with a more senior rank to you.'

'DC Blake?' Inspector Troughton was walking towards him with a look of confusion. 'What's going on?'

'There's been an error, sir. It was . . . assumed . . . Heather Knight hadn't used public transport in the run-up to her murder: she had. It was in the morning, about two hours before when we think she died. The footage from that tram journey hasn't been checked and I'm certain our man will be on it.'

'Hang on.' Troughton sat on the edge of the nearest desk, looking perplexed. 'The woman's final twenty-four hours have been—'

'Sir, I can explain to you how it slipped through. But that footage – we have to get them to send it across. Now.'

Troughton tapped a forefinger rapidly against his chin. 'Maggie? What's the best estimate—'

'Two hours. Maybe less. With a time frame that exact, they can locate it very quickly.'

'OK, I'll authorize the request.' He turned back to Sean. 'You'd better take me through exactly what you've got.'

The front desk of the police station on Brodick Street hit a quiet patch just before midday.

'Tanya, could you hold the fort? I need to put this on the system. It's been bugging me all morning.'

'I saw that. What is it, anyway?'

'A lady brought it in earlier. A spoof package, delivered to her house by a guy in a courier's uniform.'

'What makes it a spoof?'

'The fact it had nothing inside except a bit of wood and old newspaper.'

'Bizarre.'

'You've not heard of any similar incidents?'

She shook her head.

'Me neither. But there's something I don't like about it.'

He moved to the computer terminal in the corner then looked back at the plastic bag. It was an odd one. Obviously, it didn't count as evidence collected in the wake of a crime. He was fairly sure no laws had been broken. Impersonating a courier driver: was that illegal? Instead, he decided to first run a search on recent crimes. He pondered which criteria to use. Anything on the system that involved:

Confidence trick.

Doorstep delivery.

Impersonating a tradesman.

Dummy package.

White van.

He reflected on the list. It seemed to cover the way the person was operating.

He hit search and was surprised to immediately receive a notification. Seemed a DCI Ransford in the Serious Crimes Unit had put a flag on three of those criteria. There was an incident room number he was to immediately call.

FORTY-SEVEN

B y the time the single-decker bus crawled past Dawson's music shop, he was just able to make out the number on its front. 419. Was that the service that had been carrying the foul-mouthed one with her weirdly coloured hair? He thought it was.

The traffic started moving forward again and the bus edged closer. Thirty metres away, it was able to separate itself from the flow of cars and enter the lane that led into Piccadilly Gardens.

It was definitely one of the newer buses. Which meant wheel-chair passengers were catered for. Something told him a significant event was about to occur. A tickle in his spine. He wondered if it had something to do with the electronic poster on the side of a nearby bus shelter. One of the images it kept flashing up was of an immaculate woman with a mobile phone poised before her smiling face. With every appearance, she stared directly at him with encouraging eyes.

The bus now had a clear run to the turning in. He stood beside the pedestrian railings as the front of the vehicle swung past. He narrowed his eyes, trying to cut out all extraneous detail. The bus doors passed through his field of vision, then the first side window. He saw her. Her back was turned to him, but he knew it was her. Rounded shoulders. Wheelchair. It was her. Probably handing out more of those surveys.

To reach the stand for 419, her bus would have to drive past the initial stops to the far side of the gardens, follow the U-bend and head back in his direction.

Plenty of time to amble over. He could climb on board with all the other passengers then not let her out of his sight. She had to go home eventually. This felt good. This felt right. He tipped his head back and gave a grateful smile to the sky.

'That's bloody superb work, Sean.'

Troughton leaned back in his chair and looked across towards DC Morris' empty desk.

'I don't want to drop anyone in it, sir.'

'You don't?' Troughton's smile was grim. 'Leave it with me. I have no such qualms.'

Sean started to gather the printouts he'd brought over to the office manager's workstation. 'So what's next?'

'I need to call DCI Ransford and let him know. He should almost be in Hull by now. You're on quite a roll with this, aren't you?'

Sean's head filled with an image of his mum, leaning over the kitchen table, finger tracing Pamela Flood's phone records. 'One thing just seemed to lead to another.'

'Very modest.' Troughton checked his watch. 'The tram footage is due in under an hour. I'd say a coffee break's in order.'

Sean hesitated. Last time he'd offered to get Troughton a drink, he'd been blanked. 'I'll nip down there. What are you having?'

'Cheers. Americano, no sugar.'

There was a line of people waiting for drinks. It would, he realized, be a good opportunity to call his mum. Tell her that the man she'd seen on the bus was out of the country, but on a ferry due to dock in Hull. A team was on its way to pick him up. A result wasn't far off, now.

He pulled his phone from his pocket and brought up their home number. She also deserved to know her hunch had been right:

public transport had been the key. He could picture her alone in
the house. She'd be beside herself, wondering where he'd gone,
when he'd ring.

He was about to make the call when another part of him said
not to. *Don't do it. You're only acting out of guilt. How will she
ever get used to living on her own if you cave in and call her this
quickly?*

He agonized for a few seconds on what was best. Then he
returned his phone to his pocket and joined the queue. He'd
phone her later.

With a coffee in each hand, he had to push the door to the
incident room open with a foot. Troughton immediately called
him over. 'Sorry to dump this on you, Sean, but a report's just
come in. An incident has partly tallied with a flag DCI Ransford
put on the system. It needs a detective to go out and cover it off.
Can you drive over to the Lightwater Academy and interview
the principal? A woman called Katherine Harpham.'

The bus idled at the stop in Piccadilly Gardens for less than five
minutes before resuming its route. As it left the city centre and
made its way along the Oldham Road, Janet toyed with her phone.
Why hadn't Sean called? Was he that furious with her? The possibility of him never ringing occurred. It caused her sense of being
deserted to well up, threatening to engulf her. She forced herself
to sit straighter. She had to be stronger than this; show that she
wasn't a sad old woman, deluding herself that she could still do
the job of a proper police officer. Making herself useful: that
was the way to put things right. Not ringing her son and begging
forgiveness. She examined the new rows of faces filling the seats.
Dutch Pete wasn't among them.

At the journey's halfway point, she realized that she needed the
toilet. She couldn't believe she hadn't factored it in. Normally, if
she knew access to a toilet would be limited, she'd put a catheter
in place before leaving the house. The container sat in a concealed
space beneath the wheelchair's seat. *How*, she said to herself, *could
you have been so forgetful? It's this business with Sean. You're
not thinking straight.*

She glanced out the window and saw a B&M Bargains store.
This, she realized, was the place where the poor woman who'd
been killed had got on. Julie Roe. It was now all so clear in Janet's

memory. The woman's aggressive behaviour and atrocious language. The foreign guy's inability to get his words out. A stutter: of all the things to possess when faced with that woman.

Janet could recall his look of impotent rage. The woman's whiplash of a tongue that had left him belittled and humiliated. She saw once again the woman as she got off the bus before coming back to press her middle finger against the window. There'd been absolutely no need for that.

The bus came to a halt and she looked hopefully to the side to see who was getting on. Just an elderly Asian man in cream-coloured baggy trousers and a grey jacket. The bus resumed its journey.

After a few more stops, they neared the point that passed closest to Janet's house. By alighting here, it would only take a few minutes to get home. The need to urinate had now grown uncomfortable.

'Arthur?'

He half turned his head.

'I'm almost out of surveys.'

'You need to get off?'

'Yes please, at the next stop.'

'Right you are. Will I see you later?'

'When are you on until? Three, was it?'

'Correct.'

'Maybe, then. I'll have a spot of lunch and come back for just before two. A 419 comes past at ten to the hour, doesn't it?'

'It does, but it might not be the one I'm driving.'

As the speed of the bus dropped, two other people also left their seats. One was a female in a Co-op uniform. Her handbag was open and Janet could see a stack of biscuits adorned by reduced stickers poking out. Getting first dibs on any deals: perk of the job.

The other person was a man with glasses and peppery brown hair. As he waited for the bus to stop, she noticed he kept mumbling to himself. Little snatches of words, silently mouthed. The fingers of his left hand tapped against his thigh. *Looks like you're due another dose of your medication*, Janet thought.

Once the vehicle was stationary, the doors opened and the bus sank down so the floor was the same height as the kerb.

'How's that for you?' asked Arthur.

'Expertly done.' By the time she'd manoeuvred her wheelchair off the vehicle and onto the pavement, the woman in the Co-op uniform was forty metres away. Janet looked left and right for the other passenger. No sign of him anywhere.

FORTY-EIGHT

As soon as the entrance for Lightwater Academy came into view, Sean realized he'd been there before. When he was following-up on possible CCTV sources for Pamela Flood. The woman had caught a bus from right outside the college and alighted a couple of miles down the road.

He turned into the college car park, found a visitor's space and made his way to the main entrance. The building design was imposing and intentionally so. Vertical banners with words like *Resilience*, *Risk-taking* and *Respect* hung behind huge plate-glass windows. Once inside the spacious foyer, he looked up to see a clouded ceiling of yet more glass. Flat-screen TVs dotted the white walls, each flashing up statistics or footage of students hard at work.

Sean cast his mind back to his old school: a crappy comprehensive with rain-stained ceilings, cramped classrooms and long corridors with lino floors. In the summer, sections would bubble up and they would race to land with two feet on the juiciest lumps.

This place was newly built and looked like standards were high.

A side door opened, releasing a mass of squawking, swearing students. Half were hauling phones from pockets as they surged forward. A few glances went his way; mild curiosity to naked suspicion.

'Slow down!' one of the women behind the front desk snarled. 'No phones in school hours!'

They poured down a passageway, taking no notice. Sean smiled inwardly. And it had all seemed so impressive. 'Detective Constable Blake,' he said, placing his badge on the counter. 'Katherine Harpham is expecting me.'

The principal's office was on the third floor. Nice views across the college's playing fields. The room itself was messier than he'd expected. Too many folders and files lying about. He wondered if it would be a reflection of her personality. Taking a statement was always harder with less organized types.

'Ms Harpham, thanks for making time to see me.'

'No, thank you.' As she stood, he saw what an unhealthy amount of weight she was carrying. Too much time in here, probably. Her face was rounded, the hairstyle a little bizarre. A big blob of hair on top of her head and trails of it hanging down over each ear. She smiled tentatively, eyes almost obscured by a heavy fringe.

He wondered whether it would be appropriate to extend a hand. Her right arm showed no sign of lifting. 'Your facilities look amazing. When was it all built?'

'Thanks. Only five years ago. Central government money.' She retook her seat, nodding at the empty one next to him.

'And is it mainly vocational stuff?' he asked, lowering himself into it. 'I noticed a sign for the plastering centre.'

'That's right. Lots of trades: plastering, plumbing, building and the like. Health and beauty is a growing part of things. Social care, too – which was my area when I got the opportunity to actually teach!' She rolled her eyes while smiling.

It was an obvious invitation for him to ask how she'd risen to principal. He didn't take it: too much going on back at the office for that. 'Interesting. Now, I appreciate you're busy. This package. Could you describe everything to me?'

'From when?'

'I gather you weren't actually in when it was delivered . . .'

'No – my sister was. I'd popped out for some bits and bobs and when I got home, I saw a white van parked on the—'

Sean looked up. 'A white van?'

'Yes. It wasn't directly in front of my cottage, so I didn't put two and two together. Not at first.'

'Any markings on it?'

'No. Plain.'

'And the driver?'

'I didn't see anyone in the vehicle. But Amanda, my sister, said he'd gone just before I arrived. So I don't know where he was at that point.'

'Did you get a look in the vehicle's cab?'

'Yes. I'd slowed down quite a bit by then. There was no one in it.'

'Could he have been in the back?'

'I doubt it. The thing wasn't large. Certainly not high enough to stand in.'

'One of those that's similar in size to an estate car?'

'Yes.'

'Did you recognize the model?'

'No. Just one of those ones builders and the like use. You see them everywhere.'

Same as in the road next to Heather Knight's flat, Sean thought. 'Ms Harpham, do you ever travel by public transport?'

'Me? No, I mean, I should do – it would be far greener, I know. But I live a bit away from the college. The trains aren't always that reliable, so—'

'You hadn't caught a bus, tram or train in the days before this person called at your house?'

'No.'

It couldn't do any harm to show her a photo of Petr Kadlec. If it did happen to be him, they had more ammunition for his interview. 'I have a photo here.' He started to reach for his folder. 'It's of a man—'

'You'll have to show that to my sister. She saw him, not me.'

Shit, Sean thought. *Of course.* 'In which case, would you have a number I can reach her on?' He left the folder on the floor.

She was flicking through her mobile's address book. 'Should I be worried? You're a detective. I didn't expect to be visited by a—'

'We have no knowledge of burglaries taking place that involve dummy packages, if that's your concern.'

She met his eyes for a moment. 'It is. So why have you come over here to see me?'

'Certain aspects of your report tally with a case I'm working on.'

'Really?' She peered at him through her fringe. 'Which ones?'

'I can't divulge that. Not at this stage. Sorry.'

She didn't look very impressed.

'Let me speak with your sister. If necessary, I'll contact you again. But please don't worry.'

The wheelchair rolled along the pavement at a painfully slow rate. But it made following her easy.

After stepping off onto the pavement, he ducked into a little newsagent's across the street. When the bus eventually pulled away, there she was. Deposited. She was a bit older than him. A saggy posture, straggles of dull brown hair hanging over each shoulder. Dreary clothes. Despite her look of dejection, he knew her mind was sharp. The way she'd observed the entire incident from a few days before was testament to that. Not just observed it. Reported the passenger who'd stood up to the swear-ridden bitch. She probably thought she'd been so clever. Making a contribution. Playing her part. She'd soon be doing that, he thought. It would be a small part. Just one of several others. Each in their own jar in his garage.

He shadowed her from the opposite side of the road until she turned down a side street. About a third of the way along, she steered the little wheelchair onto a short driveway. He lingered until she was inside the house, then made a note of its number. Next, he checked his watch. She'd said to the driver she would have a spot of lunch then catch a bus at ten to two. It would take her five minutes to get to the bus stop. Which meant she'd be leaving the house at about quarter to two. If he was to return in his courier uniform before then, he needed to get a move on. He set off for the main road in search of a cab.

Twenty minutes later, he was climbing out of the taxi. A narrow alley let him cut through to the road that his cul-de-sac branched off. He kept up a fast walking pace, pushing off with the ball of each foot, swinging it forward so he could feel his hamstrings stretch. Left right left right left right. He emerged onto the road, and as the steady rhythm carried him forward, he rechecked his watch. Nearly half past one. It would be close.

The entrance to his cul-de-sac was now in sight. More of it was coming into view. The privet hedge that formed the boundary at the front of his garden. The russet tiles of his garage roof. The mouth of his drive.

A patrol car was at the far end, using the part where the cul-de-sac ballooned out to perform a three-point turn. The livery on the vehicle was alarmingly bright. Alien. Police cars never drove down here.

Before he knew what he was doing, he altered his step to continue straight on. As he crossed the expanse of tarmac to the far pavement, he could see the vehicle beginning to nose its way in his direction. He risked a last look. Both officers were turned towards his house. His drive. Where the new van was parked. What did it mean? Had they come for him?

He slowed to a more normal pace and listened as the car pulled out behind him. The sound of its motor shrank as it moved away down the road. He counted twenty more steps then looked behind him. It was gone.

He span round and jogged back. Now he needed to get ready even faster.

FORTY-NINE

Amanda Harpham was different to her sister. Though unmistakeably older, the extra years only seemed to lend her a certain glamour. She was a lot slimmer and her hair was tied back in a simple ponytail. Understated make-up, done with neutral colours. She wore stylish black trousers and a fitted cream shirt.

'Detective Constable Blake?'

Her voice was lower. Authoritative. A hand was being held out.

'Correct,' he said, feeling the coolness of her fingers as they shook.

'I'm so glad she made a report. Is over here OK?'

The seating area of the reception could have comfortably accommodated a bus load of people. He led the way to a couple of corner seats separated by a low glass coffee table. 'Perfect.'

'So do you regard this as serious?'

He could see something shining in her eyes. It looked suspiciously like excitement. Not excitement. Triumph. Guessing Katherine would have already spoken to her, he said, 'It's of some concern, certainly.'

'Some concern?' Her eyes narrowed.

'Shall we sit?'

She took the nearest chair and crossed her legs. 'Katherine was making light of it. Like it was one of her students. A prank. I thought it was bloody sinister.'

He took out a notepad and pen. 'The man who knocked on the door. How would you describe him?'

'He was in a uniform, you realize that?'

'Yes.' He left it at that, encouraging her to continue.

'He had a baseball cap on his head. Blue, like the uniform itself.' As she brushed at a cuff he spotted the wedding ring on her finger. The one next to it held a large diamond. 'Silver buttons. Something on the jacket, above the breast pocket. A silver emblem.'

'Do you recall the shape?'

'Wings, or a feather. Curving anyway.'

'What shade of blue was the uniform?'

'Royal. In fact, the entire thing made you think of something official. Like an airline pilot.'

'And the man himself. Weight, height, age?'

'Fifties – mid, I'd say. About five ten. Quite trim. Fit-looking, really. For his age.'

Sean tried his best to hide his dismay. Petr Kadlec was over six feet tall, heavily built and ten years younger than the age she'd just given. 'How sure are you about his height?'

'Well, I'd say pretty accurate.'

Sean thought for a second. 'You'd opened the door to him. Did you stay in the house?'

'Of course. I was standing in the doorway. He was on the path.'

'Is there a front step to your sister's residence?'

'There – ah, I see what you're up to. Clever. So: he was about the height of my shoulders. I was definitely looking down at him, and I'm five foot eight.'

'Is the step a high one?'

'Not really.'

'About six inches, then?'

'Yes, that sounds about right.'

Sean made a quick mental calculation. Allowing for the step and the fact their eyes weren't level: the man couldn't have been over six feet tall. Not even close. 'What colour was his hair?'

'What was poking out from the baseball cap was light brown, but going grey. It didn't cover his ears, so it wasn't particularly long. On top, he could have been bald for all I knew.'

'How did he sound when he spoke?'

'Manchester accent, but not heavily so. You knew he was from the region. Another thing that was odd, was how he could hardly get his words out to begin with. I opened the door and he looked nonplussed. First day in the job: nervous, I thought. Then he adopted this silly accent.'

'Silly accent?'

'Mock Indian would be the best way to describe it. I began to think, what is wrong with you? I took the package, but then he said the machine wasn't working. The thing you sign on.'

'The console?'

'That's it. There was a pen and a glass screen, which was glowing. But he said the batteries were dead. Then he shot off. Didn't want a signature.'

This person, Sean thought, was definitely up to something. It sounded almost like he hadn't expected Amanda to open the door. But it obviously wasn't Petr Kadlec. He eyed the cushion on a nearby sofa, thinking he'd like to push his face into it and roar with frustration. 'I'm going to show you a photo, Mrs Harpham. I'd like you to say if it's the man who visited your sister's property.'

'Very well.'

He removed the CCTV still of Kadlec from the folder and placed it on the table. Immediately, she frowned. 'No. Definitely not – but who is that? I've seen that face.' She looked up at him.

Sean put the sheet back in the folder. 'You may well have seen an appeal on the—'

'Oh my God.' Her voice had dropped to a whisper. 'It's the one you think has been . . .'

'Mrs Harpham, we had to eliminate him because of certain factors in your report. However, I didn't show his photo to your sister because it was only you who had seen him.'

A hand was covering her mouth.

'I really don't think it's necessary to worry your sister with this. The location of the man we're looking for is known to us and he'll be in custody very soon, if not already.'

'So . . . so what about this other person who was at my sister's door?'

'I imagine the team I'm part of will hand it back for local police to look into. Thanks for your time, Mrs Harpham.'

The magistrate put his signature on the warrant at twelve forty-seven. A call immediately went to the team who'd been waiting in the car park of a nearby pub. The vehicles raced off and, two minutes later, the front door of a two-bed terraced house on a quiet street in Chadderton was being smashed in. Officers poured through the property, shouts of *Clear* coming from each room moments later.

Once it had been confirmed no one was in the property, the search could begin.

Every drawer in the house was riffled through. In the kitchen, all containers and cereal boxes were emptied out into the sink. The toilet cistern was checked. Skirting boards were ripped from walls, as were the panels round the bath.

A laptop was carted away.

Carpets were peeled back, books shaken by their covers then thrown into a pile on the floor. The oven and grill and microwave compartments were searched. Clothes were pulled from wardrobes, pockets checked and each item tossed on the bed. The sofas and armchairs were upended and the linings across the bases cut away.

All paperwork, including letters, bills and receipts, were sealed into evidence bags.

DI Levine caught DS Dragomir's eye as she emerged from the kitchen with an evidence bag full of household bills. She shook her head: nothing significant.

'Bollocks,' he muttered. So far, they hadn't found a single thing to do with any of the victims. 'Let's hope he has another property. Or a garage somewhere.'

Magda considered how Petr Kadlec was booked as a foot passenger on the ferry. 'Anyone found anything relating to a vehicle? Insurance documents? Breakdown membership?'

'Nope.'

She lifted her eyes to the ceiling. And before entering the property, they'd honestly been expecting to find a container of human tongues in the fridge. *Strange*, she thought, *how disappointment can come in so many guises.*

Sean used both forefingers to tap against the top of his steering wheel. In front of him, a Sainsbury's delivery van was waiting to turn right. No one in the stream of oncoming traffic was prepared to let him across.

The thought bobbed up once again. It appeared Pamela Flood was Kadlec's first victim. The psychological profiler had talked about the circle hypothesis: an imaginary ring drawn around the murder locations in which the killer was very likely to live.

Not only that. Studies in some countries had shown that a serial killer and his first victim often lived close to each other. The theory was that the initial killing often had opportunistic elements to it. After that, the perpetrator began to roam more widely, actively seeking out further prey.

Yet the property where Kadlec was believed to be based was north-east of the city centre – which was completely outside the kill circle. Were there earlier victims still to be found? Or could Petr Kadlec be the wrong man? Then there was the fact he hadn't appeared in any other CCTV footage other than that for Julie Roe. It didn't seem possible.

He took his phone out of his jacket and immediately spotted the missed call icon. Mum. She hadn't left a message. Obviously assumed that, once he knew she'd tried to ring, he would crack and call her back. *Not yet, Mum. I'm busy right now.*

He brought up the number for the incident room. It sounded like the Civilian Support Worker, Katie May, who picked up.

'Is Inspector Troughton there?' Sean asked. 'It's DC Blake calling.'

'Two seconds, Sean.'

Sean, he thought. She was suddenly being friendly. The road finally cleared and he was able to let the handbrake off.

'DC Blake, are you psychic? The footage from Heather Knight's tram journey is about to come through.'

'I was wondering if it had.'

'Where are you?'

'Five minutes away.'

'Good timing. No joy, so far, from the search of Kadlec's residence. It'll be his floorboards, next.'

'When's the ferry with Kadlec on due to dock in Hull?'

'About an hour.'

Janet Blake pushed her half-eaten sandwich aside. Where had her appetite gone? She knew the answer to that: a city centre hotel, along with her son. Should she have tried to call him just now? Probably not. But they needed to talk. She needed to hear his voice. She hoped the fact she didn't leave a message would act as some sort of compromise. *I tried to get in touch, ring me back if you also want to.*

She checked the clock above the door. Just after one o'clock.

Using the walking frame for support, she got herself out of the kitchen chair. The walkie-talkie in her cardigan pocket bumped against her hip. Why had she even bothered to take if off the hallway table as she came in? Its partner was still out there. But without Sean, the things were worse than useless.

She contemplated taking hers out and throwing it in the bin. That would make him realize how much he'd hurt her. Just going off like that. Deserting her. She'd have to pay for one of those panic buttons you wore round your neck. She'd have to rely on a stranger in an office God-knew-where to summon help if she needed it. That's what modern life came to. Families broken into fragments, crowds of lonely people, all of them checking their screens, longing for some kind of contact.

Stop it, she told herself. *Carry on thinking like that and you'll lose the will to live.* She wanted to cry. Instead, she took her phone from her other pocket to see if, maybe, he might have sent a text. Anything.

FIFTY

There was no sign of Troughton when Sean got back to the incident room. But there was a voicemail from the office manager waiting for him on his desk phone. He lifted the receiver and retrieved it.

'I've been over the Heather Knight tram footage. Nothing, I'm afraid. It seemed so promising, too. But that's often the way. I'm sure you'll also want a look – it's on the system, in her folder.'

Sean kicked his desk in frustration. The noise caused a couple of heads to turn. Two colleagues, back from the search of Petr Kadlec's address, judging by the pile of evidence bags beside them.

From their faces, there was no need to ask if they'd hit the jackpot. What was it with this bloody case? Nothing would slot together.

He sat down and logged into the system. The CCTV from the tram was where Troughton had promised. Over twenty minutes of it: they'd obviously sent through footage either side of when she'd got on and off.

He opened the file, selected the full screen option and clicked Play. The usual view of the inside of a tram. People had spread themselves through the carriage to ensure the maximum distance possible from their fellow passengers. He hit pause and studied each person. Kadlec wasn't among them. He let the footage resume. A few were chatting on their phones. Others' heads were down, fingers brushing screens. One woman was reading a book. An actual book. *A rarity*, Sean thought. An elderly couple were looking out the window, lips moving. She pointed at something and he leaned into her and smiled.

One man had chosen to stay standing. He was midway down the carriage. Sean's eyes lingered on him. Unusual to voluntarily stand when seats were free. And if they did stand, people usually stuck by the area near to the doors. Sean could see that, behind his glasses, the man's eyes were closed. His head was tipped to the side. Sean would have guessed he was listening to music, but no headphones were visible in his ears.

The tram eased to a stop and the doors opened. A number of people got on, including Heather Knight. She had a face like thunder. Within seconds, she'd taken a call on her phone.

Sean watched her speak. Fingernails tapped impatiently against the handrail. This would have been when she was berating the bloke from the BMW dealership. The very moment she gave out her name and address. Where the hell was Kadlec? Was he just out of the camera's view?

A couple of young men sitting close by looked at each other. One twisted his mouth into a grimace, causing the other one to wince. She obviously wasn't keeping her voice down. The man who'd been standing midway down the aisle opened his eyes and edged forward a few steps.

Why did he seem familiar? Maybe he resembled someone off the telly. Maybe he was off the telly: the BBC and ITV had studios out at MediaCity. A weatherman, or local correspondent, maybe. The man took a small notebook out then jotted something down, by the look of it. He put the booklet back in his pocket and closed his eyes again. He looked like a lover of classical music at a once-in-a-lifetime performance. Head lolling, drinking in every tiny sound.

Heather Knight began to lower her phone. Then she lifted it again and checked the screen. Her expression softened somewhat. *The boyfriend*, Sean thought. *That's who she would have been talking to now.*

The tram stopped and more passengers climbed on board. Now the view of her was partially obscured. He stopped the footage and searched in vain for Kadlec. Where the hell was he?

He let the footage play on and by the time the tram reached St Peter's Square, the carriage was getting crowded. Heather Knight squeezed her way to the doors and disappeared from sight. Sean froze the footage again and did one last sweep for Kadlec. If he had been on board, it wasn't anywhere close to Heather.

His eyes were drawn back to the man who had been standing on his own. Now there was a young girl – somewhere in her teens – right next him. Her head was back, braided hair caught mid-swing, one hand making a stabbing motion. The other held a phone to her ear. Sean couldn't tell if she was angry or elated.

The man had opened his eyes and was staring at the back of her head. Sean felt his scalp contract: the look of untrammelled hatred on the man's face. It was shocking. He let the last of the footage play. The loathing in the man's gaze didn't alter.

The printer chuntered and whirred. *Come on*, he thought, watching the sheet work its way slowly out into the tray. *Hurry up!* At its centre was a label.

Janet Blake, 16 Juniper Street, Hollinwood, Manchester.

He placed the sheet on his dining room table alongside the package. Plain brown paper, neat folds. Seams sealed by translucent tape. He peeled the label from the sheet and applied it to the upper side of the package.

All was in order.

He put his glasses back on and cast his eye over the blue tunic draped over the back of the chair. There was quite a gathering of dust on the shoulders. The garage didn't make an ideal storage place.

After pulling a length of tape from the roll, he wrapped it swiftly round his fingers so the adhesive side was facing out. As he dabbed at the uniform, he considered the woman.

She'd driven the little scooter up the ramp to her front door. Then she'd hauled herself out of it and, using a handrail, got to within reaching distance of the door. A key had been produced. The door had swung open to reveal a walking frame in the corridor beyond.

Would it pose a problem if she answered the door while supporting herself with the frame? She'd need a hand free in order to sign for the package. He would be holding the console but he'd also need to keep hold of the package. Yes, that would work. She'd be gripping the frame with one hand and signing with the other. He'd press the button and she'd hit the floor same as the rest, mouth gaping like that of a fish. Ready for him to get the hood over her head.

He found a single hair on the tunic's sleeve and pressed the sticky tape against it. When he peeled it away, the tape protested with a little rasping sound.

'Magda! Could you take a look at this?'

She allowed the evidence bags to cascade onto her desk then gave Sean an exasperated look. 'May I log this lot with the receiver first?'

He beckoned at her urgently.

'Your knickers are in a twist?'

'No. Just . . . come here, will you?' He pulled an empty chair alongside his as she weaved her way between empty desks.

'But you do wear them?' She sat down with a smirk.

'What?'

'Never mind. What's got you all hot under the collar?'

He shot her a glance. 'When's your phrasebook from, the 1950s?'

'My father bought it for me when I was six, so possibly.'

'I'll get you a modern one. Now, tell me if I'm mistaken.'

As she turned to the screen, he opened the first of a row of tabs.

'This is the CCTV from Pamela Flood's last bus journey home from where she worked. As you can see, she was on the phone. Ian Cahill had called and they argued for the entire journey.'

'OK. I can see she is obviously not happy.'

Sean paused it. 'This man, two rows back. See him?'

'Yes.'

'Keep an eye on him, not Pamela.'

He let the footage continue.

'See how he's not staring at a screen, reading a paper or talking to his neighbour. Agreed?'

'Yes.'

'Could he be listening to Pamela?'

'It's possible.'

He opened a new tab. 'This is footage for Francesca Pinto's last journey home from work. She hasn't got on yet. Watch carefully when she does.'

The view was downwards, from the ceiling. The doors of the bus opened and Francesca Pinto came into view. She made her way along the aisle. Behind her was another woman, her neck encased in the folds of a chiffon scarf. Then a man came into view. Short greying hair in a neat side parting. Francesca found a seat a third of the way back. He positioned himself directly behind her.

Sean pressed pause and looked at Magda.

'What?' she asked.

'Look closely. Tell me if you recognize anyone.'

'Francesca Pinto: right there.' Her forefinger was reaching out to touch the screen when her hand stopped and she leaned forward. 'It's him!'

Sean let his eyes close for a moment. 'Thank God. Wasn't sure if I was going mad. Francesca is talking on her phone, yes?'

'Yes.'

'I've checked the timings from her call transcripts. She's complaining about something – and, during the call, mentions that she lives alone.'

'My God, Sean.' Magda pointed at the remaining tabs. 'These are . . .'

'Each victim's final journey. The only one he doesn't appear in is Victoria Walker's. But if you check her call transcripts, she's bickering about mortgage arrangements to her fiancé. That conversation took place just prior to her tram arriving. So she was probably waiting on the platform. Once we get that CCTV footage, he'll be within earshot of her, I'd bet my life on it.'

'How about the third victim – Julie Roe? The one with Petr Kadlec in?'

'Take a look.'

He clicked another tab. 'There you go. Julie is sitting across the aisle from Kadlec. They have their altercation. But check behind her. There he is – and he's listening to every word. He's not even trying to hide it. Now, watch. As soon as she starts gathering her things, what does he do?'

'Stands up.'

'In the transcript, she doesn't mention her address. She does say she lives on her own, though.'

'The creepy bastard! He's getting off at the same time as her!'

'And she's so busy having a go at Kadlec, she's oblivious. After that, she walks straight home.'

'And he followed her.' Magda licked her lips. 'Right. Who's around?'

'No one. Troughton's nipped out to get lunch. DI Levine's doing the house search. Ransford's over in Hull.'

She glanced rapidly about. 'We need to get hold of someone senior. I'll have to go upstairs.' She got her phone out. 'What's your number? I might need to be able to get hold of you, fast.'

Once he'd given it to her, she stood. 'Right, I've sent you a text. So you have my number now, too. Let me be clear: this man obtained the victims' details through what they talked about on their phones? The transcripts all concur?'

'All of them.'

'Once he has their address, he then calls on some pretext . . . window cleaner, courier delivery, meter reading—' She stopped speaking. 'What? Sean? What did I say?'

He felt like his eyes might pop out of their sockets. 'Courier delivery!'

'What about it?'

'Earlier today, I had to see this woman. She lives on her own . . . oh, Jesus. A man rang on her door. But it was the sister that answered . . .' He tapped a finger on the monitor's screen. 'I need to show her this.'

'You think it was the man from the footage?'

'I don't know. Her description fitted. It could be how he's gaining access to their—'

'OK, you call the sister. I'll try and get hold of someone senior.'

His mobile pinged: Magda's text. He rewound the CCTV footage to a point where the man was clearly visible, screen-grabbed the frame and saved it to his desktop. Next, he yanked his notepad from his jacket and called Amanda Harpham.

'Mrs Harpham, it's DC Blake. I came to see—'

'Yes. Is there anything—'

'Are you able to receive a .jpeg file? It's a still taken from some CCTV footage.'

'I'm at my desk now. Would you like my email?'

'Please.'

After sending it over, he bowed his head, phone pressed against his ear. *Please, please, please.* Down the line came the distant noise of an office. Behind him, a phone rang and, in the phone's earpiece, another one did the same. Parallel universes. Then Amanda Harpham spoke. 'It's here in my inbox. I'm opening the attachm— oh.'

'Mrs Harpham?' He hunched forward, now crushing his own ear with the receiver. 'Mrs Har—'

'That's the man.'

'The man who called at your sister's house?'

'Yes.'

'You're sure?'

'Yes! That's him, I'm certain. Yes.'

Sean felt like the entire building was detaching itself from the earth. His fingers gripped the edge of his desk, but it didn't help.

'Thank you. I need to go.'

'If it's possible, could you—'

He cut the call and sat back. Katherine Harpham hadn't used public transport. She drove to and from the Lightwater Academy. So how – or why – had the man in the footage targeted her? He retrieved the academy's number from his notebook.

'Hello, the principal's office, Lightwater Acad—'

'This is Detective Constable Blake. I need to speak with Ms Harpham. It's critical.'

'One moment.'

She came on the line seconds later. 'Hello?'

'Ms Harpham. I need you to look at a picture and tell me if you have ever seen the man in it.' Seconds later, he found himself on hold once again. He used the opportunity to see what Magda was doing. Her back was to him and she was speaking on the phone.

Katherine's voice came down the line. 'I . . . I'm not sure what to say.'

'Sorry?' He span round so he could face his monitor. 'The email's come through?'

'Yes. I'm looking at the photo right now.'

'And do you—?'

'Of course I know him. It's Brian Miller. He used to work here.'

'The man in the photograph worked at the Lightwater Academy?'

'Yes. Until recently, but we had to bring disciplinary— why have you sent me his picture? I don't understand.'

'Ms Harpham, why were disciplinary proceedings brought against him?'

'He . . . I suppose normal rules of confidentiality—'

'Believe me, they don't apply. What went on with him?'

'Well . . . ultimately, he lost his job because he struck a student.'

'Struck? With a fist?'

'No, the palm of his hand. He slapped her across the face. It was in a classroom, in front of everyone. Someone even filmed it.'

'Why did he slap her?'

'It was a bugbear of his. A well-documented one. She'd been talking on her phone. He remonstrated with her, she started yelling at him. It was . . . he should never have got into that situation.'

'When you say it was a bugbear – what did you mean?'

'There'd been many incidents. Many. And not only with students.'

FIFTY-ONE

Brian Miller had to drive past her house and continue for a good thirty metres before he found a space. As he reversed into it, he searched for the dashboard clock. In the Peugeot, it had been to the right of the radio's controls. In this new one, it was part of the display where the speed dial, petrol gauge and rev counter were. Stupid place to put it.

The time was one twenty-nine.

He breathed a sigh of relief. He'd made it with minutes to spare. Why did he ever doubt that he wouldn't? The drive from his house had been charmed: traffic lights had switched to green at his approach; buses had pulled over to get out of his way; vans and cars had melted down side roads. He had hardly needed to touch the brakes.

The central locking clicked in and he paused to check the vehicle was properly against the kerb. He didn't like the green paintwork. Maybe that's what he'd do next weekend: respray it. Grey, perhaps. Or dark blue. Something less obvious.

He transferred the package and console to his right hand. A bird trilled its song from a nearby roof. As he set off along the pavement, another joined it. He could hear a lazy breeze approaching through the trees behind him. The rustle of leaves got closer and he felt the air press lightly against his back. Like a hand gently ushering him forward. The trees ahead now started to shift, leaves nodding their approval. The birds sang louder and he knew then that they were singing for him. A triumphant chorus, just for him. He looked around and smiled. The world was such a wonderful place.

Sean put the phone down and looked for Magda. Her desk was now deserted, as was Troughton's. He glanced to the corner and saw several people were now in DCI Ransford's office.

Magda, Troughton, the media relations woman and someone else. It was only when he reached the door that he recognized Assistant Chief Constable Tony Shipton.

Troughton's head turned. 'DC Blake, come in.'

Sean stepped inside as Troughton turned to Shipton. 'Sir, this is the detective. The one who did so much of the crucial legwork on this.'

Tony Shipton was wearing a crisply pressed white shirt. Sean took in the diagonal cross fringed with leaves on his epaulette as the man extended his right hand. 'Excellent work here.'

Does he know? Sean wondered as their hands shook. *Does he realize I know what my mum did?*

'How's Janet, by the way? I was lucky enough to work alongside her, many moons ago.'

'She's . . . she's well, thank you. Sir.'

'Good to hear. I haven't spoken to her for far too long. Send my regards, won't you?'

Sean felt his hand being released. 'Of course.' Was this what you needed to rise through the ranks? An ability to lie this brazenly? He wasn't sure if he wanted it as his career, if it was.

Shipton now appeared to be addressing Ransford's desk. 'Carry on, Jacob. What were you saying?'

The DCI's voice came from his desk phone's speaker. 'I think we need to hear Tina's opinion. Is yet another press appeal so soon after the others advisable? We're still receiving calls about

Petr Kadlec. How will it make us look if we now ask for information on a brand new—'

'There's no need for that.'

Every head swung round and Sean lifted his notebook. 'I know who he is.'

Ransford's tinny voice emerged into the room. 'Is that DC Blake who just spoke?'

'Yes, sir.'

'Come closer. I can hardly hear you.'

Magda made room for him beside the desk.

'I just talked with a woman who was visited by the man in the CCTV footage,' Sean stated. 'He was posing as a courier driver in order to drop off a package. It seems he didn't expect her sister to answer the—'

'Who's the man?' ACC Shipton demanded.

Sean checked his notebook to be sure. 'Brian Miller. He lives at Smithy Bridge, near Rochdale. Until recently, he taught the course in Electrotechnical Services at the Lightwater Academy, Collyhurst.'

'That new one?' Ransford asked. 'On the A62?'

'Yes. He was recently sacked from it because he slapped a female student in the face. But there had been multiple incidents prior to that.'

'Like what?'

'Colleagues found him to be fixated on discipline. Several female staff had complained that he was overbearing in meetings, trying to bully and cajole them into supporting him. He was described by the principal of the academy as the type who, if he was sitting in the staffroom, you'd find a seat on the other side. Very intense, very opinionated.'

'But this incident – it was a student he slapped?' Magda asked.

'Yes. He was never happy with females being allowed to take his course. And he had a serious issue with phone usage during his classes. These two things meant the principal was dealing with accusations from a variety of students. Sexism, misogynistic behaviour, inappropriate language. All sorts. Even male students had lodged their own complaints in support of female students he'd targeted. Then came the slapping incident. Another student caught it on camera and put the clip online. He – and the college – started being hounded on all sides. The principal said that, when she suspended him, Miller went mad.'

Magda tilted her head in question. 'He wasn't expecting that?'
'No: he was expecting her to back him up – despite the whole
thing being there, on film.' Sean shook his head. 'He actually
accused her of betraying him.'

'When was he sacked?'

'Less than six weeks ago. I also ran his name through the
system. He's not on the Sex Offenders' Register or on VISOR;
understandable given his role as a teacher. I also did a search on
GMP's OIS database: two incidents, both go back years. Neither
went further than a verbal complaint, so they were never entered
on the national database.'

'And these were?' asked Shipton.

'An employee at a builders' merchants called Kingfisher. I
think it was eventually taken over by B&Q. She said Miller had
used threatening language when an order he'd placed wasn't
properly fulfilled: this was in 2003, before he moved into teaching.'

'What was he doing at that point?'

'Ran his own electrician's company. Sole trader, by the look
of it. The second complaint – also from a female – had come as
a result of work he'd done on her house. She disputed what he'd
billed her for and, in the following argument, she claimed he
backed her into the corner of her kitchen, held a drill to her face
and said he'd, quote, "fix her properly". He claimed to the attending
officer this was a reference to rectifying his work. The woman
didn't want to pursue it.'

'Tell me again, what's the connection with the principal of this
academy?' Shipton asked. 'He called at her house with some sort
of dummy package?'

'I think it's how he's gaining entry to their homes,' Sean replied.
'The packages require a signature. Their guard will be down at
that point – as they're signing it. Though I still don't see how he
subdues them so effectively.'

'Did he only train students to be electricians?' Troughton asked.
'Nothing to do with martial arts or anything?'

'Sir,' Magda cut in. 'We need to get this principal to a place of
safety: she's obviously on his list.'

ACC Shipton nodded. 'How many people are currently at the
property of this Petr Kadlec?'

Ransford's voice came out of the speaker. 'Most of the team.'

'Who's the officer in charge?'

'DI Levine.'

Shipton briefly rubbed his chin. 'OK. DI Levine needs to get everyone out of there and over to this Brian Miller's address in Smithy Bridge.' He looked at Sean. 'Is he likely to be in? If not, have we any idea of where he'll be?'

'If the CCTV is anything to go by, he's spending a lot of time just travelling around the city on public transport. It's how he finds his victims.'

'Christ. Then we need to alert the entire network of drivers, conductors, station staff. Everyone. For all we know, he's out there right now. He could be already homing in on someone else. We also need to get the principal of this academy to safety.'

Magda raised a hand. 'I can do that, sir.'

'Good. And DCI Ransford? You're SIO on this and you're currently on the wrong side of the bloody country. How long until you can be here?'

'We have Kadlec in custody, so—'

'Never mind about bloody Kadlec. How long until you can be where you should be?'

'About two hours.'

Shipton rolled his eyes. 'Are you able to direct this operation in the meantime?'

'Of course, sir. I'll liaise with Inspector Troughton and brief DI Levine. It's not a problem.'

Shipton's head turned. 'Inspector Troughton? Do you feel comfortable with the resources currently to hand?'

The office manager glanced uncomfortably at Ransford's empty chair. 'Absolutely, if I keep in close contact with DCI Ransford.'

'Very well. And keep me up to speed with everything.' He turned on his heel and strode out of the room.

No one spoke for a few seconds.

'Who's still there?' Ransford asked.

Troughton gave a cough. 'DS Dragomir, DC Blake, Tina Small and myself, sir.'

'DS Dragomir: get a move on. DC Blake: I want all of this in a report for when I get back. Inspector Troughton: set up a conference call with DI Levine, now. Tina? Stay here, I need a word in private.'

'On it, sir,' Troughton replied, leading the way out of the office.

*   *   *

Sean stared resentfully at the blank Word document that filled his screen. Yet again, stuck in the office while everything happened elsewhere. Even worse, doing bloody paperwork.

He studied the tabs still open across the top of his screen. CCTV footage for each victim. He flexed his fingers to start typing, but paused. He interlinked them instead, raised his hands and pressed his knuckles against his lips. This was tricky. When all the other CCTV was inevitably examined, what were the chances of his mum being spotted?

He reopened the tab for Julie Roe and dragged the footage back to the point where she was still sitting down. He pressed pause. There, just a few rows behind her, was Brian Miller. Lurking. Sean gave a little shake of his head. It began to sink in just how close his mum had been. Right there, just out of shot. All Julie Roe had done was talk too loudly on her phone. He realized that his mum had rung him during that same bus trip. She'd wanted to know how his first day as a detective was going.

As the realization hit home, it made him shudder. It could have been her. Jesus, he thought, it really could have.

He came back to the present as it occurred to him that he still hadn't called her back. *Damn*, he thought. *She's probably sitting in the kitchen, phone on the table beside her. Fretting about what I'm doing, where I'm staying. Why I haven't rung to let her know?* He selected the number for her mobile and pressed call.

'Sean?'

She sounded tired. Or was it apprehensive? 'Yeah, it's me. Mum, I didn't get the chance to ring you back earlier. Sorry.'

'Oh.'

'Where are you?'

'At home. Just getting ready to go out.'

'Where are you off to?'

'Just out. I need a change of scene from in here.'

He checked no one was in earshot. 'Mum, you were right. All the victims made a journey on public transport before their deaths.'

'Really? All of them?'

'Yes.'

'But you said Heather—'

'I double-checked. There'd been a mistake. She actually got a tram.'

'My God. That's . . . well done, Sean.'

He lowered his voice. 'Credit where it's due. You worked this out.'

There was a pause. 'So, where did you go last night? I got up this morning knowing you hadn't come—'

'I stayed in a hotel.'

'A hotel?'

'Yes.'

'And what . . .' She cleared her throat. 'What will you do tonight?'

'Let's talk later, OK? I just wanted you to know that your theory—'

'But, Sean. This is all so unnecessary. Surely you can—'

'Mum?' He had to stop her. He wasn't going back to live with her. Things could not continue as they were. But there was no way he could discuss it there and then. Not in the office. 'I'll give you a call later. We can—'

'You're not going to leave me, are you?'

There was a hitch in her voice that made his chest hurt. He was trying to think of what to say when he heard the chimes of the front doorbell. *Thank God.*

'You'd better see who that is. We can chat—'

'I was only trying to help you! How could I have known your boss would—'

'Please, Mum. Don't do this. Don't. It's not just that. It's time for me to . . . you know. It will be better for us both.'

The bell went again.

'Mum, you should answer the door.'

'Sod him, it's only a delivery man. Sean, listen. I realize I'm guilty of—'

'Mum, we'll speak later. OK?'

He pressed red before she could say anything else.

FIFTY-TWO

Janet angled the walking frame slightly then reached across the top of it so she could get the front door open. The man waiting at the top of the ramp was somewhere in his fifties. Glasses, clean-shaven. He had slightly mournful eyes that crinkled as he smiled. He looked rather smart in his uniform, even if it did seem a touch cheap.

'Package for Janet Blake?'

'Really? I haven't ordered—' She paused. 'It'll be my son, using my Amazon account again. It is Amazon?'

He looked down at the brown paper wrapping. 'Could be. I just make the deliveries. It's a signature here, please.'

He offered her a solid-looking pen that connected to the console by a coiled cord.

'Of course.' The phone was still in her hand, so she slotted it in the pocket of her cardigan.

'Right there. Anywhere on the glass panel.'

His voice sounded odd. Tight. She glanced up. He was staring intently at her hand as it reached out to take the pen. Something made her curl her fingers back in.

His gaze lifted and their eyes met. Abruptly, she felt unsettled.

He seemed to register this and let out a sigh. 'I'm sorry.' He glanced over his shoulder. 'It's just there's a ticket warden coming and I parked my van . . .'

She had a sudden insight to his day. Racing from one address to another, trying to not drop behind an inhuman schedule. No wonder he seemed stressed. The poor man. She straightened her fingers and took the pen. It was surprisingly heavy, the metal casing cool in her—

Sean put his phone to the side and traced circles on his temples with the forefinger of each hand. What a nightmare. The tremble in her voice; she'd sounded so miserable. So alone. Should he move out? Maybe he was being hasty.

He found himself staring at his monitor. Behind Julie Roe, Brian Miller's head was bent forward. Where he should have had eyes, there was only shadow. But Sean could tell he wasn't staring at Julie Roe. From the angle of his head, he was looking beyond her. Sean tried to imagine what ran through the man's head as he approached his victim's homes. As he knocked on their door or rang their—

There'd been someone at the front door. He'd heard the bell ring. Twice. Mum said it was just a delivery man. *Oh my God, I didn't tell her that he poses as a—*

Brian Miller, he realized, was staring towards the front of the bus. Directly at where his mum would have been sitting. He snatched up his phone and pressed redial. A lurching, sickening

sensation was ballooning up, pressing against the back of his throat.
He was close to retching. *Come on, come on. Answer.* The ringtone
repeated again and again. *Mum, for fuck's sake, pick up the phone!*
By the time her recorded message began, he was running for the
doors.

Brian Miller watched the woman slam backwards into the wall.
Somehow, she stayed on her feet. The hand that had been holding
the stylus was bent across her midriff, fingers transformed into
rigid hooks. Her other hand was locked on the handle of her
walking frame. His eyes travelled down the grey metallic legs to
its wheels. Rubber.

'*Tkkskskksssssssss*—' The sound escaped through her clenched
teeth like steam hissing. Stiff cords in her neck, stare fixed on the
ceiling.

He wasn't sure what to do. *Get in the house*, a voice screamed.
Do that first! The door clicked shut behind him.

'C-cc-caaahh—' Her eyes swivelled toward him in terrified
confusion. He was still holding the console out, stylus swinging
to and fro around his knees.

He needed her on the floor. He needed her hand off the bloody
walking frame.

She sucked in some air, used it to breath out her words: 'Hhhelp
meee.'

She didn't know what had happened! The stupid bitch had
no idea.

He grabbed her free arm and draped it over his shoulder. 'Let's
lie you down, here.' By bending his legs, he was able to lower
her to her knees. 'That's it. Can you let go of the frame?' She
didn't seem to be hearing him. 'Your hand? Your left hand?' He
placed the console on the carpet then reached out and prised her
fingers from the plastic handle. 'There we are.' Now he could
lower her fully to the floor. She slumped against the skirting board,
saliva glistening at the lower corner of slack lips.

A phone started to ring. He looked about; she'd been holding
one when she opened the door. It had gone into her cardigan's
pocket. Would the cursed things ever be quiet!

He pulled the neatly folded plastic bag from his trouser pocket
and started to shake it out. Once her hood was on, he could relax.
This had all been very stressful.

'Phow – phow—' she murmured with half-shut eyes. Her fingers twitched. A pathetic attempt at retrieving the thing.

'This?' he asked. 'You want this?' He took the phone out of her pocket, ready to hurl it against the wall. The first two words on the screen made him stop. *Detective Constable.*

He turned to the screen so she could see it. 'Why is a policeman calling you?'

There was the beginning of a smile on her lips.

He sat back on his heels and looked at the screen again. A policeman. Why would a policeman be calling her at this moment?

'C-coming,' she murmured.

'Coming? He's coming here?'

Her eyes had closed, but the smile stayed on her face.

He placed the phone on the carpet, clenched his hand into a fist and bit down on his knuckles. *No! No! No! No!* He glanced about. There was no time to do it here. Where? Somewhere quiet, somewhere they wouldn't be disturbed. He couldn't risk his garage. What if the patrol car came back?

A possibility came to him.

He looked around and saw a fold-up wheelchair leaning against the wall. That would do. He snapped it open and locked the wheels. 'Let's get you in this. I'm going to lift you up.'

He pulled her into a sitting position and hooked his arms under hers. As he raised her off the floor her head lolled against the side of his face. He felt a moist warmness on his cheek: her saliva. It took all his strength to not drop her and shriek with disgust.

Sean's car screeched into the top of his road and he immediately saw a small group of people. They weren't directly outside his house, but they were close enough. The vehicle lurched to a stop and he jumped out, leaving the engine running.

A woman of about forty was sitting on the kerb, holding a handkerchief to her head. A man was on his phone. A third person – another man – was crouched down, consoling the injured woman.

Sean's badge was already out. 'Police!' He walked sideways, heading towards his house, while addressing them. 'What happened?'

The man on the phone held it away from his face. 'I called 999!' He then gestured to his companion. That man pointed to the injured woman. 'I . . . I only heard it. This woman, she tried to stop a bloke from forcing a lady into the back of a van. He punched her.'

Sean ran up the driveway to his house. Her scooter was outside and the front door was ajar. He shouldered it open. 'Mum? Mum!'

Her phone was on the carpet, next to a blue plastic bag with a drawstring. The fold-up wheelchair was gone. He'd taken her. But she was still alive. Surely, she was still alive.

He spotted a single walkie-talkie on the table behind the door. Sweeping it up, he sprinted back out onto the road. 'Was this lady disabled?'

The woman nodded. 'He was dragging her out of a wheelchair. She didn't want to go.'

'She was alive?'

'Yes.'

Sean closed his eyes for an instant. *Thank Christ.* 'How long ago?'

'I don't know. Two, three minutes?'

'Less.' Sean turned to see a different woman hurrying towards him with a glass of water in her hand. 'A minute. Not even that. I saw it all from my kitchen window.'

'Which way did they go?'

The man on the phone nodded to the nearest side street. 'Drove his van up there.'

'Tell whoever you get through to you have a message for DCI Ransford, Serious Crime Unit. DC Blake is in pursuit of the van. Tell him it's a kidnap situation. Got it?'

'Yes.'

Sean ran back to his car. As he veered round the little group, he lifted the walkie-talkie to his mouth. He could remember the sales spiel for it on the packaging. Nautical grade. Waterproof. Shock resistant. Range 5 km. 'Mum, it's Sean. Mum? Can you hear me?'

FIFTY-THREE

The front door was hanging on by its upper hinge. 'No one in the house, sir.'

DI Levine turned away from the property. The driveway led past it to a large garage. The metal fold-up door at the front was padlocked. He scanned the side: there had been a window, but it had been bricked-up. He didn't like the look of it. Cautiously, he approached a wooden side door. Tucked between the garage's far end and the hedge beyond was a tarpaulin-shrouded vehicle. He walked over and lifted the rough material up at one corner. A van, white. 'Bring the Enforcer! Let's see what's in this garage.'

'Excuse me!' The voice quavered with a mix of old age and outrage. He looked back to see an elderly lady at the point where the drive joined the pavement. She was wearing slippers and doing her best to get past the uniformed officer stationed there. 'I intend to report your actions here, I hope you realize? What you are doing to Mr Miller's property is disgusting.'

'Are you familiar with Mr Miller, madam?'

'Of course I am. He is a friend and a neighbour.'

Levine spoke from the corner of his mouth to the nearest officer. 'Bust the fucker open, I'll be back.' He walked up to the old lady. 'Do you know when Mr Miller went out?'

'He always leaves just after eight o'clock. Why? Your colleague here—'

A harsh bang came from the direction of the garage.

'You are wilfully causing damage—'

'Madam, did you see him leave?'

Another bang, followed by several smaller impacts. *They're kicking the door in*, Levine thought.

She looked on, aghast. 'Whatever the reason for this, it's . . . it's totally unwarranted.'

'Madam? Did you see him leave?'

'Pardon? No.'

'You haven't seen him today?'

'No, I mean, yes. He did pop home earlier. But he didn't stay long.'

'You saw him?'

'I heard him. His new van sounds different.'

'He left in a van?'

'Yes.'

'You know what this van looks like?'

'Yes.'

'Sir!'

He turned back towards the garage. There was a flustered look on the face of the detective who'd called out. 'You need to see this.'

He placed a hand on the uniformed officer's shoulder. 'Have a chat with the lady here. We need to know full details.' He strode up the drive. 'What have we got?'

'Not sure exactly. But I have a nasty feeling it's body parts.'

DI Levine stepped into the garage's cool interior. The place smelled harsh and metallic. Strip lights hummed like prehistoric insects. Motes drifted through the shafts of light they were throwing down. His eyes flicked about. This was a proper workspace. Shelves overladen with stuff. Battered workbench. Cabinets. Neat rows of tools hanging from hooks.

'What am I looking for, here?'

'The shelves, sir. At the top.'

His gaze lifted. 'Sweet Jesus.'

FIFTY-FOUR

The engine sounded so loud. Every judder and bump of the tyres carried up through the thin carpet and into Janet's spine, hips and ribs. She pressed her head against the rounded metal of the wheel arch. The vibrations sent her teeth chattering. Anything to clear her head.

It had started to become obvious things weren't right when she had felt herself being wheeled out of the house. He'd ignored her attempts to say stop, her son was coming. Had someone else appeared? She'd heard another voice, she was sure. A woman's. After she'd felt herself being pulled into the rear of the vehicle, he'd scrambled back over her, one knee crushing her forearm as he'd climbed from the vehicle. There'd been a fleshy impact and the woman's voice had gone quiet. Then the wheelchair had been thrown across her legs and the doors had slammed.

She tipped her head back. A chipboard partition separated the rear compartment from the driver's cab. A small square had been cut into it. Through it, she could make out part of his ear and a section of greying hair. The baseball cap was no longer on his head.

The sides of the van were solid metal sheeting. No windows. She was partly rolled to the side as they sped round a corner, then her head banged against the wheel arch as the vehicle straightened.

She pressed her chin into her sternum. There was a window in each of the rear doors, but she was too low to see the street. Just the first-floor windows of the buildings moving steadily by. Street lamps. Guttering. The occasional chimney. Her pulse was irregular. She felt like her heart was swollen with pockets of trapped air. Too much pressure in her chest. She tried to raise herself onto an elbow.

'Stay still!'

She twisted her head. Framed in the opening above her was a single demented eye.

'If you move, I'll shock you again. Hear me?'

He shocked me. That's what happened. When had he done that? I'd been about to write on the . . . Her fingers were numb. Her wrist felt stiff. She flexed it and felt the tendons tingle. Had he—

'Hear me? I will stick that pen in your eye and shock you!'

She let her head sink back.

'Good. Stay like that.'

A few seconds passed. Faint words. Had he turned the radio on? A voice was coming from somewhere. A voice that buzzed. Her eyes widened with realization and her fingers crept to the pocket of her cardigan that held the walkie-talkie. She sought out the double lump of a side button and pressed the lower one repeatedly. The volume dropped. She slid it out and held it to the side of her face hidden from the driver's view. His voice was miniscule in her ear.

'Mum? Mum? It's Sean. Mum, can you hear me? Mum?'

He could have been continents away. She pressed the transmit button and whispered, 'Don't shout.'

His voice changed. Sharper. 'Where are you, Mum?'

She tried to not move her lips. 'In a van. On the floor.'

'I can't hear you.'

'He's very close.'

'He . . . he's very close?'

'I am in his van. On the floor. We are moving.'

'OK, got it. Can you see anything?'

'Not much.'

'Shops, houses, offices?'

'A main road, I think. We're slowing. I need to keep quiet.'

The nose of the engine fell away as the vehicle stopped. Outside, she heard the beep of a zebra crossing. They were at a red light. Should she slap on the side of the vehicle? Try to scream? What would anyone do? Maybe call the police. But she already had her son on the line.

She lifted her head a fraction. She could see what had appeared to be the pole of a street lamp. But instead of the casing for a light at its top, there was a banner-shaped sign. Capital letters had been cut into an expanse of bronze-coloured metal. She couldn't work out what it said. M. The first letter was an M. But then there was an A and an H. The next letter was completely alien. Then a 1 and a 0.

The van began to move forward, engine a quickening rumble.

'I saw a sign,' she whispered. 'It said *Mah*, then I don't know. The number one and zero.'

'Where was the sign? What was it on?'

'A street sign, at the top of a pole.'

'You saw it out of the back window?'

'Yes.'

Silence.

'So you had already passed it?'

'Yes.'

'I know where you are. You were reading it back to front. Oldham. You've just entered the outskirts of Oldham.'

Sean tried to think. He must have taken her along the A6104 then left on the A627. That led directly to Oldham. Where were they going?

'Hang on, Mum, I'm coming.'

The side road he was on led out onto the A6104. He raced to the end of it. His way was blocked by three cars queuing to get out. No siren in the vehicle. Shit! His phone started to ring so he placed the walkie-talkie on the passenger seat. It was the incident room.

'He's on the edge of Oldham! I think the A627. Pretty sure the A627.'

'Sean, it's Colin Troughton. He has your mum, is that correct?'

'Correct.' Every second he didn't move, she was being taken further away from him.

'OK, don't worry Sean. Everyone is out on this, mate. Where are you?'

'Stuck at a fucking – I'll call you back.' He threw the phone aside, put his hazards on, pressed down on the horn and pulled into the oncoming lane, praying nothing turned off the A6104. As he passed the cars queuing in front, their drivers looked across, dumbstruck. He began to nudge out onto the main road. Traffic approached from both directions. Lead cars began to slow. Ones further back began to beep in retaliation. Bracing himself for an impact, he pulled out of the side road. A red Audi skidded to a stop, then was shunted by the car behind it. Sean steered across the junction as the Audi driver jumped out. He started running towards Sean's car, waving and shouting. Sean accelerated away, reaching a roundabout seconds later. Two cars waiting to get on. He mounted the empty pavement to get round them, then took the first left up Copster Hill Road. More horns blaring in his wake. He knew the road he was now on joined the A627 at the edge of Oldham's town centre.

He grabbed the walkie-talkie. 'Mum, can you hear me?'

For a second all he got was the ocean sounds of static. Then her voice came through. 'Yes.'

Thank God. 'I'm not far behind. Have you made any turns?'

'Yes.'

Shit. 'Still on the main road?'

'I don't know. Can't talk.'

'OK.'

His phone went again. Incident room. 'Yes?'

'The A627 joins the A62. We're closing both roads, Sean.'

'She might be on the A62 already!'

'We'll find her. Every single officer in Oldham's station is flooding the town centre. He's got nowhere to go. Where are you now?'

'Just joined the A627.'

'OK. Sean? You've done a superb job, but it's best you back off now.'

'Yeah, right.' He cut the call and scanned ahead. The road was straight. In the distance, all he could see was the red of multiple brake lights coming on. Every single car was slowing.

Of course – they'd have blocked the roundabout connecting with the A62. This was all about to turn into a massive traffic jam.

'Sean?'

He lunged for the walkie-talkie. 'Yes?'

'Shop sign. Drays Hearing Specialist.'

'You just passed that?'

'Yes.'

'Hang on.'

He retrieved his mobile and opened the browser. Clamping the phone against the steering wheel, he put the name in and pressed the search button. Lees Road. His heart flipped. That was the A669. They were already off the A62 and heading east, out into the countryside. She must be three, possibly four kilometres away.

He signalled right. By cutting across Alexandra Park, he could avoid Oldham town centre and get straight onto the A669.

'Mum, are you moving?'

'Yes.'

'I'm coming, Mum.'

'We're m – sk – – t—'

'What was that?'

'Sean? Se – lt – – ing.'

Her voice was cutting up. The cars ahead seemed to be crawling along. He tried flashing his lights and beeping. All that did was cause the car in front to immediately brake. 'Get out the fucking way!' He lifted the walkie-talkie to his mouth. 'Mum? I didn't get that.'

'—ry – t. C – m—'

'Mum?'

Static. Nothing but static. He'd lost her.

FIFTY-FIVE

The browns and greys of buildings had now been replaced by greens and blues. The sky. Trees. There'd been nothing from Sean for about ten minutes. And the road was no longer flat. The van's floor tipped and dipped. Often, the bends were so sharp, only the carpet prevented her from sliding about. She knew that, in terrain like this, the walkie-talkie would be useless. She kept trying it every few seconds, anyway.

Now and again, she heard his voice coming from the cab. She could tell it was about her. She'd wondered, at first, if someone else was up front. But after a while, she knew there wasn't. It was just him, grunting and snarling. Sometimes she could hear exactly what he was saying. She didn't care how fast they were going:

the cruelty of his words made her wish she could kick the rear doors open and roll herself out.

Sean held his hand on the horn again and pulled out so his car was straddling the white lines that ran down the middle of the road. Vehicles on his side immediately slowed and swerved to the side. Eighty metres away, a car was coming straight at him. It started flashing its lights. He stuck a hand out of the window and waved frantically. *Out the way. Out the way. Out the way.* With an angry blast of its horn, the other vehicle braked sharply and edged to the kerb.

As Sean passed it, he heard a shout, speed slewing the words. 'Fucking cock!'

He pressed on, alternating between beeping and waving. On the playing fields to his right, he saw a football match, frozen. Twenty-odd kids watching him in amazement.

Then he was on Goldwick Road, jinking right down side streets until the A669 turning appeared. He accelerated out on to an empty stretch of road. Retrieving his phone, he called the incident room. 'It's DC Blake. She was heading east on the A669 about five minutes ago. Got that?'

'Affirmative.'

He pressed red and reached for the walkie-talkie. 'Mum, can you hear me?'

A terrible silence. He filled his chest full of air and roared at the windscreen, left foot stamping up and down so hard the moving vehicle shook. Tears came into his eyes. 'If you touch her,' he sobbed. 'If you touch her . . .' He bit back his words, holding the tirade before it took hold. *Get a grip. Think. He's got something in mind. He must have.*

He picked up his phone, went to Magda's text and selected the 'call this number' option.

'Sean? What's going—'

'Are you with Katherine Harpham?'

'Yes.'

'Magda, she has to think. Miller is heading east, out of Oldham. Next is Saddleworth Moor. Or beyond that, Huddersfield. Even Leeds. Did he ever say anything? Has she any idea where he might be going?'

'Hold on.'

He sped along the road, eyes cutting to the walkie-talkie every
few seconds. The roadside sign welcoming him to Greenfield
flashed past. There was, he knew, a junction quite soon. At that
point, the road split three ways: left to Uppermill, straight on
towards Dove Stone reservoir or right towards Stalybridge. *Come
on, Magda. I need something.*

It was time to face the truth: Sean wasn't going to find her. Not out
here in the middle of nowhere. Now she had to try and communicate
with the person who'd got her. Make some kind of connection on a
human level. At the moment, all she was to him was a lump of meat.
Something he could electrocute, drag around, kick and slap. And
that was just the start. Eventually, he'd kill her – like the others
whose homes he'd tricked his way into.

'Hello?'

Nothing.

'Can we talk, please? Can I speak to you?'

No reply, though she heard movement. Like he was searching
for something in the front.

'My . . . my name is Janet and I—'

'Silence!' His voice was shrill with fury. She heard something
scraping above her and looked up to see the blade of a knife
jutting through the gap. 'Open that filthy mouth again, I will cut
out your tongue!'

'Sean?'

Magda, at last. 'Yes?'

'She says he's quite a keen walker.'

Sean winced. He was about to enter the Peak District National
Park. The walking trails were endless.

'One place he mentioned that's close to you is called Pots and
Pans.'

The junction. Lights were green. 'What is it?'

'Just moorland. But there's a war memorial – it's on top of the
hills above Greenfield.'

'A war memorial?' He tried to picture anything remotely like
that. Couldn't.

'The road that goes alongside the reservoirs, she says.'

'The A635?'

Magda spoke away from the phone. 'The A635? Yes, that one.'

Sean powered straight across the junction.

'From that road, you can see it. Up on the hill.'

'And he goes there?'

'He told her once, his grandfather's name is on the plaque. That's all she can think of.'

By now, Sean had passed the little village to join the A635. He kept his eyes on the grassy slopes rearing up to his left. A gap in the trees and he glimpsed it: a black finger of stone pointing to the sky.

'I see it!'

He tossed the phone aside and turned left. Dusk, instantaneous. The tree-shrouded lane was steep and incredibly narrow, clamped in place by towering dry stone walls on either side. If he met another vehicle coming down, they would be stuck. He dropped the car into first and pressed his foot down, engine whining in pain. The lane took him to the left, causing the monument to swing away to his right. He was now going in the wrong direction. A turn appeared and he veered up that, monument directly ahead once more. The road rose for another hundred metres then he was suddenly into daylight, open heath land all around. There was a stony track to his right. It looked too bumpy for a vehicle.

He pulled over. Feet crunching, he ran up the incline as far as the first bend. To his surprise, a green van was crookedly parked further up. Silence. Not a soul around. The vehicle was a farmer's, probably. He sprinted back to the road and was climbing into his car when he spotted something black with flashes of red at the road's edge. He walked over, not wanting to believe it. His mum's walkie-talkie, casing fractured, stubby antenna snapped off.

'For pity's sake, leave me!'

The wheelchair bucked and tilted as he dragged her backwards. They were now in a dip of the rough track, view around them swallowed by a thin line of scrubby bushes. Forty metres further down, the green van's bumper was folded into a stone post. When he'd driven into it, the impact had squashed Janet up against the chipboard partition. Now she could hardly turn her head.

It had been the second sudden stop in less than a minute. The first had been when he'd spotted her speaking into the walkie-talkie. The vehicle had skidded to a halt and, moments later, the rear doors had opened. 'Give it to me!'

'Let me go. They'll find you, you realize? There will be—'
'Give it to me!'
The look on his face was petrifying. 'No.'
He'd grabbed her left foot, pulled the shoe and sock off.
The nasty-looking knife appeared from nowhere and he pressed
its serrated edge into the tender arch of her foot. 'I'll flay you to
the bone.'
Sobbing, she'd thrown the walkie-talkie in his direction. A hand
had swept it out of the doors. He stamped down on it then kicked
out with his foot. She'd heard it clatter across the pits in the road.
The track was now getting worse. For the third time, he had to
tip the wheelchair right back onto its rear wheels so he could
negotiate an especially severe ridge. His breathing was ragged and
desperate with the effort of what he was doing.
The wheelchair stopped and he appeared in front of her. 'Sit
up,' he gasped, beckoning with the knife. 'Sit up!'
'I . . . what do you mean?'
Beads of sweat glistened in his eyebrows. Drips were making
their way down his face as he took in gulps of air. 'Sit forward.
Reach towards me.'
The moment she extended her arms, he grasped a wrist. Pulling
hard, he got her over his shoulder. Almost crying out, he began
to stagger forward. By arching her head back, she could just make
out a tall dark structure on the bleak skyline.

Sean drove on for another few seconds. Farm buildings on his left.
The monument was now to his immediate right. Surely, it was
impossible to drive any closer? Up ahead, a footpath sign pointed
to a thin trail leading across the heath land towards the stone tower.
No white van. Where had he parked? Was there another way to
the top? Perhaps on the far side of the hill? Bollocks. His foot hit
the brakes with such force, he was thrown against the seatbelt. As
he jumped out of the car, dogs began barking from beyond the
farm's privet hedge.
Had he parked the van in their yard? He started down the gravel
drive, dogs now going ballistic on the other side of a wire fence.
He looked around desperately. A jeep of some description. A
Mercedes estate and a battered old Ford. Back on the road, he
assessed the footpath. Too narrow and uneven for a wheelchair.
He must have missed an easier way to the top, but there was no

time to try and find it. Half scrambling, half jogging, he started up the slope. The footpath was barely wide enough for a sheep. A steady breeze ruffled the hair on the back of his head. Crystal-clear sounds from the valley far below were being carried on the flowing air. A motorbike's hacking coughs as it went rapidly through the gears. The bleating of a sheep. A train's horn.

From somewhere up ahead came the sad and tremulous sound of a curlew. He had to pause and get his breath. Glancing back, he could see the faint dim tower blocks of Manchester dotting the flat land that lay beyond the slopes. His position on the path meant he was now tucked in beneath the crest of the hill; only the monument's pyramid-shaped tip showed above it. A last section of slope to scale.

Would they even be up there?

He cupped his hands to his mouth. 'Mum! Mum!'

Did he hear her voice? Or was it the wind mocking him?

Ignoring the aching burn in his thighs, he set off once more.

Janet felt him bending forwards then she was flung down on some stone steps. She was at the monument's base. He fell back onto the grass, eyes shut, hands curled against his sternum, knife blade resting on his chest. He sucked desperately at the sky.

Tentatively, she lifted herself onto an elbow. How had he carried her up that final stretch? Something terrifying had given him the strength. She looked around, knowing the same dark force would soon be turned on her. She estimated her legs had about fifty metres in them before they failed. A foot-dragging, shambling totter. Wind whipped her hair about. There was a grit stone outcrop off to her right. Large enough to hide behind, but he'd soon guess that's where she was.

Lying on the step beside her was a little wooden cross. It had been stamped with black letters. *In remembrance.* More had been blown into the grass beside him. Slightly further away was a semicircle of bright red. Poppies. She looked behind her: there were several more wreaths at the monument's base. They formed a line directly beneath the green copper plates inscribed with the names of fallen soldiers.

Each wreath had been weighed down by a single stone. Pushing a strand of hair from her eyes, she checked him. Still panting heavily, eyes shut. She shuffled backwards up the shallow steps

and closed her fingers round the largest rock. About the same as
a bag of sugar. Enough, if she brought it down hard enough, to
cave the bastard's skull in.

Slowly, she got to her feet. *Thought I couldn't stand? Thought I
couldn't walk?* Carefully placing her feet down, she edged onto the
grass. His head was two metres away. She took a couple more steps
then raised the rock up to shoulder height. As she focused on the
bridge of his nose, something light and insubstantial brushed against
her ankle. A split-second later, wind tumbled the wreath against his
side and his eyes opened.

Just below the crest of the hill, Sean heard a scream. *Mum.* He
started pumping his knees in a desperate attempt at running. His
feet slipped and he fell forwards. Hands grasping at tufts of wiry
grass, he hauled himself forward. With every stumbling step, more
of the monument came into view.

She brought the rock down at his face as a scream escaped her.
His head twisted and the rock smashed against his ear, flipping
his glasses off. The rock sank into the long grass and his hand
shot up. Fingers hooked into her hair, as his other hand locked on
her upper thigh. She was pulled forwards, balance immediately
lost. The pressure on her leg released, instantly replaced by fingers
on her throat. She felt the ground slam into her back and next
thing his face blotted out the sky, eyes boring into hers. The remains
of his ear flapped against his jaw and spots of blood began to
pepper her face. She flexed her fingers. No rock.

'Whore!'

He straightened his elbow, driving his weight down on her
windpipe. She tried to struggle as a pulsating roar began to fill
her ears. Her vision began to slowly redden and she felt her tongue
being pushed out through her lips. His maniacal stare slid down
her face and the knife appeared. She tried to retract her tongue.
Couldn't.

He brought the knife closer to it, grinning.

Sean saw a wide base of steps at the base of the blackened tower.
They were on the grass beside it and he was kneeling over her.
She was pinned to the ground by her throat and a knife was almost
touching her mouth.

He felt a guttural roar erupt from deep inside his chest. Miller's chin lifted, whites of his eyes plain to see. The entire left side of his face was slick with blood. Now on flatter ground, Sean was able to charge forward, the sound pouring out of his mouth.

Miller staggered to his feet, took a couple of unsteady steps back then turned and fled.

Sean reached his mum, fell to his knees and pressed a palm to the side of her head. She was coughing and clawing at her throat, trying to remove an invisible band from the blotchy skin.

'Are you OK? Can you breath?'

Her voice was an unintelligible rasp. Tears squeezed from her eyes, as she started to nod.

Dots of blood covered her face and chest. Hers or his? 'Did he cut you? Are you bleeding?'

Her head shook.

Thank you, God. 'Easy, Mum. Easy. You're safe.'

She coughed. Attempted to swallow. 'Geh . . .'

Sean looked up. Miller was now about a hundred metres away, a lone figure in a sea of moorland. 'He's gone, Mum.'

A hand closed over his and she looked at him properly. 'Get him,' she whispered.

'What?'

Each word came out as a separate breath. 'I. Will. Live. Get. Him.'

He checked again. Miller was slowing, head turning from side to side. He felt his fingers being squeezed and he looked down.

A fierce light was in her eyes. 'Go!'

FIFTY-SIX

The grass formed a spongy layer and with each stride he felt like he was being lifted high into the air. He pictured the way wolves ran across the tundra in pursuit of prey. Effortless. The word formed a rhythm in his head, as he quickly closed on the older man.

Miller looked like he was spent. Twice, he stumbled and fell, hands pushing against his bent knees as he got back up.

'You've nowhere to go!' Sean yelled.

Miller's head turned. His face was haggard. The collar of his courier's uniform had come away. One sleeve was ripped. The jacket's left side shone with blood. To his side, the land lifted a fraction. He made toward a cluster of grey rocks that showed through the grass.

By the time Sean also reached the top of the modest rise, Miller had turned to face him, knife held by his side. *The knife he would have used*, Sean thought, *to saw out my mother's tongue.* Sean spread his hands and smiled at the man through his rage. 'What now?'

Miller lifted the blade. 'Stay back!'

Sean kept walking, the smile broad on his face.

'I said get back!'

Sean nodded. 'You get one try. Maybe you slash my face. But then I'll be on you.' He lifted his thumbs. Wiggled them. 'I'll find a pressure point and the pain will make you pass out. You'll come round in cuffs.'

Miller retreated a step, and said in a wavering voice, 'I mean it.'

'So let's see what happens, you sick fuck.'

'I'll jump! I will.'

Sean slowed. *Jump?* He realized that the colour of the terrain behind Miller was a degree fainter. And it was peppered by rocks that had been shrunk with distance. There was a wrinkle in the land. A hidden fissure. The other man was on the edge of a drop, but how much of one, Sean couldn't be sure.

Keep going, part of him said. *Let the bastard jump. Why not?* Sean slowed to a stop, unsure what to do.

Janet felt like the inside of her throat had been scrubbed with wire wool. Every intake of breath ignited a molten wave of pain. She lay still, trying to assess her other injuries. Left shoulder: a needling spike, but small in scale and already losing strength. Her right wrist: throbbing. Bent back, probably, when the rock had thudded into the grass. She switched her attention lower, aware of a hot feeling between her legs. *Oh no*, she thought. *Please don't let me have wet myself.* She lifted a hand from the grass and tapped tentatively at the insides of her thighs. The material was hot and wet. Drenched. She became aware of an ache deep in her hip and when she lifted her fingers she saw they were dripping in blood. *His knife*, she realized with dismay. *When he opened his eyes and grabbed me, the knife had been in his hand.*

*   *   *

As Miller looked off towards Manchester, Sean saw his ruined ear. The crimson swathe that coated his neck.

'This,' he announced, with a reverent look around, 'this wonderful silence. I tried to make the world a better place.'

The desolation in his voice caught Sean by surprise. He didn't know what to say.

'I tried.' The man's voice was barely audible.

Sean dredged up the closing slides of a distant training course. Dealing with suicides. *Don't allow silence; silence let's them think.* 'How?'

A twitch played at the corner of Miller's lips. 'I had plans. Such plans.'

'You did? What were they?'

Miller shot him a look of contempt. *Shit*, thought Sean. *I'll have to do better than that.* A pulsing throbbing sound intermingled with the breeze. Sometimes quicker. Sometimes slower. Sean spotted the far-off helicopter in the sky above the city. Dark insect in a roiling sky. He looked back at Miller. The man's eyes had lost focus. He was slipping away. 'We all want to make the world better, don't we? The woman back there? She was in the police, once. Got injured while doing her job. Doing her bit to make the world better. Same as your granddad.'

He saw Miller's knife hand half drop. The comment had got through.

'Is it his name on the monument back there? World War One?'

No reply.

'Where did he die? Somewhere in France, was it?'

A succession of barks and Miller's eyes shifted. There was the sound of voices, too. Sean glanced back to see a line of officers working their way up the slope. The noise of the helicopter came back stronger, engine whine now intertwined with the blades' deeper thrum.

'We all try to make the world better,' Sean said. 'People like us. Especially people like you: teachers. That's all you were trying to do, wasn't it?'

The other man twisted his head to check behind him. Then he calmly placed the knife in the grass and inched backwards.

Sean lifted both hands. 'Mr Miller! You didn't tell me about your grandfather. Tell me about—'

'I'm sorry.'

Sean was about to wave the apology away. But Miller wasn't talking to him. He was talking to the sky. *His granddad?*

'I'm so sorry to have failed you.' The man's eyes were still on the clouds as he let himself fall back.

For a second, Sean stared at the spot where Miller had been standing. Cautiously, he approached the edge. The land was scarred by a deep cleft. Five metres down, Miller lay with closed eyes across a jumble of boulders. If it wasn't for the dark red lines nosing their way across the stone behind his head, he could have been asleep.

Sean turned and looked back to the monument. The first officers had already reached his mum. As he started walking, he wondered why they were standing around while she lay in the cold grass. *Come on, at least sit her up.* He narrowed his eyes. *What the hell are they doing? Why is Mum's head to the side? Is she looking at me?* He began to form a wave. Someone moved and he saw another officer. This one was on his knees, leaning over her, fingers entwined as he pumped the heels of his hands against her chest. He remembered a patch of grass beside a trampoline and the wind filled with ice, as he began to jog. He was within shouting distance when one of the officers reached down and placed a hand on the kneeling one's shoulder. *No. No. No.* The mouth of the officer who was standing began to move. *Don't say it. Do not tell him to stop. You mustn't.* The one on the ground lifted his hands from her chest. Then he sat back on his heels and bowed his head.

EPILOGUE

Three weeks later.

As Sean turned his phone over and over in his hand, the sounds of the canteen dissolved to near silence. Each time the screen was uppermost his eyes slid across the name displayed there: *Mum.*

What to do with the traces of her that remained?

The bereavement counsellor had said decisions like that varied with each person. Some chose to delete, close down and cancel, even as they were dealing with the practicalities of the funeral. Others needed more time to process. A few could never let go.

At least, he said to himself, *I haven't been tempted to call her number.* He almost had in the first few days after she was gone. Hear her voice, even leave her a message as requested.

The house was too big. Cold and silent, like a mausoleum. The knee-high power sockets, ramp at the front door, stair lift: all were unwelcome reminders. He'd started looking at flats. First in Fairfield then closer to the centre of town.

A cup of coffee appeared on the table before him. Suddenly self-conscious, he slipped the phone into his pocket.

'So,' Magda announced, taking the seat opposite, 'what do you think?'

'I . . .'

'Ransford said he'd give it his approval.'

'It sounds—'

'And, obviously, Inspector Troughton backs it, seeing as it was him—'

'Magda.' He found her nervousness strangely touching. 'Can I get a word in edgeways here? I think it sounds great. And thank you.'

'You do?' She grinned. 'That's good news!'

'Well.' He hunched his shoulders up to his ears. 'It'll get me away from that cramped corner where I am now.'

She spun a sachet of sugar in his direction. 'Cheek like that . . .'

He plucked it from a fold in his shirt. 'I'm really chuffed, Magda. It means a lot you were happy when Troughton suggested it.'

'We'll work very well together. You'll see.'

They wandered up the corridor, drinks in hand. Coming through the doors to the incident room, Sean couldn't help glance over to where DC Morris used to sit. He realized all the other desks were empty, too. Everyone was congregated at the top of the room.

Sean sent an uncomfortable glance at Magda. *Are we missing a briefing?* A couple of detectives peeled off from the gathering, their smiles jarring sharply with the sadness in their eyes.

In the gap they'd created, Mark Wheeler was visible. Sean was still registering the fact he was in a wheelchair when their eyes met. The other man's half-smile fell away. The sudden change in his expression caused heads to turn in Sean's direction. A few murmured words and people began to step aside, opening a channel between them.

Sean was aware of Ransford, Troughton, Levine, everyone. All watching. *No one had mentioned he was coming in*, Sean said to himself. He kept moving forwards. The dad was behind the wheelchair, also staring. Fuller alongside him. *Christ*, thought Sean. His shoes felt like they'd been chiselled from granite.

He was now a couple of metres away.

Mark's mouth began to twist at one corner and Sean braced himself for a snarl to emerge. Abuse and accusations.

The other man's right hand was shaking as it lifted slowly from the wheelchair's armrest. Sean realized it was this attempt at movement that was causing Mark to grimace. Immediately handing his drink to Magda, Sean dropped to a crouch and took the other man's hand in his. The room looked on in silence as they shook.

'Sorry about your mother,' Mark said, labouring over each word.

'Thanks. It's good to see you looking so much better.'

'Hardly—'

'I heard they've got you spending a lot of time in the pool.'

'Yeah. Treadmill next. In a few weeks, I'm hoping.'

Sean could see how much weight had vanished from the other man's frame. Angular shoulders beneath his T-shirt, bony knees jutting against his jeans. 'I bet you'll be on it sooner than that.'

It was rumoured Mark wasn't coming back, even though he was expected to regain most, if not all, of his movement. The decision to leave the police had been his.

The corners of Mark's mouth lifted. 'Legs and arms are one thing.' He broke their grip to wiggle his fingers. 'Need to practise getting a baton to open.'

The back garden, Sean thought. *That's what Mark had been trying to do when Cahill had dropped onto the trampoline.*

'You did your best there, mate,' Mark added, renewing the handshake. 'My fault, that.'

The father stepped forward to place a hand on Sean's shoulder. 'Thanks.'

Sean searched his mind for something to say. He glanced up to nod his appreciation to them both. Fuller was further back, eyes averted.

'Right,' Ransford said, breaking the silence. 'We're due up on the top floor, Mark.'

Sean straightened up. Around him, people were wishing Mark the best as they began to disperse.

'The rest of you,' Ransford added, 'those cases ain't solving themselves.'

Sean could now see the display boards on the end wall. The photos of Pamela Flood, Francesca Pinto, Julie Roe, Victoria Walker and Heather Knight had long been taken down. New faces had taken their place. The usual family snaps or images sourced from social media. Mouths smiling, eyes happy, expressions optimistic.

THE END

AUTHOR'S NOTE

For the sake of drama and pace, I took certain liberties with what the police can access from a murder victim's phone, and how fast. I'm aware of these inaccuracies, so please don't email to tell me off!

I'd also like to thank Jim K and Ray R, my two trusty plot advisors, for all their deft suggestions.

Join Chris Simms' Readers Club to get latest news, special offers and an exclusive novella absolutely free.

www.chrissimms.info/readersclub